ORDINARY BOYS

And Favorite Sons

Thank you for
for me something really
cool—

Sandra Lowen

Book self-published through lulu.com, ISBN 978-1-304-96440-3-90000. For further information, including possible discounts for bulk purchases, contact lulu.com.

ACKNOWLEDGMENTS

To author Sydney Taylor (1904-1978), whose *All of a Kind Family* book series introduced me to a world of Jewish life and tradition when I was just a little girl;

To Rabbi Joseph Gelberman (1912-2010), whose gentle kindness and warm reception welcomed our family to study and experience the Faith;

To John Lowen, who stayed up nights to help edit and read through this manuscript again and again and again and…

To Dr. Brian Saunders, longtime friend, who frequently set his oratorios aside and employed his superior French cooking skills to make sure I ate;

To countless acquaintances, friends and relatives, from whose collective sharing this compendium of fictionalized lives arises; and

To Iulia Mund, Bina Rosengard, Geula Putziger, Julius Fischer, and a host of others whose long-ago wisdom, acts of kindness and personal sacrifice made this story possible.

PREFACE

I am not Jewish. Nobody in my family of origin is. So I am sure many readers will be doubtful of my ability to convey well the history and feelings of Jewish characters, even in a work of fiction. Well, I thought I would try my hand at it anyway, so let's see how this works out.

Back when I was an eight-year-old, I spent every hour that I wasn't doing homework or housework after school at the library. Having exhausted her supply of regular books for me to read, the librarian handed me the first in a series of Sydney Taylor's *All of a Kind Family* books. I was fascinated by the descriptions of holy days and practices so different from those of my Christian upbringing that I studied them intently.

By the time I was fifteen, my brother and brother-in-law were beginning to explore different belief systems. Their feeling was that Judaism was 'best', because it was at the root of all Western religions. But who was there to introduce three Black would-be proselytes to Judaic culture?

The Sixties unlocked all sorts of inter-ethnic doors. People began tearing down the barriers of race and religion to meet the people that were on the other side. I went to school, to summer camp and to work with people of every possible background.

One day in 1988, while caring for six children that represented my entry fees to grad school at Columbia University, I found myself on the upper east side of Central Park, near the pavilion in which Rebbe Menachem Mendel Schneerson was hospitalized with a serious illness. When his well-wishers told me what had happened, I stopped; the children gathered around me, and we prayed with his faithful. His recovery soon after was just one more proof to the children that a benevolent God watches over people of every race and creed. Following that impulse, I began having a series of 'experiences' with the great man, from which I learned a great deal not only about myself, but also about caring for the planet and its people.

Not all of the stories were wonderful; how could they be? After all, this is life. I couldn't, for instance, figure out how to weave in the story of real-life friend Lois' mom, though some of her is Beryl's mother. I went to visit Lois when I was seventeen. She served lunch, and I volunteered to help with the dishes. The family had a double sink, which, since we had one at home, too, I assumed was to 1) wash the dishes and then 2) rinse the dishes. They also had these cute little sponges, one shaped like a milk bottle and one like a veal cutlet. Lois never said anything, so I began scrubbing the plates with a will, when her mother came in. She screamed at Lois for allowing me to wash the dishes, and then at me, just for living. She grabbed up the entire set—a beautiful set of china that she swore, between everything else that she was swearing, was Meissen—and heaved the entirety of it into the nearest trash receptacle. As she stood breathing heavily over the exertion and contemplating her next move, Lois suggested discreetly that this might be the moment to terminate my visit. Nor was there a vignette I could come up with to portray Ellen's mother and her upsets over her husband, who turned out to be a devout atheist. He loved to aggravate the poor woman, who, despite the tattooed numbers on her arm had persisted in her beliefs, by frying pork bacon every Sabbath, the only day on which he made a point of eating it.

Benyamin, the main protagonist, was very forthcoming about his life story. He told me that I should write it someday, and even recorded parts of it on VHS. Again, I changed not only names, but also details; hopefully enough that his children and grandchildren will not come after me.

So I hope it does not mean so much that I, a non-Jew, have written a story about Jews that I hope Jews and non-Jews will read and appreciate. As the late Rabbi Joseph Gelberman asked the first time he met me, "Who are you?" I told him my name, but he said, "That is what your mother named you and the last name of the man you married. Who are you?" I tried to put intelligence behind my response, but now even the question puzzled me. He asked again: "Who are you?" After I stammered out every possible answer I might give from my ethnic background to my chosen profession, he smiled his beatific smile and said, "Why is that question so hard to answer? Don't you know that, before anything, you are first a child of God?"

So are we all.

Sandra Lowen
November 27, 2013

CHAPTER ONE

Benyamin would have told anybody, had anybody thought to ask him, that his life was going to be ordinary. Gymnasium for sure; and after that, university, he supposed. He'd never apply himself enough to do well at Leipzig, as his father, the *ganz grosse* gynecologist and obstetrician Eliezar Rosenthaler, MD, had. Something local, probably; the University of Cologne or, more to his liking, the Fachhochschule Koln for Applied Sciences, if he could escape his mother's plans for him to become a doctor. Maybe he would study in Bonn, though he'd just be doing that for his mother's sake; he didn't give two pins for school. More than likely, he'd wind up in his Uncle Reuven's lumberyard – or should he say, his Aunt Ayelet's lumberyard, since she was the one mostly running it and it bore her family's name. Uncle Reuven, who'd been sick as long as Benyamin had been alive, was usually just lying there, pale and breathless, on the sofa in the office. Benyamin wondered if he could even work at the lumberyard. He didn't think he had the head for business figures as his aunt did, but he lacked the ambition to do much else. Right now, his main goal in life was to get his ten-year-old eye to the keyhole before his brother Herschel did. Anya was about to step into her bath.

Anya, the Polish maid, who by day wore her hair either in a tight ball at the nape of her neck or caught up in two braids that met in the middle of her head; Anya, in her starched gray dirndl under her crisp white apron, her face streaked with housework sweat. Could that same reserved maidservant who woodenly obeyed his mother's every whim during most of her waking hours possibly be this exquisite pink creature, her golden hair swirling around her shoulders like sun-kissed clouds gone mad, her cheeks rosy from the steam rising from her bubbly galvanized tub, her ample hindquarters glistening from the soap, her breasts – ah, her breasts –

"Enough excitement for you, Bennychen!" Herschel was big enough to hoist him up and catapult him onto his bed. "This is nothing for little boys to see!" Herschel, still squeaky from his ablutions, took up his station at the keyhole. His hands were under his nightshirt, moving fast. His hulky butt wiggled with delight.

Something wet and heavy hit the door. It sounded like the big yellow sponge that Anya washed her soft pink body with. "To bed, you boys!" Her voice always had a laugh in it when she talked to them, even when she was supposed to be mad. That made it hard to tell, right now, if she was angry or if she was delighted at their sport. She knew – *had* to know, because Herschel was making so many moaning noises and bumping the door now and again with himself. Benyamin frowned. Herschel was almost a full four years older than he, and had been bar mitzvahed last spring. He was supposed to be a man. He was *supposed* to be a responsible member of the community, to whom Benyamin could now look for guidance. Well, he might have made it through the training and he might be a man, according to the teachings, but it didn't make any difference in the way he acted. Benyamin had to agree with Oma Rivkeh – maybe Herschel was just plain stupid.

Benyamin figured he himself could probably do all right in school; be as smart, even, as Eisenbart, who everybody knew was Herr Reichstetter's mascot and pet. It was just that usually his daydreaming all but precluded his studying. Sometimes ciphering offered Benyamin a challenge; he got to match his own brain against those of his teachers. Herschel, though, couldn't cipher his way out of bed. He couldn't read very well, either, and he wrote some of his numbers and letters backward or upside-down in an unsteady and labored hand.

Their mother, Eliana, would stroke Herschel's head, sometimes, and look sad. "I ate salt," she would say. "I ate salt the whole time I was pregnant with you. I ate salt and I slept in on the Sabbath instead of going to Temple. That's why you're simple. It's *my* fault." Other times, though, she would lose patience with their father, Eliezar; especially when he was sitting in the parlor after dinner with his feet up on the fringed and tufted green velvet hassock, enjoying a cigar with his coffee and reading one of his tomes of medical practice. "How can you sit there, Elie," she would enquire of him, "smoking and smiling as if all was well with the world? You need to *fix* him!" And Elie would turn the page of his book and mutter back, "Fix your *tone*, Woman! I am a gynecologist, not a miracle maker. Besides, did I not strictly instruct you as to your diet during your pregnancy? 'Fresh fruits and vegetables', I said, 'and fowl, not fish'! How often did I have to chastise you about the wurst on your plate? And you've lost your figure entirely. Bonbons and tortes! You are not a young woman anymore, Eliana. You must stop eating like one!" Thus chastened, Eliana would retreat to the kitchen and castigate Anya for some non-existent fault with the Sabbath soup.

How old was Anya, Benyamin wondered. Certainly she was no more than seventeen. Twice his age, nearly; but the chance that he might marry her someday was not totally out of the question, at least not for him. She was Polish, his mother would say with a little disdain, and surely not worthy of doing much more with her life than being a servant. Yes, Eliana would have admitted if anyone asked her; there were Polish doctors at the Hospital who were as brilliant – or almost so – as her own Elie. But – well, no well-bred *Jewish* woman would serve in the home of another woman. Benyamin knew of none that would. He could not imagine his mother struggling beneath the weight of a steaming tureen of chicken soup, turning out challah for someone else, slaving over the kettle of boiling linen and scrubbing at the carelessly dropped grease stains on her mistress's dinner napkins with the caustic soaps. Seeing Anya perform all of those tasks and more, Benyamin felt bad about the times he accidentally spilled food on the table linen while sitting stiffly at Sabbath meals with Herschel and his mother and father and his Uncle Reuven and his Omas, Bina and Rivkeh, when they came to visit. Otherwise, his parents rarely celebrated the Holy Days. His mother would have liked to, he was sure; but with her husband rushing out to the hospital on a moment's notice, she did not feel equal to the task of managing the prayers and the candles and the food and the readings and all it took to celebrate properly. Nor was she even going to consider turning the task over to Herschel, even though as a newly-bar-mitzvahed man, he was qualified to officiate, no matter how deficient his brain might be.

Benyamin more than suspected that his father was not as religious as he might have wanted the world to think. In fact, his father seemed happier on Sundays than on Saturdays. He always got up late on Sundays, and sat in the parlor in his heavily brocaded red-and-gold silk robe with fox fur at the neck and cuffs, and smoked his cigar and read his papers and periodicals over coffee and the delicacies Anya put before him – fresh-cut fruits, sable fish and eggs, fresh-baked bread with jam. Then he stood before the picture window in the parlor and looked with satisfaction at the Christians going to the Kolendom with its soaring majestic twin towers, almost directly across the street. Every Sunday, the pealing call to worship from the South Tower bells filled the house with the tunes of Christendom.

Eliana said it was an abomination to be that close to the Gentiles' heathen palace, and that they should move closer to the Temple. Elie only chuckled at that. "Those Gentiles pay for your dresses and your soups and your fine furniture, and the chocolates I know you nibble no matter how much I protest," he would say. Eliana would mutter that the family did not go to Temple nearly enough, but she would do her sulking quietly, lest her husband hear her and raise his voice. She never forgot that she had been arranged—affianced to him, not chosen by him, as she wished she had been, so that she could feel more carefree and confident in their relationship. She had given him sons, but liberal times were coming, her mother always warned her; and a woman who had married above her station in life and no longer had her youth, beauty, wit or bedroom skills to recommend her had best hold her tongue. "He treats you well," her mother would always say, "and he still seeks you out for sex. Many who moved from their homes in the country to the towns only grunt when their wives address them, and leave their sheets cold and dry while they warm themselves in other women's beds. Keep your mouth shut and be grateful!"

Benyamin and Herschel would come dressed to the parlor and wolf down their breakfasts, waiting for Anya to emerge from the kitchen. And she would come, all signs of the washtub vamp effectively vanquished; her hair pulled back in a tight bun at the back of her head, her gray cloak around her shoulders, masking her shapeliness. The boys would look to their father, who would say with a shrug, "Go, you little heathens. Soak up some Christianity. Their Jesus was a Jew, after all."

And so they would trail off, following Anya, out the massive carved oak door, down the fourteen stone stairs to the pavement, and across the broad Ringstrasse to the Kolendom. They would tour the nave and the chapels as if for the first time, staring at the Tomb of the Three Kings and the tall colorful windows depicting the lives of the saints they knew only snippets about. Then they would sit close up front with Anya, and try to pretend that they did not realize that the same tall young man always came and sat on the other side of them, and that Anya and the tall young man winked and blushed at each other over the boys' heads.

They also pretended they did not know that, five minutes after their departure, Elie peeled Eliana out of her clothes as if she were a banana and fell upon her in their big oaken bed upstairs. It was their only time together, and it did not always happen as often or as tenderly as Eliana desired. Sometimes in the middle of everything there would come an urgent ringing of the doorbell, and Elie would wrap himself in his brocade bathrobe, plod downstairs in his scuffed leather slippers, and speak a few words to a courier's anxious face at the door. Then he would hasten upstairs and drag on his trousers, a fresh shirt, his tie and great-coat, and disappear into the morning, leaving Eliana in whatever interrupted pre-coital state she might be. At such times, the boys would come home to find Eliana bitter and irritable, and anything every other living creature in the home did was wrong in her sight. If, however, there was no interruption, or Elie was able to return to his bed and then to the parlor and his periodicals, Eliana would most likely spend the rest of the afternoon humming songs from her childhood as she darned their socks and knitted in the fringed green velvet chair next to her husband's.

Sabbaths were different. Elie was often up and away from the house long before the sun rose. It seemed that every woman in Cologne who counted herself fortunate enough to be a patient of Eliezar Rosenthaler's chose the Sabbath for her gynecological or obstetrical crises, he remarked often to his boys. "They do it because I'm Jewish," he always said with a laugh. "And I have to deliver their babies, which is a mitzvah. But I also violate the Sabbath, because I am doing work, which is an abomination. Now, boys, here is a puzzle for you: What do you think? Is it better to deliver their babies and risk alienation from God, while I am also earning a blessing, or should I leave it up to some *goyishche* doctor without my skills, so that I can stay at home and observe the holy day, but expose the poor woman and her child to possible injury, which would be a great evil?"

Benyamin remembered the story from the Christians' Bible that the priest had addressed just the other Sunday in his homily about Jesus, the Christians' *Meschiach*. There was some animal that had fallen into a ditch on the Sabbath, and Jesus had said it was better for the observing Jewish men to get it out than to leave it in there until the sun had gone down and it was no longer a sin, but the animal might be dead, which would be wasteful and therefore a sin. Benyamin quite agreed with Jesus on this point, and had he been at school conversing with his Gentile friends, he would have pushed the point most mightily until they agreed with him and their own god. But he knew better than to express such a heretical statement at the dinner table. His mother would fling her plump hands skyward and insist that the children were learning entirely too much heathenism at that abomination of a church across the street, and that they were not to go anymore or they were likely to lose their own religion altogether, and then the Lord God would rain fire down upon them as He had on Sodom and Gomorrah in Abraham's time so long ago.

For Benyamin the tragedy would be that he could not go to the church with Anya; not so much that he could not go to the church, although he loved its marble-and-stone coolness even on the hottest of summer days, the gentle creak of its wooden pews as people rose and sat, the paintings and friezes and statuary that made it like going to the museum, even though the depicted women were modestly garbed. In that respect the women were not like the museum at all, he considered. At the museum one could view uncovered breasts and even, rendered in marble or delicate paints, that downy hair-lined place between a woman's legs, where his father went numerous times a week to bring forth new life into the world. Anya had hair there; golden hair that crimped and snarled. It looked rough to the touch, and Benyamin's hands twitched, wondering what it would feel like to the fingertips. He had no hair there. Herschel had hair, though Benyamin would never have even thought of asking him to touch it. There was an older boy at school – Seubert was his name. He was – *odd* like that. One or two of the boys were curious about him, but most laughed and called him "Girly Fritz". Benyamin felt sorry for him. He seemed a nice sort, who studied hard and kept mostly to himself.

Oma Bina usually came to Sunday dinner. A tall, portly woman with an older version of Elie's face, she had worn black almost since Benyamin could remember. He had a vague recollection of her husband: an Opa who had dandled him on his knee and then had looked longingly and lovingly at him from a narrow bed as he played with his toys on the parlor floor, and then had disappeared into a long wooden box over which Oma Bina and his mother had draped their sob-wracked bodies. Since then, Oma Bina had worn black. She had sat in her dark parlor with the curtains drawn, mourning for years – or maybe not just mourning. Herschel said that she had a real head for business, and that she retained her husband's mercantile contacts and continued to build their friendships and businesses abroad, perhaps with even more skill, if it were possible, than their Opa had done.

When Oma Bina came to the house, Anya served briskly, and more than once Benyamin saw a dish jiggle anxiously in her hands. Oma Bina inspected everything: the glaze on the baked bread, the seasonings in the soups, whether or not the kitchen was really being kept kosher, with this Polish *shiksa* touching everything. She inspected the boys' linen chests and she sniffed around the parlor, hunting under the chairs and around the lamps for dust. She made certain to use her nose well in the water closets. There were, after all, three males in the house, and they surely did not always have the best aim. No one, however, should ever know it, she said loudly and angrily to Anya on one occasion. Benyamin noted that Anya gave special attention to the water closet after that. He was tempted once or twice to wet there just before Oma Bina came, but he dared not. He did not want to see Anya sent packing.

There were only two rooms in the house that Oma Bina did not inspect on a regular basis. Anya's room was one. Oma Bina peeked inside once, but said she only wanted to see that the girl was being well provided for. Benyamin thought secretly that she did not go there anymore because of Anya's statuary, which included a small art piece called *Pieta,* a model of the Christians' *Meschiach's* mother Mary holding her dead son. There was also a large wooden cross that Anya had nailed into the wood where the rafters met over her bed. "A pagan," Oma Bina had said to her daughter-in-law once. "A pagan *and* an idolator! Well, she came well-recommended to me, and that is why I sent her to you. My Liesl is more discreet about her religion. She knows she is in a Jewish household and she knows how to live there without offending us."

The second room was Elie's office, which occupied the ground floor of the three-storey house. His patients could come to visit him without ascending the fourteen stairs that led to his home's main entryway. The boys knew that floor was absolutely not to be entered for any reason, on pain of punishment so severe that they could not imagine it and therefore they risked it only in the case of dire emergency. Anya went there only to empty the trashcans and to very carefully dust the surfaces or carry away the soiled linens from his examinations and surgeries. Once or twice she took down coffee for him and a visiting physician, or a meal, if he was working late. But she scampered up the back stairs as soon as she could, carefully closing the door behind her. Because Elie had declared his ground-floor rooms sacrosanct, Oma Bina complied with his wishes.

Oma Rivkeh went down there only once, when Elie was out on a consultation somewhere in the hinterlands. She just wanted to see it, she said above Eliana's objections, and she was horrified at what she saw as its disheveled condition. Tools and instruments lay in no order that was apparent to her, books were left open with pages of notes stuck in as page markers, and it happened to be a day that the dirty linen barrels were overflowing. She recruited an anxious Eliana and a terrified Anya to clean the whole office. They boiled instruments and laid them out in an order constructed by Oma Rivkeh's concept of how they should be, covering them with a sheet to keep the dust off. They dusted bookshelves until Eliana's sneezing called for a new task. She was sent off to boil the linen and Anya to re-order Elie's desk and set the medications in neat rows. Oma Rivkeh, meanwhile, attacked everything; from the framed diplomas and the case on the wall holding his Iron Cross from the Great War to the deep stains in the floor. The women sweated and labored for several hours to right the perceived wrongs Oma Rivkeh found in her son-in-law's office. Finally Taskmaster Rivkeh was satisfied, and the women, wrung-out from more work than they had done in some time, stumbled up the stairs and collapsed on chairs in the kitchen.

"You have been neglecting your man, Eliana," Oma Rivkeh said. "His office should look like his home; it should be spotless. You must do this routine every week." Then, turning on Anya, she thundered, "I cannot believe your master's office looks so horrible! He pays you well. Why don't you carry out your duties as you should?" Anya dared not speak. Oma Rivkeh had not hired her, but she could very well tell Oma Bina that she was doing poor work. Oma Bina could be very severe: severe enough to terminate her, if she wanted to. There was little honest work in Germany for a teenaged Polish girl whose father had not returned from the Great War and whose mother had died so far from home, and Anya was grateful to her benefactor. Had not Oma Bina, with a large handful of Reichsmarks, rescued her from slaving in a household with a master that had more than once put his drunken hands on her? Anya bit her tongue.

When Elie came home and discovered the violation that had taken place in his sacrosanct space, he had been more than irate. "It will be weeks – *months* – before I can find anything!" he had shouted at the height of his fury. "There is to be no more cleaning – none – in my offices! *Not ever again!*"

"But Doctor – But it was *awful* down there!" Oma Rivkeh had defended her actions. "I do not know the woman who would want to wade into that awful morass without some sense of – of *repulsion!*" Oma Rivkeh had appealed to Oma Bina the following Sabbath, and to Elie's surprise, his mother had agreed that the place was probably overdue for a thorough cleaning. Although Elie had continued to scowl, he knew she was right, as Oma Bina was about so many things. She was right, that he should get a car and hire a chauffeur to drive him out to the hinter places where women seemed to choose to bear their brood, far away from the modern conveniences a hospital offered. She was right, that they should consider apprenticing Herschel to a journeyman or sending him to her other son Reuven and his wife Ayelet to learn the lumber business instead of insisting that the boy had the brains to do more than flounder at the Gymnasium. And she was probably right about the office, too. He let out a long sigh, allowing his blood pressure to return to normal. "All right," he said, his tone softer. "Anya may clean the vestibule and my waiting room. But no touching my books!" he said to the trembling girl in a louder tone. "And don't go *near* my instruments!" He then struck up a cigar, strode into his office, and slammed the door.

"You see!" Oma Rivkeh had said in triumph to her daughter as she regained her composure from enduring his wrath, "It took only the act of doing it for your man to see the value of having everything neat and clean. You must take better care of him, Eliana. It is not every woman who is fortunate enough to marry a doctor!"

And Eliana agreed. She was the fortunate one of her sisters. One, who was wed to a farmer, had a life that was harder than Anya's. The other – ah, poor thing! Her man, a blacksmith from England, had fallen on hard times with the advent and growing popularity of the automobile. He fixed the odd wagon wheel or farm utensil, but there were few horses that still needed shoeing. They would probably have starved in their threadbare little shop, but Oma Bina had finally convinced him to become involved in some vague project with one of Opa's business partners in England. Eliana's poor sister had packed up all of her things and wandered off behind him to that foreign land, where people barked at each other in a strange tongue that she could not initially understand. Occasionally Eliana received a letter from her, the envelopes regaled with strange stamps. Fewer letters had come over the past few years, however; and she noted the errors that had crept into her sister's formerly perfect German. For instance she would say "It seemed strange to me" instead of "for me", as German dictated and Eliana could not help but notice that her sister described some things rather than name them, or failed to use the correct word. She hoped, when they met again – *if* they ever met again – that her sister would not have forgotten her German entirely, or how would they communicate?

Eliana's days were mainly filled with the things she loved best. Tea and perhaps even shopping with her friends, talking to her mother when things troubled her, badgering Anya to do what she herself did not wish to do around the house—that being pretty much everything, munching contraband sweets, and spoiling her two boys. She liked to sit by the Victrola, listen to the new music that was making its way from America, and write letters to her sisters and girlhood friends far away. The garden made her sneeze, but she went there periodically anyway. She would walk with her boys to the park, though they were becoming far too rambunctious for her to handle anymore when they wanted to romp around, and Anya usually accompanied them in their play while Eliana admired the little babies trundled to the park by their nurses or looked about to see if any of her friends might be passing by.

She worked with the boys on their studies, fretting that neither seemed to have much of an inclination in that direction. Herschel – well, she had heard from her mother-in-law that there was a school that taught skills to young boys that could not cipher or read well; oh, but that would be such a humiliation for her! She could imagine her friends clucking their tongues when she was not around: "Poor Eliana! Her husband is *so* intelligent! To think she would give birth to a fool of a boy that can't even learn!" She had tried very hard, with the second pregnancy, to do everything Elie told her to. It was indeed hard to be married to a gynecologist. If he caught her nibbling on a bonbon – even one – he would flail his arms around as if he was having a case of fits, and yell at her in his loudest voice, "You are eating for our *child!* Do you want to develop diabetes and have him die inside you? Or worse, would you have him come out with a head full of water and flaccid limbs, missing organs and a feeble mind?" This always terrified her, but not enough to make her change her ways. He gave sharp instruction to the woman who was in the kitchen before Anya, that Frau Rosenthaler's taste for chocolates and sweets and heavy meats was *not* to be indulged, upon pain of dismissal. But it was hard for a servant to obey two masters; and when Frau Rosenthaler insisted that she must have those very same forbidden items set before her and without delay, the woman could only obey, and hid the evidence of her disobedience from discovery by her master for as long as she could. Despite Eliana's dietary sins, Benyamin had come out fine: a roly-poly boy who fed well and showed no signs of the colic that had plagued Herschel, and thus the whole household, every night for fully half of his first year of life.

Eliana had marked Benyamin to be a doctor, like his father. She hoped he would make up for Herschel's slowness in school, which she thought could mean only that the older boy was indeed an imbecile, despite his facility with his hands and glibness of tongue. Benyamin, however, showed far less interest in books than Herschel, who pored over them ceaselessly, attempting to unlock the secrets they hid from his uncomprehending mind. What, she thought, if Benyamin did not want to become a doctor? A lawyer, then, or—Oh! Or a *Rabbi!* But Benyamin showed less than a passing interest in Judaica, and even less in religion. Every now and again his father would pose a question from the Torah to his progeny at the dinner table. But Benyamin seldom responded with any real enthusiasm. She sighed. What was to become of her boys?

Elie had decided, above her protests, that they did not need any more children; and since he was a gynecologist, he knew the secrets of contraception, and she knew no arts to counter his precautions. She could not help but wonder if a third child might not have had more of a chance to excel academically. Alas, she would never know. Occasionally she would pose the question to Benyamin: "Wouldn't you like another little brother to play with? Or maybe a little sister?" She wasn't sure why she asked him. Maybe she hoped he would give an assent that the heavens would hear, and then a miracle would occur. But Benyamin's answer was always the same: "Another brother! Herschel is enough. And who wants a girl around? *They're* no fun!"

Except for his cousin Liselotte. She was more daring than her brother Ezra, and when Benyamin went every summer to visit with his Aunt Ayelet and his Uncle Reuven – well, mostly with his Aunt Ayelet, since Uncle Reuven could do little more than smile weakly over his equally weak tea and watch the children frolic among the cords of wood stacked for pickup. Liselotte, or LiLo, as everybody called her, was more daring than Benyamin. She didn't care about a skinned knee or a bump. She didn't go screaming her head off if a little blood came out of her. What she lacked in physical beauty she more than made up for in enthusiasm and stamina. She could play all day and half the night, despite her mother's warnings that she had to let the boys sleep. LiLo could swim, too; better than any of the boys, even Herschel. Every summer when Aunt Ayelet closed up the business and they set out for a week at the lake, Benyamin determined that *this* season he was going to out-swim LiLo. But she had strong limbs, and her smaller body allowed her to move quickly through the water. She was like a fish with arms and legs, he thought often.

Aunt Ayelet and Uncle Reuven had an office out of which they did all of their selling. Each wall was completely paneled in wood: the oak planks ran horizontally on the north wall, the pine vertically on the east wall, and the cedar ran diagonally on the south wall. The cherry wood was parquetted, like a floor; and though its wall, which faced west, was almost all windows, the parquetted effect was there. The floor was done in tile; black and white, like a chessboard. Sometimes Benyamin and LiLo would leap about like chessmen for Uncle Reuven's amusement. Benyamin could see that Reuven was a handsome man, taller and better-looking than his brother, Benyamin's father; but with very pale flesh, from his heart illness and from getting little to no sunlight, except for what filtered through to him from outside. He took all of his meals in the office, and slept there during the day as well. When the Germans came to make their deals, though, he propped himself up at his huge wooden desk to speak with them. "Never show a German that you are weak," he always said to the children. "He will crush you if you do." Benyamin was not sure why Uncle Reuven always said that. Surely the Germans knew Uncle Reuven was not a well man. Nor did he seem to have much business sense; misreading a client's ability to pay and insisting that everyone present cash up front, which they sometimes found offensive. Most of their clientele preferred to do business with Aunt Ayelet, who could recognize that she should give a break to a man whose company might send him back to do further business. And they did come back. The Salzenstein lumberyard was well known for its quality. One did not get knotted wood hidden in the middle of solid planks from the Salzenstein lumberyard. The wood was insect-free and well cut. Wood with the Salzenstein stamp was good wood. And if the German businessmen who came had difficulty dealing with a woman, particularly a Jewish woman, they learned to mask their feelings well. There were always pick-up trucks coming and going through the Salzenstein gates.

Nobody hovered over the children at the Salzenstein home. Thus they ran wild all summer. When Herschel and Benyamin went back to Köln well tanned, the hair on their arms and legs blonded and the rose of health on their cheeks, Eliana could not help but feel a little jealous of her sister-in-law, who apparently not only had business acumen, but also the ability to raise children to be strong and healthy while allowing them the freedom to grow with the wildness of well-nourished weeds. On the rare occurrences that they were at her home, she dared not let the children out of her sight, or at least out of Anya's sight. She was always fearful that some major catastrophe would befall them, and then there would be Eliezar and his mother as well as the Salzensteins to answer to.

Certainly, had LiLo and her brother visited regularly, they would have spent the entire time at some carefully planned activity: going to the museum or to the manicured city parks, or perhaps to the university grounds. Assuredly the synagogue would have been on the itinerary. Although the family rarely went, except on high holy days, Eliana always *talked* about going, and she periodically met with the Rebbetzin to do some project or another. Benyamin, on the other hand, would have preferred to take LiLo to the Kolendom, to admire the beautiful statuary and the paintings and to feel the cool, quiet serenity that the Catholics enjoyed on a hot Sunday morning, but he was sure his mother would never allow it.

Benyamin was glad that they were not Catholic. Werner, one of the German Catholic boys in his class who actually attended the Kolendom, told him once that if one missed a week, it meant one would go to hell. "Of course it does not matter for you," Werner had said. "You're a Jew, so you will go to hell anyway." "No I won't!" Benyamin had declared. "I will *not* go to hell!" Werner had insisted. "You Jews killed Christ," he said. Benyamin was outraged. "Who said that?" he demanded. "We didn't kill anybody!" He could not imagine his mother or his father killing the Christians' god, no matter how abhorrent the Christians' religion was to his mother. "Not just you Jews," Werner declared, "But the Lutherans, too, and the Moslems and the Chinese. Everybody who isn't Catholic is going to hell." Benyamin had laughed. "Why, that's precisely why I will *not* go to hell. Because I am not Catholic," he replied. "Has it occurred to you that perhaps heaven and hell are dilemmas only for you Catholics?" He told LiLo about the conversation some time later, and she told him he was probably right.

Benyamin could recall only two or three times that LiLo had come to Cologne. One time was when Herschel had his bar mitzvah. Reuven had been too ill to travel so far, and so Aunt Ayelet had driven the huge black car the more than two hundred kilometers to Cologne with the two children. The family had left soon after the service. Although LiLo confided later that she had wanted to stay in the Rosenthalers' big house, she knew her mother would take her home because of her father. LiLo thought her mother was afraid that if she were gone too long from Reuven he would have one of his heart spasms and die, and it would be her mother's fault for leaving him so long when she knew how ill he was. LiLo had never seen him have one, but she said her mother talked about it all the time. Her mother was always telling her to be quiet around her father, but since Reuven liked to see her running and laughing and jumping over things – things he would never do ever again – she did them for him, making just as much noise as she could.

No, Benyamin did not want a sister. But if he had to have one, he would have wanted LiLo to be his sister. And since she was already his cousin, she could not be his sister. So he always gave his mother an emphatic 'no'. Eventually Eliana stopped asking.

There came the day in his twelfth year that Benyamin had been dreading: his own bar mitzvah was less than a year away, and he spoke no Hebrew at all. "Why do I have to learn Hebrew?" he asked at every opportunity. "Because it is the sacred language," his mother would always answer. "The songs are in Hebrew and the readings are in Hebrew, and the prayers. And you must give a speech in Hebrew." "Why can't I speak in German?" he asked. "We live in Germany. Why do I have to learn Hebrew?" He opened a book and looked at a page. "It's hieroglyphics, like the Egyptians wrote," he muttered. "How am I supposed to make sense of this?" He complained to Herschel, but for once Herschel did not support him. "It's our religion," Herschel said. "You *have* to learn it." Benyamin frowned. The Rabbi had made special considerations for Herschel because of his trouble with reading and writing. But Benyamin knew there would be no special considerations for him. He was supposed to be the bright one; the one who would be able to learn everything and make a good showing.

Rabbi Hirschfeld began coming to the house, as he had done four years before, when Herschel was bar mitzvahed. But this time he was coming for Benyamin. Benyamin did not like Rabbi Hirschfeld. The man smelled of garlic and cigarette smoke. His nearly white beard was yellowed and stained, and more often than not bore identifiable traces of his latest meal. He wore the black flowing garb of his calling, which, Benyamin observed, made some Germans turn around and stare at him with more than curiosity in their eyes.

All of this could have been forgiven, Benyamin thought, but the man had absolutely no sense of humor. He never smiled, or even looked pleasant; and any error a struggling student made, no matter how small, was met with wrath. Not a word of German would he allow after the first three sessions. And once, when Benyamin's multiple errors proved that he had not studied at all since their last meeting, the Rabbi took his omnipresent cane that seemed to Benyamin to be as big around as a tree limb and just as heavy, and rapped him across the knuckles with it. Benyamin had shoved away from the dining room table and, ignoring the severe caveats about entering his father's offices, had stormed down the back stairs to his father, who had shocked him by sending him back into the room with the advisement that he not only needed to apologize to Rabbi Hirschfeld, but that Benyamin would get the same treatment from *him* if he ever gave the Rabbi reason to give another bad report.

That night in their room Herschel tried to soothe him. "You know that silver pen you like that I got from Papa's patient?" he asked. "Papa has a lot of clients: rich ones; *German* ones. They will give you so many things. A bar mitzvah means you are a man, and people give men things. I'd help you if I were a better reader," he said. "I will talk with you in Hebrew, though, if that helps; here in the room, anyway". And then Herschel had gone to his drawer, gotten out the pen, and given it to him. "It'll be easier to write in Hebrew if you like the pen you are writing the letters with," he said. "Anyway, I am not such a good writer. I don't think I've had this out more than once or twice."

Benyamin went to bed that night clutching his new possession. Herschel was all right, he thought. He was a pretty good brother to have, even if he couldn't read so well and his own grandmothers thought him to be a dimwit. Maybe he wasn't really stupid. And his mother, he was convinced, loved him. If she was over-protective it was because she did not want anything bad to happen to him. He had to admit he didn't really understand everything she did, or why she asked him silly questions sometimes; but then, he concluded, she was just a woman, and he could ignore most of what she said. He loved and feared his father, the *ganz grosse* Doktor. And he knew his life was better than those of most of his classmates. He ate better food and his house was grander. The family had two servants, Anya and now, thanks to Oma Bina, Fischer the German driver and gardener, whereas a lot of his friends did not even have one. He sighed contentedly to himself as he snuggled deeper into his eiderdown. His life was good: ordinary, but good.

CHAPTER TWO

Herschel flung the bedroom door back on its hinges so hard that the doorknob left its imprint in the plastered wall. He hurled his books at the opposite wall and plunged into bed with such force that the box springs squealed in protest. Benyamin, who had been struggling with the mysteries of the Hebrew alphabet until his brother's entrance, turned in his chair to stare at him. Herschel was all-over red in the face, his fists knotted into twin hammers that bludgeoned his pillow. And he shrieked; so loudly that Eliana burst out of her bedroom and Anya rushed in an instant later. Fischer, who had been lollygagging with her in the kitchen, took the back stairs two at a time to summon Elie.

It took several minutes for Herschel to speak intelligibly. Elie sent Anya back downstairs for the brandy bottle and she brought it up with a glass. Elie put it to Herschel's lips and the boy's raving slowly subsided.

"Now, Son," Elie said, and Benyamin knew something very serious was happening, because Elie called Herschel 'son' and not by his given name. "What is the matter? What could possibly have happened to upset you so?" Herschel took another swallow of the brandy and then spoke.

"Herr Knacht," he said. "He stood me up in the classroom. 'Stand up, Rosenthaler,' he said. 'Come up here, to the front of the class.' Well, I went up. You see, I'd done rather a good job on my geography assignment. That was rare for me, and I expected he was going to point out my accomplishment to the whole class. Instead—" Herschel gulped another swig of the brandy and then took a deep breath. "Here," he said, making a passable imitation of the professor's voice, "'we have an inferior person. Note his eye color; his skin tone: dark; almost dark enough for him to be a Turk or even a *schwarznegger*. Note the craftiness of the gaze;

the long fingers, ready to grasp money, or worse, to touch your mother or your sister in *that* way. And what makes Rosenthaler inferior?'" Now Herschel was almost fully metamorphosed into Herr Knacht coaching his class. "'Come, children; it is so obvious.' Hans Furmann raised his hand. 'He is a Jew, Herr Knacht?'"

"'He is – *a Jew*! And you are so right, Herr Furmann! That is what makes him so inferior. This riff-raff and rabble live among us for now, but it will not be so for long. That is all, Rosenthaler,' he said. 'Go and sit down. And now we will open our Algebra books to page one-fifty-two...'"

Herschel was himself again, and, as if he had returned to the event in the telling of it and had just come back, he began to shiver. Elie felt his son's head. He felt a bit warmer than he should have. Elie gave him yet another sip of the brandy.

"Well, Herschel," he said, ruffling his older son's hair. "You've upset yourself into a fine fever. Maybe you've picked up a little cold. You'd better stay home tomorrow, so that the other boys don't catch it."

"I'm *never* going back there," Herschel said through clenched teeth. "*Never!*"

"Nonsense," Elie said. "Of *course* you will go back to Gymnasium. Why, you've done so well! Far better than we ever expected!" he added, without meaning to say that last bit aloud. Fischer was a born teacher, and he had done a wonderful job of tutoring Herschel, Elie thought. The boy had leapt ahead despite his disability. "You stay in bed tomorrow. Friday too," he said. "*I* know! Let's go to Temple this Sabbath, shall we? It's been ever so long since we've been, and with Bennychen studying with the Rabbi for his bar mitzvah –"

Herschel flung himself back against the pillows. "Temple!" he cried. "Here I am being called 'an inferior Jew' and you want to take me to *Temple?*"

Elie sighed. "Now, Son," he said, "Be reasonable. It's just silly talk your teacher's making. We are Germans, too. Why, you know I fought in the Great War. I have my Iron Cross downstairs, framed in my office. I earned it. I earned it for this country. I risked my life for the Fatherland. I am a German and you are a German. You're as German as Herr Knacht," he concluded. "Here, look at you. You are still in your school uniform. Let Anya wash you and get you into bed properly. He patted Herschel's leg as he rose. "Anya, give him a little massage to relax him, if the brandy does not," he said as he departed.

Anya looked at Fischer, who shook his head. Fischer was a German, whose mother Elie had saved by divesting her of her womb when other doctors had insisted on leaving the cancer-riddled diseased organ in her and abandoning her to die. Once out of her body, the offending organ had lost its ability to poison her, and so she still lived. Fischer figured Herr Doktor had added twenty years to his mother's life, and she bounced around her little apartment with vigor, now, whereas before it had been a trial for her even to sit up in bed. Fischer himself had taught at a Gymnasium, but he had not liked the boys he taught. They did not want to learn. They were spoiled, like their wealthy parents that gave Fischer little respect when he gave their arrogant, bratty darlings failing grades. "He is too young," parents would say to his headmaster, "and too modern for our children. He makes them do too much work and he has them thinking about politics and things they do not need to know." Despite the usual respect teachers received, Fischer soon found his students as well as their parents challenging him. One or two of them even called him a

Bolshevik. His mother advised him to resign. He had happily accepted the position of driver for Herr Doktor, and he had volunteered to help Herschel study for Gymnasium and to tutor him at home so that he could keep up with the daily lessons.

Fischer believed that Herschel was not dull, but due to some faulty neural wiring, he did not perceive of the world as others did. He did not think the boy's writing was flawed. He was convinced that Herschel wrote precisely what his brain told him it saw. Herschel had real facility with his hands. When the car smoked under the hood or when Fischer perceived odd grinding sounds that he was sure should not be there but for which he could find no source, he would summon Herschel, who would go under the hood with him and invariably solve the problem. He was a genius, Fischer believed; just not a genius in the areas his parents would have preferred. Let them have their Benyamin, he thought, and let them mold his mind into what they would. Herschel would surprise them all someday with his mechanical acumen.

Fischer looked at Anya again with meaning in his glance, but she avoided his gaze as she shepherded Herschel toward the bath. They both knew it was becoming hard for Jews in this new administration. Jews, even those in professions, were losing their jobs, and more and more sanctions were being issued every day. The rope around Jews' necks was growing tighter and tighter, and now it had intruded into this family that Fischer cared so much for. He wondered how tight the rope would have to become around their throats before they realized it was no necktie, but a noose that could so easily strangle the life out of them.

He had tried once to tell Herr Doktor that he really needed to take the boys out of Gymnasium. The teasing was going to turn into baiting pretty soon, and move rather quickly from baiting to bullying, and the next thing anyone knew, one of them would not be returning home from class unharmed. But Herr Doktor always said the same thing: yes, Fischer was doing a wonderful job with Herschel; and no doubt Benyamin, whom he thought was a great deal smarter, would also prosper under private tutelage. But why, when there was a perfectly good German school system that turned out bright young men every year, right here in their own hometown? Surely, when it came time for the boys to go to University, Herr Doktor insisted, they would find completing Gymnasium to be a requirement for admission. Besides, everyone would wonder if there had been something wrong with them, that they had to be tutored at home. In exasperation, Fischer had told him that it was a bad time for Jews, bad and growing worse. Didn't he know –?

And Herr Doktor had cut him off sharply, speaking through clenched teeth as if to a stubborn child that would not listen to reason. "I served in The Great War", he had insisted. "I am as German as you. 'Jewish' is a religion, not a nationality. And this is my nationality: German. I know, Fischer, that I am right about this!"

Fischer had not thought it tactful to disagree with his employer at this point, and so he had said nothing more. In fact, he knew that a great number of Herr Doktor's German clients were coming to him in secret. Some of the latest edicts forbade Jewish doctors to practice in hospitals. Already Herr Doktor, along with his Jewish colleagues, had been told they were not welcome at the clinics anymore. Jewish doctors, especially gynecologists, were not to touch German women by law; and even though his treatment room downstairs remained packed most days and his doorbell still rang at odd hours to admit in secret some Aryan woman who would have no other doctor but the esteemed Doktor Rosenthaler,

Fischer feared that the day would surely come when the Doktor would pay dearly for accommodating them.

It was this new Fuehrer, this Adolf Hitler. He had risen over the last fourteen years since his failed Burgerbraukeller putsch. Now he was in charge of the entire country. His proponents had thought it would be a good change when he rose to power, and it appeared that he had glorious plans to lead the Reich to new heights. New heights, Fischer thought, as he watched Benyamin return to his Hebrew studies and quietly slid the door closed. Yes; but might the next step of these 'new heights' be off a precipice?

That Sabbath, as promised, Herr Doktor bundled the entire family, including a protesting Herschel, into the car. Fischer drove them to synagogue. There were fewer than half the usual number of cars out front, and the tally of families arriving on foot was far less than the popular synagogue usually boasted. Parked half a block away and leaning against the car with his chauffeur's cap carefully cocked to the side, Fischer lit a cigarette and pretended not to notice.

Inside the temple, Benyamin noticed. Where was Mendel? Where was Avi? And where were their parents? Mendel's father was usually cantor for the service, but he was not there today. And while there were enough men to make a minyan, there had not been enough until just a few minutes before the service was to begin, even counting Herschel. The huge hall with its intricately carved ceiling and mosaic-studded walls was very nearly empty, and the sacred words echoed hollowly from the stones. There was only a smattering of women in the balcony reserved for them. Where was everybody? Was there illness in the town? He had heard of nothing.

Rabbi Hirschfeld was there. He gave Elie and his sons a baleful glare that Benyamin surmised was supposed to be a friendly nod, and began the service. Benyamin supposed he ought to be listening, but he wasn't. He was too busy craning about, looking for his friends. Once or twice he caught his father frowning at him, and more than once Elie pinched his arm and nodded toward the front of the room. But he could not help it. He wanted to know where all the people were.

"Where is everybody?" he finally whispered to Herschel, who did not look at him. "Shut up. Follow the service," was all he said. And Benyamin turned his attention to the text, stumbling with his formation-level knowledge over the fire-letters of his faith.

His father said very little on the ride home. At the table, however, Eliana remarked to her mother, who was visiting, "What is happening to our community?" Oma Rivkeh did not respond, but Oma Bina looked up sharply. "Why?" she asked, "What do you mean?"

"Practically no one was there," Eliana said. "I couldn't believe it. I thought there might not even be a minyan, until practically the last minute. I'd say there were no more than twenty-five families there, all told."

"Maybe people are sick," Oma Rivkeh said. "Elie, is there anything passing around in the community? Fevers? Influenza?"

"Not for a long time," he said, then blushed. "We haven't been attending as regularly as we should. I've been so busy—"

"You're not at the hospital anymore, are you?" Oma Bina asked. "I hear they're kicking out Jewish doctors right and left."

"Rumor," Elie said. "They've had cutbacks. It's not because I am Jewish. Some Gentiles were let go as well."

"But why a doctor like you, someone as talented as you? Why not some of the young fellows?"

"Economics," he replied. "The younger fellows cost less money. If you can get a good doctor for half the price of a *great* doctor, you take the good doctor." He put down his fork. "Frankly, I'm relieved. I have so much to do as it is. Without the hospital I can at least keep up with my cases and have a little more time to spend with my family."

Herschel could contain himself no longer. "Oma Bina, did you hear what happened to me in school?" She braced herself on the edge of her chair, hoping not to have to hear some tale of Herschel's maltreatment because of his poor head for academics. His story concerned her deeply, but she said nothing. She would have preferred to hear that someone had cracked him with a ruler because he didn't understand what was going on in the classroom. But she could see that Herschel understood all too well. She wondered why his father chose to be so blind.

CHAPTER THREE

Slowly, slowly for Benyamin the alphabet became clearer. Rabbi Hirschfeld scowled less and his features softened to an expression of mild dyspepsia.

Benyamin awaited the day that he would become a man.

He had his fears – that he would muddle the prayers, or that his memory would fail him entirely, and the letters he had painstakingly learned to string into words with only an occasional stumble would return to the fire from whence they had come, leaving him choking on their smoke, breathless and panicked in front of all of his friends and elders. He also had his hopes – a pile of presents bigger than the one that Herschel had gotten. He hoped it did not seem unkind; his brother had been so nice to him, giving him extra help with his Hebrew and memorization, giving him the silver pen from his hoard. But he expected he would get better presents, because he was *smarter* than Herschel. Reading in German was easy, and Benyamin could cipher with the best of them. He had won academic medals almost without trying; at least before things had become so biased at school and he had found himself shuffled to the back of the classroom. Hebrew seemed the same; at least when he and Herschel practiced in their room, it seemed easier than he had anticipated, and it grew simpler by the day. What would it be like on his personal great and terrible day of reckoning?

Indeed, the great day went by without a hint of failure. He wore his new black wool suit and shiny black shoes and the beaded yarmulke his mother made for him. He had practiced over and over how to drape his tallis and he did it perfectly, without his father's help. He did not drop the

Torah, despite his worst nightmares. He recited perfectly, and thought he detected a sigh from Rabbi Hirschfeld, comparable to a wild, leaping dance of uncontrollable pride from anyone else. He saw happy tears in his mother's eyes and a smile on his father's lips.

But where were his friends? Kruger, who usually ate lunch with him, Eisenbart and Werner, Baum and even the timid little Girly Fritz – not a single one of them was there. He had sent out the invitations, and checked with Anya again and again to make certain that they would arrive on time. He had even checked with a couple of them at school. Yes, they had received his invitations. They congratulated him on his achievement of manhood, and he expected lavish presents from them. But they hadn't come, and neither had his anticipated wealth. He'd scanned the audience periodically, looking for Eisenbart's blond hair or Baum's freckles, but they never appeared. Anya and Fischer were there, but Anya remained with the women preparing the feast, and Fischer stayed outside; keeping an eye on the automobile, he said.

The banquet afterward was lavish: very carefully kosher. He invited in two poor passersby, who ate voraciously. Having performed a mitzvah in his very first hour as a man, he felt peace in his heart as he surveyed the bright pile of gifts – books and pens and more money than he had ever possessed at once, even without the anticipated German hoard of presents. Oma Bina suggested that she invest the money for him, and he knew better than to protest. Herschel gave him a silver Passover wine cup that Benyamin suspected he had not picked out. Fischer gave him a pocketknife, which he promised to keep secret, since his father had insisted that no matter how much of a man he might be, he should not have one, lest in trying it out he should cut himself or damage something precious.

And Anya – That night Benyamin got into his nightshirt as usual and fell asleep earlier than he expected, probably due to the quantity of wine he drank at the bar mitzvah. He gradually became aware of soft breathing on his neck and the unmistakable scent of her soap, her soft arms around his middle…

"Shhh," she said. "Shhh. Don't wake your brother."

Anya had massaged him before, when he pulled a muscle or became overwrought about something, and he was used to her hands on him. While her ministrations always soothed him, he had always wished for something more than what she gave. Tonight she went beyond anything he had imagined, her hands working a magic he had never known before. But she would not allow him to touch her. "You are a man," she whispered in his ear. "I cannot allow you what I can give only to my husband."

It was a few days before he could separate dream from reality, and when he did, he asked Herschel about it.

"Yes," Herschel said. "She gave me the same 'present' after my bar mitzvah. She said that now I would *really* be a man."

CHAPTER FOUR

It was during summer vacation that Benyamin saw Adolf Hitler.

LiLo had come down with influenza, and Oma Bina had brought Ezra to stay with the Rosenthalers for two weeks, until she recovered. "Goodness knows," Oma Bina had said, "Ayelet cannot look after two ill people *and* this robust running-around child. He will be no trouble, and plenty of company for your boys."

Benyamin wished it was Ezra home ill and LiLo by his side as they frolicked in the park. But Ezra was a good enough companion, and Benyamin enjoyed being able to tease Ezra about his Hebrew pronunciation, telling him what a 'baby' he was and how fortunate it was that Benyamin, now a man, still deigned to play with him. Ezra was still half a year from bar mitzvah.

On this particular day, Fischer had given reluctant permission to Herschel to escape his studies and take a few minutes of air, and so he joined his brother and cousin. The boys had just headed down Ringstrasse in search of sweets at one of the many shops when they noticed that a crowd was gathering. Quickly the boys fell in with the press and found themselves pushed to the front by the throng.

Now they could hear, in the distance, the thrumping of drums and marching feet, the pinging of glockenspiels, the blaring of brass horns and above it all, the growing swelling and cheering of the crowd. "It is the *Fuehrer*, someone shouted. The *Fuehrer* is coming this way!" Benyamin saw Herschel's face muscles go taut. The older boy seized his brother and cousin by the hand and attempted to drag them away, but Benyamin fought him and broke free. "I want to stay!" he said. "It's a parade, Herschel! I want to *see*!"

And indeed, it *was* a parade. First came the flag bearers, with the German colors, then row after row after row of a startling flag; red outer panels with a white center, upon which was emblazoned a symbol; not X, not Z. Behind these many flags stepped young men that Benyamin could describe only in superlatives. Each was tall and most were blond. They wore armbands on their brown shirts, smart caps and jodhpur pants. Each carried a rifle slung over one shoulder and each wore the most beautiful shiny black boots. They lifted each leg high, almost to ninety degrees, and looked neither to the right nor to the left.

Benyamin's eyes left those magnificent men reluctantly, to survey the central person in all of this fanfare. Several cars preceded and followed his, but there was no doubt as to who he was.

Hitler stood up in his open-top car, which made it clear that he was the person of note. He was dressed in military uniform. His dark hair was in sharp contrast to the Nordic marchers that had preceded him. Although standing in the car placed his head above those of the spectators, Benyamin wondered how tall he really was. His face was sunburned and his eyes were partially hidden by his military cap. He wore a short mustache, trimmed closely, so that it appeared little more than a vertical slash of black under his nose. He raised his hand in a beatific pose, almost as if he were Christ blessing the people, like in the Kolendom's stained glass windows. The throng cried out in almost a unified voice, "*Sieg Heil! Sieg Heil!*" Women were holding their babies up so that the little ones could see the important man in the car. Men threw their hats in the air. People were screaming. Near him a teenage girl swooned.

"Hey! Hey!" Benyamin called out, and raised his hand to wave. Herschel pulled his arm down. At that moment, the man looked in their direction. Afterward, Benyamin could never be sure if Hitler had actually directed his gaze upon him; and if he indeed saw him personally, if he had smiled or sneered at him. But he caught sight of the man's eyes: twin jet-hued daggers that bored for a micro-second into his own face with such force that Benyamin staggered backward from their intensity.

Behind Hitler's car came more music and more flags and more of the young, high-stepping men. Males from the crowd broke free of the throng and fell in behind the marchers, eager to be a part of them; to join their ranks, if they could. Even old men marched for a short space with them. The air was electric with celebration. Herschel did not wait around to celebrate, however, He took both boys firmly by the hand and propelled them back in the direction of home. As they reached their stairs, Ezra looked up quizzically and squeezed Herschel's hand.

"We Jews are waiting for a special person to come to liberate us from bondage and lead us into an age of prosperity," he said. "They say such things about this man. He is not the *Meschiach*, is he?"

"Far from it," Herschel said. "He is the Devil."

After the parade, Benyamin became aware of the changes around Koln. They seemed to be everywhere, these handsome young men in their dashing uniforms. Anya's beau no longer met her in the Kolendom, but afterward, in the plaza for only a moment, if he met her at all. Herschel would not linger about with her as he might have years ago, but quickly dragged Benyamin away before the young man reached them. What a sight the fellow had become! He was always attired, now, in the Nazi uniform, with its jodhpurs and incredibly shiny black boots. How Benyamin envied him those boots! How many nights he dreamed of himself strutting along behind Hitler's town car or swaggering across the plaza to meet some young golden-haired fraulein in just such boots!

"You can't get them," Herschel told him. "They're only for the Nazis."

"Then I'll become a Nazi," Benyamin said. "I want a pair of those boots. I wish I hadn't given all of my bar mitzvah money to Oma Bina, or I'd get Anya to take me to get a pair right now."

"You can't be a Nazi. You're a Jew," Herschel said. "And now you're a Jewish *man*. Only Aryans can be Nazis."

"Papa was a hero in the Great War," Benyamin said. "He won the Iron Cross. In his pictures he has on big black boots. Our father wore them and he is a Jew. So it's not true that only Nazis wear them."

Herschel sighed. "The times have changed, Chen," he said. "They don't give Jews big shiny boots anymore." Then almost to himself, he added, "They just put them on and kick Jews' asses with them."

Benyamin decided to ignore his brother. Herschel was, after all, not that smart. He still was no great student, no matter how fantastically Fischer said he was doing. He had been put out of the Gymnasium; he *said* because he was Jewish and Knacht wouldn't allow him into class anymore because of 'policies'. Benyamin suspected otherwise. He had watched his brother bent over his texts far into the night. He knew how much trouble he had; how much preparation he made for the simplest examination, and how miserable he was after each low mark. So where did his great awareness of international affairs come from? True, he spent a great deal of time in discussions with Oma Bina, and when they went to visit the lumberyard, he talked mainly with Aunt Ayelet and Uncle Reuven. The three of them were always listening to the radio these days, and discussing their conclusions in hushed voices. Benyamin sat in with

44

them once or twice, but he became bored and did not seek to be included anymore.

Despite being a man, now, Benyamin still preferred to run and rip through the lumberyard and surrounding woods with LiLo. She never bored him with politics and world affairs. She usually occupied him with things that involved climbing and jumping and hand-to-hand strength tests. She had acquired an archery kit for her latest birthday, and they must have spent whole afternoons perfecting their aim at the bright red circle in the middle of the target. He showed LiLo the knife he got from Fischer, and they practiced whittling; first with bars of soap (that got them into trouble) and then with discarded wood. Sometimes they read stories, or listened to the radio, but only to the music stations; not the boring news.

Benyamin asked LiLo about the boots, and was shocked when *she* told him he couldn't have them. "You're Jewish," she said. "The shiny black boots are just for Nazis, now. You can't wear them. You'll get in trouble." He didn't respond. Surely she was wrong. But then again, what did she know? She was just a girl.

One Sunday as autumn approached he decided to raise the question with his father. Elie sat in the parlor in his favorite chair in his favorite smoking jacket, a stack of periodicals on his side table, looking across the street at the spires of the Kolendom. He puffed thoughtfully on his cigar, which filled the parlor with its leafy fragrance. An empty wineglass and plate sat on the table next to him and the remains of smoked salmon, pickled pearl onions, and crackers, his father's favorite snack, stained the plate. Benyamin decided that this was probably the best time to ask for his boots. He had his speech all ready, and positioned himself in his father's line of sight. Elie lowered his gaze and looked enquiringly at him over his pince-nez.

"Papa, I see the men in the street," he said. "They have shiny black boots, like you had in the Great War. I was wondering – winter will be coming soon, and I would like a pair."

He waited, fully expecting his father to give him a beneficent smile and then order Anya to take him immediately to get his heart's desire. Instead, his father's affable expression disappeared. "You can't get that kind of boots," he said.

"But Papa, I *want* them," he said. His father was scowling now.

"Quiet! I won't hear another word about those boots! You can't have them and that is that!" He rose out of his chair and stood over Benyamin, who was shocked at how much taller he seemed and how angry he was. Still, he wanted the boots so badly. He could see them on his legs. He could feel the leather, warm and supple beneath his fingers. No matter how angry his father got, he *had* to have them.

"Papa –"

"No, I said; NO!" His father's face was purplish. "They are Nazi boots. No self-respecting Jew wants to wear Nazi boots!"

"Then," Benyamin said, "I don't want to be Jewish anymore. I will run away and become a Nazi!"

The blow was so sudden that he was picking himself up from the carpet before he felt the pain in his cheek. His father looked as shocked as he felt. "Oh, Son!" he cried out. "I didn't mean to – I didn't *mean* –"

Privately Benyamin exulted. His father had crossed a great line, a barrier that he had never traversed with another human being in his life. He had struck his son in the face, struck him out of anger, and now he felt horrible about it. Surely, Benyamin thought as he clutched his face, he would get the boots now. He hoped his face would swell or at least bruise, so that his father would feel doubly guilty until the boots arrived.

His father took him down the back stairs to his sacred domain, settled him on the examination table, and swabbed at his cheek with liniment. He checked Benyamin's joints all over, unguent at the ready, but aside from the cheek, nothing had been injured. He pressed an ice pack against Benyamin's cheek and then ushered him back upstairs. Then he pulled Anya aside and had a few words with her. She threw her cloak on and immediately rushed out into the street.

"She is going to get my boots," Benyamin thought, and settled happily back on his pillows, pressing the ice pack to his offended cheek and seeing himself in his mind's eye, marching along the streets, planting his feet heel-first, lifting his legs high, as the Nazis did; as much to show off the boots as to show his national pride. Anya returned a few minutes later; not with boots, but with chocolates.

"I am so sorry, Son," his father said as he held out the box to him. "I promise, I will never, ever strike you again."

Benyamin took the box and made the expected responses to his father; appeasement words, but he did not feel them in his heart. Every bite of the chocolates was like sawdust. He took them up to his room, an action that was usually verboten, but which his father did not forbid today. He handed them to Herschel, who wondered what he had done to deserve such a gift.

Benyamin climbed into bed that night, his spirits at low ebb. He certainly knew better than to pursue the boot issue anymore. He lay beneath the eiderdown, contemplating the ceiling, listening to Herschel's even breathing. What was a Nazi, and what really was a Jew? He realized how much he didn't know about the world, how little he had understood as he plodded through his bar mitzvah lessons. His eyes grew heavy and he dozed.

He caught her scent before she crawled into his bed. Anya, with her sweet-scented body, molded herself to his back. He felt her wet lips on his cheek, her breath on the back of his neck, her soft hands, moving, moving. The shiny black boots faded from his mind under the gentleness of her caresses.

Herschel had to go to school somewhere. Eliana wasn't happy with his just being tutored by Fischer. "Who's going to accept him into University without Gymnasium credentials?" she asked. "No offense, Fischer, but you haven't taught in a classroom for some time." Anya shot Fischer a quick look as he opened his mouth, and he fell silent. There were, he realized, things Frau Eliana and Herr Doktor were just not ready to hear, and maybe there would not come to be such a time when they could.

Oma Bina had recommended this particular school, which was run by her own cousin's husband, a German, in Frankfurt. It was a residential shop where young men learned to build and repair machines; and though it was some distance away, she was sure that, at nearly seventeen, Herschel could manage the separation. "Younger boys than he leave home," she told a tearful Eliana, "He will do quite well, I am sure."

"But why so far away?" she asked. "Why can't he work with Reuven and Ayelet at the lumberyard? He'd at least be with family."

Oma Bina sighed and folded her hands. "How much work do you think they are getting there, with the boycotts? The private contractors still come, but the government contracts are all but dry. Ayelet can hardly keep the shop going and Reuven gets sicker every day. They just couldn't manage another mouth to feed." Eliana was shocked. She had not realized Reuven and Ayelet's situation. Everything always looked so *—orderly —* when she went to visit. She began to suspect that her mother-in-law was now supplementing the Salzenstein Lumberyard's income.

"Bad business decisions," Elie said. "Comes of having a woman at the head. Ayelet is a good woman, and strong; but she can't run a business. Men don't like to work with a woman. They should think about getting a man to run things there."

Oma Bina looked at him for a long time. "Ayelet is the reason the business did not go under long ago," she said. "That woman is an amazing person. She can do anything she puts her mind to and everything she touches turns to gold. But she can't do anything about the laws Hitler put in place. He says Germans can't buy from Jews and I don't know a Jew who is short-sighted enough to build anything in Germany right now."

"Nonsense," Elie said. "It's just poor management. Who checks the books?"

"*I* do," Oma Bina said. "And every receipt, every expenditure, every single thing is correct. But the business is failing because of these crazy laws."

"I have total faith in the government," Elie said. "I'm sure they'll get it right soon. They are new, after all, and at least we aren't looking at a billion *Reichsmarks* to the dollar, like in the days of the Chancellor."

"There are rumors that they'll come after us Jews, like in the days before the Great War," Oma Bina said. Elie just laughed.

"That's foolishness," he said. "Even to *imagine* that the pogroms could come back is foolishness. These are civilized times. Besides, we are not *poor* Jews. I am a doctor and a German citizen. I was decorated with the Iron Cross in the Great War. If they come after me at all, it will be to urge me to serve our country again, as a doctor or a soldier." He drew himself up to his full height, and added, "And I shall be ready!"

Oma Bina threw her hands into the air. "I wish you were right," she said. "But the reason your son is not in school and the reason you don't work at the hospital anymore are certainly not because of choices *you* made."

Herschel left two days later, bathed in a lather of tears from his mother and Anya. Fischer drove him to Frankfurt. "I'll write to you," Herschel called cheerily to Benyamin. Benyamin wished it were he and not Herschel leaving for an adventure in a new town. But he was to be the scholar of the family, and to be a scholar one must remain at Gymnasium.

CHAPTER FIVE

A year passed, and a little more. On the rare occasions that they ventured to the synagogue they found fewer and fewer men occupying the polished mahogany pews. Once even Benyamin was counted to make up the minyan. Boys were disappearing from his Gymnasium classes, too. Sometimes, on his way to school, he passed one of them. The boy would stare at him for an instant, and then scurry off on some errand of apparent urgency. Sometimes Benyamin would call after them: "Hey, Greenbaum! Avi! Wait up! Why aren't you coming to classes anymore?" but they would not stop to tell him.

And then came the biggest blow of all: Anya was leaving.

With Herschel gone, she had spent many a night in his bed, snuggled up to him and working her magic beneath the eiderdown. He was never allowed to reciprocate, however, and there was one place she would not take him or allow him to go: she said she was saving that ultimate gift for her wedding night. Not even the University student could go there, she said, and she had defended that sacred space even from her lecherous prior master. According to Anya, she wanted to marry the University student some day, and with no dowry or personal wealth of any kind, she had only her purity to offer him as her dowry. Benyamin had not seen the University student at the Kolendom for some time, but then Benyamin had not gone there for some time himself. Anya had simply stopped taking him, and finally she herself had stopped going, even though he had gleaned from his half-attention to the sermons that missing even a single week could send her to hell, poor Christian girl! On the rare occasions that she did leave the house, he assumed, though he had no proof, that she might be trysting with her University student somewhere. He felt jealousy, though he knew she was not meant for him. He tried not to think of her twining her hands around someone else's body, kissing someone else's neck.

Her eyes were red and her lashes haloed in tears the last time he saw her in the house. She hugged him hard, and he pressed his gift: a gold pen, one of two he'd gotten for his bar mitzvah, into her hand. Elie gave her a sum of money and Eliana gave her linen and table napkins. Fischer offered to take her to the train station, but she said her University student was coming and he would see her safely there. Fischer begged her to meet her young man outside the house, and said he would carry her trunk and its dolly to the pavement so that he would not have to come into the house to get it. He asked if he should accompany her to the station, or even drive them both there, but she said 'no', she thought the University student would be insulted. Besides, it was not so far. She stood at the bottom of the stairs with Fischer until the young man came.

Benyamin sobbed in his room. He did not know how he would live without his Anya. He stared blankly at his desk clock for a while, and then it occurred to him: he knew where the rail station was. He could say 'goodbye' once more; just once more. Quietly, so as not to alert his mother, his father or Fischer, he slipped into his jacket and down the back stairs, through his father's office vestibule, and up the four stone steps to the street. Then he ran as if pursued; all the way to the station, mindless of the painful stitch in his side.

The train was not yet in. She stood tall and straight on the platform, her yellow hair loose and resplendent in the afternoon sun, her yellow print silk dress blowing about her shapely legs. Next to her, equally blond, equally handsome, stood her beau. He wore the full Nazi soldier's uniform. He carried weaponry and wore the Swastika armband – and upon his feet were the shiniest black boots Benyamin had seen to date.

Anya looked up. "Benyamin –" she started, and then looked anxiously at her beau, who looked questioningly at her. "He is – was – He lived in the house where I worked," she said. Benyamin noted that she trembled.

"They were *Jewish?*" the student asked. "But they came to church with you every Sunday. I didn't know! You mean, the man that handed over your trunk to me was not your employer?" Then he nodded. "Ah, the Nuremberg laws. So it wasn't as you said, just a deep desire to be with your family that is sending you to Poland. They are *Jews!*"

"I don't work for them anymore."

"Of *course* not," the student said. "They are Jews. *Jews!* You shouldn't have worked for them in the first place! It is illegal now!"

"Benyamin, why did you come?" she asked. "It's not safe. Is Fischer with you? Go home right now!"

"I came to say 'goodbye' again," he said, mindful of how high and thin his voice sounded; how young it made him seem. He had never imagined that she would send him away so abruptly, and had envisioned some impassioned adieu on the railway platform, with many tears and more kisses. The worst that he had thought might happen was that he would have been too late for the train and that she would have been gone. In his scenario of bidding her one more 'goodbye' he had failed to script in the University student, this grand fellow decked out in his uniform, that made Benyamin look so childish, even though the Jewish faith said he was a man. Nor had he even considered that the formerly innocuous suitor to Anya could look on him with such hatred, caressing the weapons on his belt as he glowered down at him. Anya grabbed the young man's arm.

"But it is all right now, Hans," she said. "I don't work for them now. I will go to my family in Poland and when you are ready you will come for me."

Hans pulled away. "Polish bitch!" he hissed. "To think I wanted you— to think I even thought of marrying you! To think I put up with not having you; of respecting your wish to stay pure, when you've been wallowing in a sty with swine! You are filthy! Do you hear! *Filthy!*" He turned to Benyamin.

"And you—" he raised a fist and waved it in Benyamin's face. Benyamin was too frightened to run. "I could break your little neck! You—you—*Jew!*"

Tears began to roll down Anya's cheeks. "Don't hurt him, Hans!" she cried. "It's not his fault; *please!*"

Hans' face was purple. "You made a fool of me!" he said. "But I should have known; you're Polish. You're a Slav! You're an inferior! And who knows? You *say* your parents are dead; how do I know you aren't a Jew yourself? There are blond Jews!"

"Please—please, Hans," she said. "I am sorry; so sorry. I'm going back to Poland. You never have to see me again. Just don't hurt the boy. Please. For me," she said, and her eyes filled with tears once more. "Promise me you'll see him home safely, so nobody else hurts him. I have money--" She fumbled inside her bodice for her money-purse.

Hans smiled suddenly: a lopsided snarl of a smile that was worse than his scowl. "You're going to pay for his safety," he said, "but not with your filthy Jew money!" He seized her wrist. Then he turned to Benyamin. "Sit on this trunk for a moment, fellow," he said. "We will be gone for just a little while." Then he turned to Anya. "I'll keep him safe—for now—for a price," he said, wiping his lips with the palm of his hand. "The *ultimate* price. And *now*. Otherwise—"

Her lower lip quivered and tears spurted down her cheeks, but she nodded numbly. He yanked her toward the end of the platform where there was a remote alcove in the wall and shoved her into it. The two or three other people on the platform moved quickly away. Benyamin had a good idea of what he was making her do for the price of his own safe conduct home. He tried not to think of it and he tried not to weep, even when he heard her cry out in fear and pain, even when he heard Hans snort and chuckle and curse at her for her tears. Hans half-dragged her out of the niche and back down to Benyamin and her trunk as the approaching train sounded its whistle. Anya wiped at her tearstained cheeks, smoothed her ripped and rumpled dress, drew Benyamin into her arms and gave him a hard squeeze. "Hans will not hurt you," she said. "God protect you, Bennychen." She stepped onto the train. Hans handed up her trunk to the porter and with a chuckle waved to the train windows, but she did not appear.

"Come, my little *Jew-kind*," Hans said to Benyamin. Benyamin was terrified to go with him, but he did not know what might happen if he disobeyed. The two of them walked away from the station, toward the Ring. Despite what he had made Anya do, Hans smiled and made jokes most of the way. He talked about Anya as if she was the smuttiest woman on earth; Benyamin could not be sure, because he had never heard a man talk about what he did to a woman before. Hans said that, when he finished his military service, he intended to fetch her from Cracow and bring her back to Cologne as his workhorse and love-slave, whether she wanted to come or not; and if she resisted him he would beat her and then tell everyone what she had done on the train platform with him, and embellish the tale so that no other man would ever want her. "Thank you, little Jew-Boy," Hans said with a chuckle that made Benyamin feel odd in his belly. "Do you know what she did for me to save your worthless hide? I would never have gotten that going-away present without your coming to the station! I guess I owe you something, so I will not put a gun to the back of your neck and do what I promised her I would not. She paid for you and she paid well, so never forget that!" Then he turned to what he considered more pleasant topics.

"So," Hans said. "Do you have a little Jew-girl that you like?"

If he had asked on yesterday, Benyamin might have said "yes" and extolled Anya's virtues as those of some Jewish girl he was yet to meet; Anya, no matter what this fellow thought of her, was still his ideal for a wife, spoiled or not. But something made him hold his tongue. Anya was no Jew. She was a golden-haired Aryan princess, and there were laws about consorting with such princesses if one was not a golden-haired prince. He shook his head dumbly, and tried not to listen to the man's overly-descriptive diatribe against Anya and all women.

And now they reached his street on the Ring. People were about their errands, or working, or just sitting in their parlors. Many of his neighbors, he knew, were not Jewish. But as he passed home after home, he realized that suddenly the parlor shades were being drawn; that people were rushing into their houses and closing the doors; that people were driving away. It was as if he had brought a pestilence with him: a Nazi in full dress. It could not bode well, and indeed, he wondered how he would shake the man once he reached his door. He wondered even if he should go to his door. If the man knew where he lived, would he come back, now that Anya was gone, to hunt him?

56

He was not aware of Fischer until he felt the grab at the back of his jacket.

"Where have you been, Benyamin Rosenthaler?" Fischer screamed at him, his face red and angry. He looked at the University student. "So much trouble, these Jews! I am a neighbor; I—I helped the young girl with her trunk. This boy's mother has been troubling us all, banging on our doors looking for her little brat! Horrible people! I can't believe that girl was actually working for them!"

Hans said nothing to him, but he bent to glare with his blue-black eyes into Benyamin's face. "I will come back for you someday, my lovely boy! And I will roast your Jewish behind!" He straightened, took a step backward, and gave Fischer the Hitler salute, which Fischer returned; he knew better than to refuse. He took his stand in large crowds; he had even defied the law and folded his arms at the launching of the *Horst Wessel*; but he knew how to mimic a good Nazi when he needed to.

As he watched Hans stomp away from his doorstep and down the street, Benyamin realized he no longer had any desire for the boots. He didn't know much about the Nazis and their philosophy, if one could call it that, except what he had heard from snatches of conversation between Oma Bina and Uncle Reuven and Herschel at table. The National Socialist Party had been in power for nearly five years, now, and they had done a lot of things against Jewish people. The Salzenstein lumberyards were now in the hands of German 'businessmen', and Aunt Ayelet complained almost every time he saw her about how the quality of wood had gone down. Their business had been seized, and was being run by Germans. Their family had been kicked out of their wonderful wooden house, and they were now living in an apartment somewhere closer to the city with no income and only what they were able to grab before the bank froze their accounts. Uncle Reuven had taken a turn for the worse, and Oma Bina was talking about moving with him to a better climate. His father was seeing only a few German patients, stealthily and late at night when the streets were empty. And then there was what happened to Ezra.

It happened three blocks from his home. He was coming back from synagogue. Suddenly a van drew up and swept him off the street and inside. He rode, crowded up against other Jews that had as little idea of why they had been apprehended or where they were going as he did. For two weeks his frantic family had no clue where he might be. Then had come the letter, on official paper. Ezra was being held at Dachau, the concentration camp outside Munich. He would be returned unharmed – provided the family sent a sum of money: a large sum even for the doctor and the former business owners. With Oma Binna's help, they had scraped together the necessary funds. A week later, Ezra had come home; dirty, sick and much leaner, but intact.

Elie had insisted to the entire family that Ezra must have done *something*; that the government would not just scoop up innocent people off the streets, and that Ezra should be made to pay back the ransom money. It was at this point that Fischer had been unable to control his consternation. "Don't you know what is going on? Can't you see it? Herr Doktor, how plain must it be? They won't stop until you're dead – until you're *all* dead!"

Fischer had held a mild interest in the new leader when he rose to power, and so he had invested in his books, and read them, first with curiosity and then with alarm. If the man – no, the *fiend* – did even half of what he proposed –

But who would do such preposterous things? Fischer had long ago thrust the books and their propositions out of his mind. Now what he had tried to forget flooded back afresh. The latest reforms – the restrictions and boycotts, the quiet deaths and disappearances in the night – he was convinced. His mother had put it best: "They burned books," she said of the action five years before. "Heinrich Heine said 'when books are burned human beings are destined to be burned, too.' Mark my words, they intend to kill the Jews, every mother's son of them." Fischer believed his mother. She had never, ever lied to him, and he knew she was not lying now.

But how could this otherwise intelligent doctor stand in front of him and insist that everything that had happened had some very logical and even benign explanation? There was only one possibility; he could see it, but if this man chose not to see it, what would become of this family that Fischer loved so much? How could Herr Doktor see the signs of his mother's cancer quickly enough to save her life but not perceive what was happening to his people in time to save his own?

"Herschel is being educated in Frankfurt," Elie said to his chauffeur, "so there is no tutoring task for you here. And I am quite capable of driving myself. Perhaps, Herr Fischer, we no longer require your services here. And certainly we do not need to hear you railing against our beloved Germany and its leaders. You may go—now!"

Everyone stared at Elie. Fischer had been nothing but helpful to them, and his outburst had come only because of his concern.

"*Eliezar!*" Oma Bina had cried. "*Surely* you will not send away your faithful Fischer! How will your household manage?" She knew that Fischer helped Eliana with the cooking and the household chores—no, performed them himself—now that Anya was gone. She recognized that Fischer also had his finger on the pulse of what was happening in the

Aryan community. He knew things and he shared them with her. He was her barometer. She could not lose him.

"It would be a terrible mistake to let Fischer go," Eliana added. "I need him here. Surely you can understand that his objection is not political, but out of concern."

Fischer said nothing. He nodded to Elie, tipped his chauffeur's cap to the ladies and rumpled Benyamin's hair, even though the child was a man now. He turned and went up the stairs to clear out his things.

"Go up there, Benyamin," Elie said. "See to it that he doesn't take anything. And Eliana, do not ever disagree with me in front of the servants again!"

Oma Bina scowled at him. "How can she?" she asked. "You *have* no more servants!"

"We will have them soon enough again; as soon as this instability is over and the government settles in."

"It has been five years," Eliana said. "Perhaps Fischer and your mother are right; perhaps this is no 'settling', but the way the Fuehrer will be doing business with us Jews." Eliana's mother shushed her, but Elie hardly noticed.

"Benyamin!" he said, "Go upstairs with that man now and watch everything he does! He will not leave this house with a splinter or a spoon that he did not bring here!"

Benyamin followed, but he did not spy. He sat mournfully at the bottom of the man's bed and watched as Fischer packed his linens and his books. "Do you really think the Nazis will kill us?" he asked.

"Surely," Fischer said, "unless you get out of Germany, and that soon!"

60

CHAPTER SIX

The Gymnasium grew tenser and emptier. Benyamin could not help but note the absence of every other Jewish child in his classes. Nor could he ignore the proliferation of brown shirts and accompanying hard stares from his classmates. Eisenbart growled at him when he offered him Hamantaschen from Purim, though only a year ago the boy had drooled over the sweets until Benyamin gave him several. With all social avenues closed, Benyamin actually studied his lessons. Trigonometry, recently such an agony for him, began to make sense, as did the teachings of the philosophers. He still daydreamed—sad little musings chiefly based on Anya and her terrible last moments with him—but mostly he studied.

There was no sense in telling his father about the changes at the Gymnasium; he simply would not listen. "If they are making you sit in the back of the classroom now, if they are failing you despite your hard work, then you are not working hard enough!" Elie told him. His mother listened, but only shook her head. "My poor baby!" she would say. "My poor precious baby!" Craving neither derision nor pity, Benyamin stayed in his room, drawing bridges and the fantastic houses he saw in his imagination, and coming down only for meals or when Oma Rivkeh came for her Sabbath visits. He saw Oma Bina on Sundays now. She never came anymore on the Sabbath; "Too many people are watching where people spend their Saturdays," she said.

Oma Bina listened to Benyamin with more attention than he realized. "You don't say!" she would comment. "Three more this week than last, in the brown shirts? What do you think of that?" When he reported Girly Fritz's disappearance from class, she agreed that it was probably because his classmates had reported him to the authorities, or that his parents had sensibly sent him out of country, even though as far as anyone knew, he was a hundred percent German. Suspected homosexuals and the mentally ill, she said, were not welcome in Hitler's world. There were reports of institutions for 're-learning' that such people went into, but never came out of, and even of trucks with suspicious hoses emerging from them that people climbed into the backs of to go for a ride they never returned from. Elie remarked that she needed to check her sources; at a time that the administration was looking for brains and manpower, how could she be so foolish as to believe that it would put people to death that might recover and make the nation great?

Oma Bina remarked casually one Sunday afternoon that she thought Elie looked pale, and maybe he should consider a vacation. "The seashore might be nice," she said. "Or maybe a trip abroad. I am going with Reuven to Switzerland for a few weeks," she said. "I'm thinking about seeing America too, before I am too old to travel. What do you think?" Elie only frowned. "You mean, you're running away! You're thinking about leaving Germany and never coming back! I can't believe you are leaving," he said. "This is a time when Germany needs its best, and what is happening? Its best are deserting!"

"Goodness, Elie!" Oma Bina said. "It's not like we're not coming back *ever*! We're off to see a specialist and maybe a different part of the world, and then we're back here as quick as you please. Say, why don't you come with us? Benyamin's school is on vacation in a matter of days, and Eliana says you have far fewer patients –"

Elie shot Eliana a withering glare. "Eliana does not run my affairs," he said icily. "She has no idea whom I see and whom I don't see. Anyway, I'm fine, and I cannot leave my practice."

Oma Bina cut her visit short; she said she had to make arrangements to leave. She slipped quickly into her car and was gone.

Benyamin took the charcoals his grandmother had brought him and slipped up to his room, but he did not take out drawing paper. Instead he lay on his back, staring up at the blank white ceiling. For an instant he considered decorating it as Michelangelo had done the Sistine Chapel ceiling, but he could think of no explanation for such a thing that his father would accept, and besides, he could think of no topic for so grand an opus. Eventually he fell asleep, but his dreams were of running and hiding and war and the man in the open touring car and the man in the black shiny boots on the train platform, both with the same killing black eyes.

His dreams became reality only a few days later.

The boys were in the classroom, packing their things for the spring break. Benyamin was jubilant: three weeks without ice-blue glares from his classmates' eyes. Carefully he loaded his rucksack with his books, heaviest on the bottom, so that nothing got squished; and he sprinkled his pens and compasses among them. He wished he'd pushed a little harder to go to Switzerland; but he supposed he'd wished it too late, since Oma Bina and his Uncle Reuven would be leaving the next day; and though it would be the Sabbath, he understood why they would travel on that day. If they were to convince the authorities that they were not Jews—that they really were the Germans their fake passports said they were—they must be about when Jews were not, no matter what their personal thoughts about violating the Sabbath might be.

Surely there were happier people in Switzerland; people who wouldn't glare when they passed them on the street. Here in Cologne, people who only months before, or maybe it had just been weeks before, had smiled pleasantly at him, now glowered threateningly at him. The headmaster did not wave to him or call out a cheery, "Have a great vacation! Be safe!" to him as he did to the other boys. Solitarily Benyamin pushed open the heavy oaken door and stepped out into the sunshine that shone without prejudice upon all.

He missed the boys that used to walk alongside him: Eisenbart and Fritsch and Heuer. He missed their occasional forays to the local cake shops, where they sipped tea and ate sweet cakes and talked about this girl or that passing on the cobbled streets outside the window. Herr Brecht's shop was shut, now: its sweets all gone, its huge glass window marked with a *magen david* carelessly scrawled and beneath it the single word **JUDE,** which explained why such a prosperous business was no more. Herr Brecht was gone, too: gone with his family to Holland, it was rumored, though there were some that said he had been Disappeared, meaning he would not be returning, even after this nasty business with the government was over. He missed the Jewish boys, too; rushing home on a Friday to prepare for Shabbas, mulling over the mysteries of the Torah, taking a break to discuss with academic earnestness the physical attributes of this or that young lady passing on the street.

He wondered if he would ever walk these streets again as a friend to boys his age, rucksacks on their backs, heading for boyish adventures. Would Eisenbart ever beg him for Hamantaschen again, or would Schick ever ask for his help with composition? Would Voegel and Schwartz come back to class, so they could play chess during lunch? Would Poetzl ever finish his tale of courting Liesl Frey? Would –

"Benyamin! Hey, Benyamin!"

His heart leapt. Eisenbart, Schick and Poetzl lazed against the butcher shop wall with two boys he didn't know. His classmates; his friends. He'd come to regard their brown shirts as corollary to the school's gray shirt and blue tie uniform. He'd even wondered if *he* might show up one day in a brown shirt. He wore plain Oxfords, short gray pants and black socks, while all five boys wore those formerly coveted shiny black boots, brown long pant cuffs tucked inside them. Lucky! He thought it aloud. Lucky, to have been born German and able to wear such great clothes, while he was denied. But wasn't he a German, too? His father said so. His father had fought in the Great War, and had been decorated by the Kaiser himself. His shiny medal hung carefully mounted in its frame in his office; Benyamin had seen it himself. Who could deny him his right to citizenship in this country for which his own father had risked his life? Surely people understood that!

He grinned and headed toward the boys with a grateful trot. It wasn't until he was almost upon them that he realized he was the only person smiling.

"Stupid Jew!" Poetzl said, with venom in his voice. "*Jew!*" one of the unknown boys said. "Let's get the Jew!" He stood, a truncheon in his hand, measuring its weight against his open palm. They loped casually toward Benyamin: one boy swinging the truncheon, one gripping something Benyamin could not make out.

It took a moment to register: they were going to beat him; *him. He* was the Jew! So Fischer was right, and the Jews that had left already were right, and his father, the Grosse Doktor, who swore he was right about everything, was wrong. He felt the fear rising in him, and he felt something else: an anger; an outrage that, he never knew until this instant, lived somewhere private deep inside him but was now awakened and incensed. He snatched the truncheon from the surprised boy's hand and swung it with the mad accuracy of some Maccabean ancestor. *Crack!*

Crack! Crack! The other boys drew back in shock and horrified awe as Benyamin swung again and again and again at the boy's head. Blood gushed from a wide gash in his skull. Then Benyamin began his assault on the others. Two fell in their rush to get away from him, and he swung on them until they did not move. Still gripping the cudgel, Benyamin let a snarl out of his throat that terrified even him, and tore across the cobblestoned streets to his house, past a shocked Eliana at the door, up the stairs and into his room. He slammed the door and stood trembling and vomiting in his bathroom.

His parents pounded up the stairs and thumped on his door. "Benyamin! Benyamin, whatever happened to you? You're covered with blood!" his mother yelled through the bathroom door. "Let me in, Son!" his father called in his most professional voice. "You're hurt. Let me dress your wounds."

"It's not *my* blood!" he screamed back. He felt like – like *Benyamin*. He was Benyamin Rosenthaler, the Jew, who had just bested five murderous Brown Shirts on a side street in Koln, Germany; *his* Germany. The bloodied truncheon lay sticky with the German boys' blood in a corner where he'd thrown it. He rolled it with his foot and it left a tacky maroonish trail on the white tiled floor. Had he been a Wild Indian in that moment, he thought or a Mau-Mau in some feral jungle village, he would have licked the truncheon clean, or at least painted his face with his victims' blood. Perhaps this stain on the white tile would suffice; a trophy that would show forever that Jews were not to be trifled with.

"Benyamin, you really must come and let us see that you are all right," his father said to the door. Slowly the heroic moment passed and his feet touched solid ground. He watched his features metamorphose as his visage returned to normal. Slowly he stripped out of his blood-spattered

66

shirt and let it drop to the floor. He splashed cold water on his face. He felt normal again; more in control of who he always was and had been, until a quarter of an hour ago. The Malkhut in him disappeared. He was again just Benyamin Rosenthaler, age fourteen, younger son of Eliezar and Eliana Rosenthaler, bar mitzvah'ed seventeen months ago, younger brother of Herschel Rosenthaler, who had recently moved to Frankfurt to apprentice to a machinist. As the minutes passed, Benyamin felt less the warrior and more the boy that he was: a child, no matter what Rabbi Hirschfeld called him, who had only a faint fuzz on his testicles and no facial hair at all. Slowly he slid the lock back and opened the door.

His father glimpsed him for only an instant. The telephone jingled urgently, and Eliezar Rosenthaler never ignored the telephone. He rushed down the stairs and picked up the receiver.

The conversation was one-sided, but his father's face when he came upstairs again told a terrible tale. "Benyamin – " he said. "You put a boy in *hospital*!"

For a moment, Warrior Benyamin returned. He half-hoped he'd killed the brute. Then he began to shake all over. "Hospital—" he quavered.

"That was Doktor Hauer on the telephone," his father said, his own voice quivering. "You hit a boy in the head and half-killed him." Benyamin opened his mouth to explain. "Do you know what you've done, what you've called down upon yourself?" his father thundered. "That boy's father is a member of the Nazi Party; *very* high up!" He took a deep breath before he spoke the next line. "Doktor Hauer is my friend, and he told me he could be in very serious trouble for warning us, but Benyamin, he said we must get you out of town now; tonight, because they are coming to arrest you in the morning, and you are to be Disappeared, he is sure of it!"

His mother was already on the telephone with Oma Bina. Half an hour later they were all there: Oma Bina, Aunt Ayelet, Ezra, LiLo, and some relatives he had not seen since his bar mitzvah. Even Uncle Reuven came, clutching the stone bannister and leaning on his wife as they crawled up the stairs.

"Benyamin's done us all a favor," Aunt Ayelet said. "We should have left as soon as we started having trouble at the lumberyard."

"I'd say we've waited too long already," Oma Bina said, stroking LiLo's hair. "We can't get out of here too quickly."

"I just don't think we good Germans should leave our nation at such a sensitive time," Elie said.

"When *do* we go, then?" Reuven asked. "When they come kicking down our doors? And what becomes of us then? Where do they take us and what do they do to us there? I listen when I go to the hospitals. Jews are getting hurt out there. I watch the German doctors turning them away. When one of them stuck his face in mine and said I would be dead in a couple of years anyway and he could make it a lot sooner for me so I'd stop taking up a bed a good German could have, I got out of there fast!"

"So one German was mean to you," Elie said. "Just the fact that Doktor Hauer called, instead of letting the Nazis come and drag Benyamin away proves there are Germans that still care. We would not even be in this mess if Benyamin hadn't attacked that boy."

"There were five of them, Papa." Benyamin spoke of what had happened for the first time. "They were going to kill me."

"But they didn't touch you, did they?" his father shot back. "You took a brickbat and beat that boy in the head with it. You did it in cold blood. I should let them take you to the police station; it would teach you a lesson!"

"You can keep him here until tomorrow, if you never want to see your boy again," Oma Bina said. "You talk about 'caring Germans'. Yes, many care; just not enough of them to save us from what is coming. But we are wasting time. They say they will come tomorrow, but the Nazis lie, and they could be here in an hour or less. Benyamin, go and pack quickly. You have five minutes, and then we must be gone."

He went to his room and picked out a few items to throw into his mother's tapestry valise: a few changes of clothes, the silver Kaddish cup Herschel gave him for his Bar Mitzvah, Herschel's silver pen, his pocketknife and a few other keepsakes. He hesitated, then scooped up the truncheon in a snowy towel and tossed it into the top of the bag. He grabbed up his rucksack and jacket and took a quick look around his room. When would he ever come back here again? Oma Bina called out his name, and he flew down the stairs.

They drove in two cars, out to the forest overlooking the city. It twinkled below them, a fetching jewel in which nothing bad seemed capable of happening. Aunt Ayelet, LiLo and Ezra dug the hole at the base of the designated tree. Looking at the heads of the three of them that went deeper and deeper into the hole as the mound of dirt they raised grew higher, Benyamin wondered if they would keep at it until they came to China. But at length they stopped, and the rest of the family hauled them up. Then, almost without words, everyone in the circle began lobbing things in: gold household items, jewelry and trinkets they loved. Anything of value went into that dark place. Benyamin watched as his mother slid her fantastic collection of jewels in their ebony wood box over the side. She hesitated, looked timidly at an iron-faced Elie and then slid off her wedding ring, slipped it into a little velvet pouch and nudged it into the great hole. Her engagement ring, however, she kept back; she could not bring herself to let go of the beautiful ring her husband had placed on her finger so long ago. "Besides," she said half-aloud, "if times become hard, I can always sell it. It will be like my little bank."

"Put it in, Eliana," Oma Bina had said, not without a bit of sternness in her voice. "The goyim will be wearing it, not you, if times become much harder than they are now." Eliana slipped it off, but only feigned putting it into her little velvet jewelry pouch. Instead, she palmed it and secreted it in her undergarments when no one was looking.

Benyamin peered into the hole. There was the Kaddish cup, he thought. He would like to keep it, but what use would he have for it? On the other hand, the thing he was *not* going to give up was the silver pen Herschel had given him. Carefully he drew the cup out and wrapped it in the towel with the truncheon. He watched them disappear into the dark hole. He thought of what a great tale he would have to tell his children when he was older. The larger significance of the truncheon and the Kaddish cup wrapped together escaped him in the moment.

"You've all seen where we are," Oma Bina said. "Those of you who survive – whatever is to be survived – you come back here and get our treasure and bring it to whoever is left." She took a knife out of her clothing and made several long, seemingly random gashes in the wood of the nearest tree trunk, scarring it. Then everyone began pushing the dirt into the hole and tamping it down and strewing about the dried leaves and dirt until the forest appeared as it had before they arrived.

Benyamin's mother came over to him and embraced him. "When you get to—wherever you are going," she said, "remember to represent yourself well. Don't go out without a handkerchief. Take flowers to your hosts; they will appreciate you more. And *do* always be polite." His father said nothing, nor did he embrace him. Benyamin could not help but feel—quite rightly—that his father was still angry with him for all of this trouble.

He watched his parents head toward Aunt Ayelet's car, and he started after them, but Oma Bina blocked his way. "You will come with us," she said, holding open the back door of her Dusenberg.

"Mama – " he called out, but Eliana strode away quickly and did not look back.

"Papa – "

His parents climbed into Ayelet's car and sped away with her, LiLo and Ezra. He got into the car with his uncle Reuven and Oma Bina, hoping against hope that it would follow Aunt Ayelet's car back to the city and his home, but he knew it would not. Tears stung his eyes, and he longed for his room: for the security of his eiderdown, for the brown-soap freshness of Anya's enfolding arms, for the sound of Herschel's even breathing. He stared at the back of Oma Bina's neck, which he could just make out in the darkness of the back seat as they bounced over the open roads. He half wished, as his eyes closed with weariness, that something terrible would happen: that Uncle Reuven would grab his chest and fall over dead, or that Oma Bina would run off the road and the car would blow up and then he could escape back down the rutted road to the city.

But it was not to be. The city lights drew further and further away until they glittered as distant and remote as the stars, and then the dark woods closed in on all sides, and then sleep overcame him, and still they drove on.

CHAPTER SEVEN

Uncle Abner and his mother's sister spoke that language that Benyamin came to know as 'the King's English'. Benyamin understood not a word of it, so English just sounded like barking to him. The Gymnasium had dropped the study of the 'Enemy' languages – English and French – over the last couple of years, and he had been so busy learning Hebrew that he would not have been able to study anything else anyway, he figured. His uncle still possessed the rudiments of the German language, and his aunt could manage to blunder through a German conversation with him, but mostly he found himself isolated, unless they deigned to use their waning language skills to speak with him.

"You really should try to learn English," his aunt told him. "You never know when you may need it. " But Benyamin determined that he would *not* learn. "Why should I?" he would ask her. "I'm sure this trouble will be over in a few days or weeks at the most, and then I can go home." She would look at him sadly and shake her head, unwilling to discuss anything else about the subject, including what his return date might be.

Once or twice he received a painfully scripted letter in Herschel's halting handwriting. He liked the school in Frankfurt, where he found himself comfortably situated, thanks to Oma Bina's generosity, but he complained constantly about his apprenticeship. He was under a German, who constantly belittled him and punished him for the sin of being born Jewish. Paradoxically, the man was an excellent teacher, who prided himself on being able to pass his skills along to anyone, even an ignoramus of a Jew like Herschel. As a result, his brother said, he had become more skilled than anyone had expected him to be, and even the

German had to admit he was the best at repairing the complicated machines and figuring out schematics that no longer existed.

"Hurrah!" Benyamin said sarcastically. His brother was enjoying his life, even in Frankfurt, which was surely closer to danger than little Koln. Why couldn't he be at home? Herschel was no less Jewish than he was, and yet he could walk among Germans, and even be instructed by one, while Benyamin had to play hide-and-seek here in England. He exhausted the texts he'd brought in his rucksack eventually, and his uncle brought him the few books he could find in German, but most were college-level texts. Out of boredom, Benyamin actually read some of them, with growing interest.

Otherwise he drew, and watched the post for letters from his mother. These came infrequently, were addressed to her sister, not to him, and always contained the caveat that he not respond. The police had actually come to the house before light on the morning after he escaped. They had demanded that Benyamin be brought out immediately; and when she told them he had fled, they had ransacked the house looking for some trace of him. Fortunate it was that his mother (or his father—he knew not which—) had wiped up the blood from the antiseptic white tile, or he feared the sight of that Aryan stain on their Jewish floor might have driven the police mad. There had been nothing to find but his hastily tossed room. Finally they had gone away, but not before telling her she must bring him to the station immediately to answer to charges of attempted murder, should he turn up, and that they would keep a watch out for him themselves. She had been most worried that they had demanded a photo of Benyamin, and wondered if they had the power to bring him back from England, which put a whole new worry into his thinking.

It occurred to him that he may have saved his parents from arrest by bringing the truncheon away and burying it in the woods, instead of leaving it on the bathroom floor or secreting it in the belongings he brought to England, from which he might be snatched at any moment. In his mind, he saw the soldiers behaving as rabid dogs would: sniffing the air for the scent of it and then jumping up and down, insane at the sight of blood, especially German blood, on the floor of a Jewish household. Part of him realized that he might be even now in the back of some police van, being trundled through the streets of Munich toward Dachau, which Ezra had described in graphically chilling detail. The other part of him, however, wondered if a few Reichsmarks pressed into the right palms might have 'exonerated' him, as they had Ezra. He would probably not have been able to return to school after the break, but at least he would be free to move around in a place where he understood the language.

In her next letter, which didn't come until some months later, she told him about what had just happened. His father had been summoned to the center of town to successfully deliver a particularly recalcitrant infant, and had been making his way home in his car when suddenly he had rounded a corner and found himself in the midst of hell.

"Police and soldiers were running through the streets like crazy people, breaking Jews' store windows and setting fire to synagogues and burning books in the streets," she wrote. "There was so much confusion that at every turn he had found his way blocked, and finally he had had to abandon the car and try making his way on foot." There had been arrests, too, she reported; and it had not taken his father long to observe, from the shadows to which he had wisely retreated, that all of those being rounded up were Jews. He'd known that flattening himself in the shadows was not going to save him for long, and so he had scurried down side streets with other Jews, seeking open doors to duck into and barriers to hide behind. But he didn't know anyone in that quarter, and it was too far back to his patient's house. Gunfire rang out. People were screaming and falling around him. Wounded? Dead? He was too terrified even to consider providing anyone with aid, and he had stood, frozen with fear in a niche in a wall for he did not know how long, viewing the scene with bulging eyes. Suddenly a man had grabbed him; with a strong grip, but a gentle and familiar voice:

"Herr Doktor," the voice had said. *"Kommst du hierein, bitte"*. He had turned, startled, and looked into the quiet eyes of Fischer. Fischer, his ex-chauffeur, had spied him from his bedroom window and dashed out to rescue him. The man had clapped a hand over his former employer's mouth, hustled him up a flight of stairs into the apartment he now shared with his mother, and stuffed him atop the box of the dumbwaiter in his kitchen. *"Not one word!"* he had hissed. Moments later there had come a pounding on Fischer's front door, and the place had filled up with soldiers.

"Are you hiding any Jews here?" an angry voice had demanded. He heard heavy things being tossed about, and then the door of the dumbwaiter flew open. Elie observed the top of a military cap through the slit of light that his position afforded him, and he held his breath, lest he should make a sound and give himself away.

"Jews!" Fischer had yelled back. *"Certainly* not! I wouldn't let a filthy Jew into my house! They smell and they steal! And I would not let them anywhere near my *mother!* What kind of man do you think I am?" He heard Fischer offer to join the fracas outside and round up "the vermin", but the policeman told him to stay inside, or he might be accidentally

shot. The officer said a few pleasant words to Fischer's mother, then slid out with his troops to complete their business in the streets.

Elie had crouched, quivering in the dust atop the dumbwaiter cab for what seemed like a millennium. After what seemed to be an eon later, Fischer brought the car down and helped the doctor out.

"I tried to warn you, Herr Doktor," Fischer said. "I *told* you these days were coming. Many Jews died tonight and many more will die before morning. Get your family out of Germany; out of Europe, if you don't want them to die, too. There is nothing here for you. Crazy men rule the streets now. Get away while you can!"

Frau Fischer, Elie's old patient, came to her bedroom door. Elie strode, hand outstretched, to greet her, intending to enquire after her health; but she regarded him without words, and with a look with which she might have considered a cheap garment. "Max!" she called out to her son, who was struggling into his overcoat. "Where do you think you are going?"

"I am taking Herr Doktor back to his home," he said. "He cannot stay here, and it is not safe for him to go alone and on foot."

Her usually sunny blue eyes were dark, as if a storm was brewing behind them. "Are you mad? They are killing people on the streets, and you want to go *into* the danger? For what? For the sake of this ass of a Jew that doesn't have the sense to stay low or run away?" She turned her baleful glance on her former savior. "Why are you still in the country?" she asked. "Do you realize we could be arrested? We could be imprisoned because of you?"

Elie could not believe his ears. He had saved this woman's life; she would be virtuously and self-righteously rotting away in some Christian cemetery, were it not for him. His impulse was to remind her. But he bit his tongue.

"Well," she said, turning to her son, "be quick about it. Get him out of here before those hooligans come back looking for him. He'll put us all in danger, and I am not risking death for the likes of him! Get out, Herr Doktor, and don't come back! I'm not ungrateful for what you did for me, but I won't risk my life for you." She hesitated for a moment, then added, "And besides, you *did* fire my son!"

Elie felt like a child; or worse, like an unwanted animal. This woman had been so grateful for his ministrations to her. She had paid him handsomely—as handsomely as a widow could—and she had completely recovered. Had she no gratitude?

Fischer took his arm and hustled him into the back seat of his car. "Do not mind Mother," he said. "She seems to grow crankier and crankier every day. It is the political situation," he added. "Please forgive her words tonight. I know she is grateful for everything you did for her."

Elie, however, was not in a forgiving mood. His head was abuzz. What he had endured tonight! And he was one of the lucky ones; he had not been arrested or killed. Three-quarters of an hour's exile in the dust of the dumbwaiter's top had rendered his clothing with nothing that a good dusting could not fix. But there were others—

And Fischer's mother! How could she turn on him so? How could he go, in her eyes, from the skilled practitioner whose hands she had taken in both of hers and kissed in gratitude for her life to an 'ass of a Jew'? What was going on with the world?

They traveled in Fischer's car through the splintered glass and smouldering ashes and blood-stained streets, Elie covered with a heavy blanket. He did not breathe easily until he viewed the spires of Kolendom through a rip in the wool.

"God was merciful to you tonight," Fischer said as he pulled back the blanket. "He may not be a second time. Get out; *now!*" He deposited the doctor on the street and sped off. Elie scurried up the stairs and into the house.

His wife had been beside herself, and fell upon him with many kisses. He pushed her aside.

"Call my mother!" he said. And from Switzerland, where she still 'vacationed' with her ailing son, Bina began making what arrangements she could.

Benyamin's mother concluded her writing by saying they were looking desperately for a way out, but it was not easy. Some Germans were not above taking money from trusting Jews, then disappearing with their funds, leaving them nothing but despair in return. What Jew was going to retaliate? And to whom were they going to complain; the police? Many had given away all of their life savings and were beginning to sell their jewelry, their furs, their household goods; anything they could do without to get away. In a postscript she said she might not be writing again, because there was a rumor that the Germans were opening letters posted internationally.

Benyamin closed the letter. Suddenly he was not so anxious to return to Koln.

CHAPTER EIGHT

Benyamin never met Meira, but she was the reason he had parents still. A distant cousin had slipped off to Buenos Aires some years before, with Oma Bina's support, and he had married this woman, a native of the country. By all accounts she was a beauty: young, slender and dark-eyed in that stunning Argentine way, with olive skin and long, long, glossy, thick, raven-colored hair.

It was she that went to the officials to get visas for Elie and Eliana to enter her country. "Benyamin is safe, for now, in England; so we need not worry about him just yet. But his brother in Frankfurt is still in harm's way. Try to get a visa for Herschel, too," Oma Bina had instructed her.

The young girl took Oma Bina's money and every bit of cash she and her husband could lay hands on and went to the building. She did not have much hope. Others who had preceded her had come away empty-handed; some without the money they entered the building with. Still, she had a sliver of hope and much determination. She would get whatever she could to help her family.

It was late before she came before the desk of the proper official, and she realized that there was nobody behind her in the line. Many of the clerks were already tidying their desks to leave, and she feared she would be turned away until tomorrow; but after waiting for so many hours, she was determined to see at least if the man serving her line would see her and hear her story.

She begged the official to allow this very eminent and skilled doctor and his family to find refuge in his country. "You know the political situation there," she said, with tears in her eyes. "They will die if you don't help, and it would so benefit our nation to have them here. Please, I have money—" she said, fumbling inside her blouse to retrieve and unwrap the parcel of bills she had hidden in her undergarments.

The man was fiftyish; he had no immediate family and cared little for his position. He was very open to being corrupted with bribes. But seeing the lovely Meira and noting that the others in his office were already covering their typewriters and packing up for the evening and that there were many empty rooms in the place, he hit upon a better price.

"Step into this side room," he said. "And if you can show enough – *compassion* – for your relatives, I may be able to bring one or two of them over. We'll see. It all depends on how much sympathy you show me you have for them. If we—get along, I may even be able to give you an extra one—or two." He reached out and fondled a lock of her hair, but the chill of his intentions went through her entire body.

Meira considered. She also knew that the office was just short of being unoccupied, and that the man was quite capable of taking by force and without remuneration of any kind what he was offering a visa authorization or two for. He was not an attractive man by any means, and she was not a little repulsed by the large wart on the side of his lip and the gray hairs growing out of the backs of his hands. He was fat and sweaty and the neck and cuffs of his yellowed shirt were filthy. He slobbered a bit as he grinned at her, his open mouth revealing tobacco-stained, rotting teeth. Her impulse was to rush out the open door and down the stairs into the refreshing air of the street. She wanted to bury her head against the strong, clean chest of her beloved husband and let him stroke away the filth of this man's very gaze upon her. Maybe *he* could come in the morning and pay the man enough for the visas.

But she considered again. The line had been so long, and those who received even one visa each were few. Here was this man, no matter how repulsive he might be, offering life—*if* she acquiesced. *If* she did whatever he asked and maybe a bit more. No matter what disgust she felt in the moment, she reasoned, it would be over in an hour. She was a wife, now, not a virgin girl; and his violation would not mean so much to her, because her cause was noble. He wasn't going to kill her, after all. Besides, her husband need never know, and she would be saving her relatives' lives. She smiled a weak smile at the man and followed him into the side room, determined to please him to the best of her ability.

Two weeks later Oma Bina opened the small package addressed to her German alias and stared in pleased surprise at the returned money and the six documents in her hand.

Herschel traveled that very night to Dusseldorf and a reunion on the dock of the first ship sailing, with his parents and his cousin Ezra, who were also traveling to Buenos Aires. Oma Bina owed a debt to many people in the city, but she could not save them all. Rivkeh had begged for passage out of Europe, but she refused to go in any way but first class, which meant she wasn't willing to pose as a German and take the train or travel third class or supplement the ticket price to provide for a more esteemed cabin on the ship. Well, Rivkeh would have to find her own way out. Bina could give the gift of safe passage to a new life to only two more people. Reuven should have gone, but he would be too far away from Ayelet and LiLo, who had already found passage to France and were anticipating visas to the United States any day. Besides, she feared how his health would stand up to the rigors of an ocean cruise.

Benyamin collected their occasional letters from the various places from which his relatives wrote and wondered: What was going to become of him? Was he doomed to remain in England with these barking British people? Why couldn't he go to South America too?

He would not have long to wonder.

CHAPTER NINE

War crept closer. It was all anyone talked about now, and Benyamin could pick up threads of what was happening, even in the rapid-fire English conversations. Not that he went outside much. He hung around his aunt and uncle's shop, performing only the easiest of tasks. His aunt swore that he was just 'sensitive', but his uncle's designation, surely closer to the mark, was that he was a lazy, spoiled brat of a boy with no idea of what was going on around him or how fortunate he was still to be alive, after the 'stunt' he pulled in Cologne. When he spoke to him at all, Abner spoke gruffly and in English, further annoyed that the boy cared little about understanding his words. Finally the man could bear it no longer, and sent a letter to Oma Bina, asking what he was to do with 'the item' she had sent him, as it was defective and non-functioning.

She said she would arrange something as quickly as possible.

A few weeks passed. There was talk of sending children to the countryside, perhaps to help with food production while the farmers kept them safe; but Benyamin would be useless, his aunt insisted, working on a farm. He was not made for such work, he had no experience for such work and he certainly had no interest in it. She was convinced that he would not do well and would probably fall ill. A few hours of his insolence, his uncle added, and any farmer they sent him to would be ready to serve him up on a silver platter to the Germans. Better he should take his chances here in Coventry, even though their Christian neighbors were starting to glare at them as if the impending war was their personal fault, and this pettish new arrival from the country that was threatening to make war on them was hardly acceptable to them.

What Benyamin really wanted, he realized, was to go to Argentina where his family was. He missed Herschel's bantering with him in the bed next to his. He missed his mother's fussing over him and the smell of his father's cigar. Even if LiLo would not be there, he could make do with his cousin Ezra. Yes, that was best, he thought: that he should go to South America and live with his parents. He waited to hear that they were sending for him. Every day he expected the summons.

Oma Bina's letter arrived, with a few hundred English pounds and instructions to put Benyamin on the next ship floating West. At dawn the very next morning Uncle Abner strode without knocking into Benyamin's room, which was tucked under the eaves of his uncle's shop; a crude affair, Benyamin thought, after his pleasant little room in Cologne. There were cracks in the plaster, the bed was hard and the covers sparse. There were no pictures on the walls, which curved in so that he could hardly stand up straight when he went to bed. As well, there was no bathroom for him alone; only what his relatives referred to as a 'clo', which he had to share not only with his uncle and aunt, but also with their other employees during business hours. He had to go downstairs to use the clo. It was not always tidy, and he did not improve its state when he used it, being careless about his aim. Often he left towels and even his dirty clothing in the middle of the floor, where his disgusted aunt swept them up to be laundered. He kept the few items he had grabbed up before he left home in his tapestry valise, rather than in the little dresser in his room, so certain was he that he would have an imminent departure to South America. He wanted to be ready whenever the call came. He never made up his bed, since Anya or his mother had always done it for him, and it lay open all day, since his aunt refused.

"We will go to the steamship office today," his Uncle Abner said in his broken German, to be certain that Benyamin understood. Benyamin's heart leapt with joy, then sank with his uncle's next words: "You will leave for the United States on the next ship."

He was not going to be with his parents? He was not going to see Herschel or Ezra? At times he felt so alone in the world. "Will you and my aunt be coming with me to the United States?" he asked. "Will you set up shop there?"

"No," his uncle said. "You will be on your own there, with some people that will look after you. Your Grandmother Bina has arranged everything. I am to take you to town and we are to buy you what you need and you are to get on the ship with a family that will watch out for you and you are to be met at the shipyard in New York by your new caretakers." His grandmother had discovered distant relatives in North Carolina that would put him up, he said.

Benyamin took the news indifferently, until he remembered that LiLo and her mother were supposed to go to New York, if they weren't already there. Maybe, he thought, they would be settled soon, and then he could run away from wherever Oma Bina sent him and find them. No matter what the Americans spoke, he could speak German with his relatives all day long, instead of sputtering along in Yiddish and Hebrew or learning to tangle his tongue up in English. Maybe the Americans didn't feel so angry about Jews. Maybe he could resume Gymnasium there, and go to an American university; preferably one at which everyone spoke German.

As for leaving England, Benyamin was thrilled, when he thought about it. He hated his uncle's ironworks shop. He hated the stares of the men that worked for his relatives, and was certain that they would be in front of the mob that came to drive them from their home, if that time ever came. He felt, however, a certain fondness for the smell of the machines and the heat they threw off when they were running. Something in their humming was soothing to him. Still, England was not Germany. He had set his mind on hating England, so he would not allow himself to like the shop. He hastily threw his few belongings that were scattered about the room into his bag and glanced at himself in the mirror.

He could not help but note that he was handsome. His chestnut brown hair was not bushy like Herschel's, but waved from his forehead to his nape, where it curled itself into soft ringlets. His eyes were beer-bottle brown, and gleamed with health, reflected in the pale rose of his cheeks against his olive skin. He had begun a growth spurt, and now stood almost as tall as his Uncle Abner. He was slender, but not thin. Despite his lack of hard labor, he was well-built through his shoulders, and he had recently begun to think he might have promise as a gymnast. He thought about Max Schmelling, and wondered if he had the nerve to be a pugilist; after all, he had singlehandedly whipped five of Germany's best. But he considered: he was too good-looking to put his looks at risk in that way. One well-placed fist might split his perfectly-formed lip, or smash in his handsome nose.

"*Today*, Benyamin!" Uncle Abner called. Benyamin ripped his face away from the looking-glass, grabbed up his valise and rucksack and bounded down the stairs.

Though the sun was barely up, his aunt had already prepared a basket for them by the time he arrived in the kitchen. "We'll eat on the way," his uncle said. Benyamin gave his aunt an obligatory hug around her still-narrow waist and followed her man into the street, grumbling half-aloud that they had wanted so much to divest themselves of him that they had not even afforded him the luxury of a final breakfast under their roof; they were going to force him to eat on the run as if he were a refugee.

By eight they had reached the Charing Cross landing, and they headed up the Thames toward the Port of London. It was not hard to find the Cunard Line office, and his uncle announced that his tickets and papers were filed with the purser and Benyamin would have his own stateroom, next to a family called Clark that had two daughters. Everything was set, and —

Benyamin sat in the office, looking at a photo of the *Queen Mary*. It was gargantuan: a veritable behemoth. He was going to be in a stateroom by himself, tossed on the mighty ocean! What if the ship sank, like the *Titanic*, or got torpedoed, like the *Lusitania*? Would he be able to get to a lifeboat? What if he fell overboard? What if someone robbed him? What if any of a number of unknown occurrences that could happen to a fifteen-year-old boy on the high seas occurred? Fear gripped his insides, making him feel as if his gut had turned to jelly. He felt his stomach churning and bile rising in his throat. He was determined, however, to look brave. "I don't like this ship, and I am not going on it," he said hoping there was no tremor in his voice.

His Uncle Abner almost grabbed his lapels and shook him. "Insolent cur!" the man wanted to shout. "We save your life and you tell me this!" But he curled his fists inside his pockets.

"What upsets you, Bennylein?" he asked, deliberately making his tone a little too smooth.

"I won't go—not unless—unless there is a swimming pool!"

At this the purser beamed.

"Ah, of course! And you will be happy to know that we have a *beautiful* swimming pool!"

"Olympic size?" Benyamin asked, thinking of a magazine article his father had shown him some years before. He absolutely would *not* admit to his uncle or this fop of an Englishman that he was fearful of crossing the water and perhaps even more fearful of what lay ahead when—*if*—the ship docked.

"But of course," the purser said. "This is the Queen *Mary*, Sir!"

As he had promised, his uncle took him into town and purchased new underthings for Benyamin, as well as socks and a pair of shoes. He bought him two swimsuits, a dress suit, and a coat and cap, in case the American winters should prove harsh. The rest, he thought, Benyamin's American sponsors could provide. He gave Benyamin fifty pounds for any items he might want to purchase on-board (an awful lot for the little fool, Abner thought), and he presented to the purser an envelope containing fifty pounds to make certain Benyamin stayed comfortable, an envelope containing an equal amount for the Clarks for their trouble, and a hundred pounds for Benyamin's caretakers in America. The other hundred and thirty-four pounds he pocketed, feeling that the money more than compensated him for "the annoyance of having had to put up with the little blighter".

CHAPTER TEN

The ship set sail at five PM, affording its passengers the best view of the sunset on the water, once England lay behind them. Benyamin stood on the deck next to the Clarks. He did not wave to the well-wishers on shore as the Clarks did. He was sure that his Uncle Abner, having given him a perfunctory handshake, was now three-quarters of the way back to Coventry. He also did not wish to possibly attract the attention of some Nazi pursuer from Cologne that might have tracked him to the dock.

Eustace Richard Henry Clark, PhD was an Englishman and an Episcopalian. He was a professor who had been at Leipzig until a few months ago. Now he was moving his family to safety, back to his wife's homeland. He was a tall man with a toothbrush mustache, which, sensing that people would equate it more with Hitler than with Charlie Chaplin, he shaved off as soon as the ship set sail. He spent a great deal of time in his stateroom or in some quiet part of the deck, reading his tomes and scribbling notes onto a pad. He was not a man of many words, and Benyamin was never sure if Dr. Clark even understood that he was supposed to be looking after him.

Mrs. Clark, on the other hand, was loquacious to a fault. She was a slightly faded and frowzy blonde, who apparently thought that she could make far better color choices for her hair than God had, though her black roots showed signs that she had not visited a salon recently. While she had been born to a Jewish family and was, by race, Jewish, she had converted to Christianity to accommodate the wishes of her in-laws, once she and Mr. Clark fell in love and determined to marry, and she was raising her children as bona-fide Episcopalians. She wore dressing gowns of the most outlandish hues and patterns over her swimming suits, and entirely too much makeup. She prattled on in German, which pleased Benyamin initially; but when she failed to quiet down after a time, he found himself bored with her, and it was only with great difficulty that he managed not to yawn in her face. He learned, after a day or two, to avoid her, as her daughters did, or suffer the consequences of being drawn into one of her endless soliloquies.

The elder of the two girls, Davida, was pockmarked and scrawny. Her skin was sallow and her hair was stringy and a shade that seemed unable to decide if it was red or brown. Thick glasses perched atop her sharp nose, making her watery blue eyes seem enormous. She appeared very nervous, and tended to study with her father a great deal, perusing her own volumes and scribbling her own notes. The younger, Sheila, however, was an ivory-skinned beauty, with dancing dark eyes and coal-black ringlets that bounced when she walked. He always expected to hear her curls tinkling like bells when she moved about. Sheila had a slow, easy voice; and since she spoke impeccable German, they spent a great deal of time together in the pool and in his stateroom and in lounging chairs on deck.

Dr. Clark did not like their closeness. He felt they were too near in age to wander all over the ship unescorted, and insisted that someone should always know where they were, lest they should slip into some unguarded space and do what boys and girls in such circumstances did. Since he did not designate anyone, however, and since Mrs. Clark was usually running someone else down to talk to, they continued to have the run of the ship.

Benyamin asked Sheila about America. She was, after all, a citizen, and he supposed she would know something about the place. She had not, however, been there for at least seven years, and recalled only the things she left behind when she was very young, or what she had gleaned from picture books. "Everyone lives in flats," she said, "and they all go to theater in the city." She remembered the yellow taxis and underground trains, and she remembered that "there were so many lights and a lot of noise; very exciting," she said, "with tall, tall buildings reaching into the sky." She said she had gone to the top of the tallest building in the world, the Empire State Building, which had more than a hundred floors, she thought. Benyamin said he didn't believe her; a building that tall would be an architectural impossibility. They almost argued over that, but she told him he would see when he got there, and then he would know she was right. He agreed to wait and see.

She told him he had better learn English, and she offered him a few phrases to learn, so that he could introduce himself to people when he got there. He was an apt pupil; partly because it was beginning to dawn on him that he needed the language to survive and find his relatives, and partly because Sheila was so lovely. She awoke in him feelings he had not had since his golden days with Anya.

How could he have forgotten Anya's soft hands on his young body? He thrilled at the memory. Surely, he thought, if a Polish *shiksa* years older than he could awaken such feelings in him, the sensations a girl his own age would arouse in him would be incredible. Sheila was thirteen: almost marriageable age, by his reckoning. She ought to know about tenderness and touching, he thought. Maybe there was no boy that had touched her yet as a girl ought to be touched. He would be the very boy to initiate her, he decided. She spent so many hours with him. Didn't that prove she cared for him? She would be thrilled, he concluded. And who knew? Maybe—just maybe—she would want to be his wife, and he could take her into the deep, mysterious world that Anya had not allowed him to enter, because she was saving herself for her future husband, but wound up having her virginity torn away in order to save Benyamin's miserable life.

At times he felt Anya had made a big mistake, saving herself. In the end, the prize she guarded so carefully had been ripped away from her; he more than suspected, given her tears, without a shred of kindness or regard. Too many times, her face appeared in his dreams: an Anya face that was drawn and tear-streaked. He didn't like thinking that, if he hadn't run down to the train station like a callow fool, she might still be a virginal girl, with a sacred gift that she had saved for her wedding night. He wondered what, with her virginity gone, she had to give her husband when she got married, or if she ever would. Maybe he would tell Anya's story to Sheila, and even convince her that maybe she should give her virginity to *him*. Not like Hans got Anya's, though. It was wrong to just take it. Nights he lay in his narrow bunk, dreaming of Anya; only now, in his dreams, it was Sheila's face and Sheila's hands that caressed him and brought him ecstasy.

One quiet evening when the *Queen Mary* was about two-thirds of the way across the Atlantic, Benyamin decided the time had come. He crept stealthily to Sheila's door after her parents' lights were out, and invited her to his stateroom for chocolates. Being a great lover of chocolates, Sheila threw on her robe and swished next door, careful not to awaken her sister, lest she should have to share. She settled herself on the foot of his bed and smiled up at him with great anticipation. Benyamin's mind, however, was not on the chocolates. A quivering had begun in his loins; and knowing no other way to quiet it, he placed a soft kiss on Sheila's surprised lips and tenderly placed his hand on one of the twin lumps just under her robe.

His cheek burned from the blow. Sheila rose from his bed and screamed at him. "Don't you *ever* do that, you—you—you dirty Jew-boy!" she yelled. "I hope they send you back to Germany! I hope you go back there and die, if you ever do that to *anybody*! They'll kick you right out of America. They'll *do* it, you know! *You're* not an American! They don't have to let you stay in America! I hope they kick you out first thing, when we get to the docks! And Mister Hitler himself can stomp you to death, and when you are dying, you remember it was because of what you tried to do to me!"

Summoned by Sheila's shrieking, the now very attentive Dr. Clark banged at the door. Tears streaming, Sheila took up a handful of chocolates, flung them in Benyamin's face, threw open the door and rushed into her father's arms. She sobbed out a story Benyamin could not begin to follow; it was all in disjointed, staccato-fire English. Dr. Clark, however, appeared to understand it very clearly.

The next morning, almost at first light, the purser entered his stateroom without knocking, unceremoniously gathered up Benyamin's scattered-about things, dumped them into his rucksack and his mother's valise, and moved him to a room on the other side of the ship. He caught an occasional glimpse of the Clarks, but they ignored him. Only Davida slipped close to him one morning when the others were not about. She twined her arm in his and whispered in his ear, "You picked the wrong Clark girl. Why do boys always go for beauty? I would have done whatever you wanted and more! And I still will, if you like." Benyamin felt his skin crawl. He pulled away from her and retreated to his room.

He was puzzled. Anya had initiated everything with him, and he thought *all* girls would initiate, or at least respond to him, once he was close. He stared at himself in the mirror. Look how good looking he was!

Maybe there was something wrong with Sheila Clark, he thought, but then he considered: maybe American girls were different from Polish girls.

He thought, too, that Sheila just might be right: if he was not careful he just *might* be sent back to Germany: to Cologne, where truncheon-carrying Brown Shirts would bash in his brains or blow them out with their guns. He must, he thought, control himself, or he could wind up dead in this prosperous new place. For the last three days of his trip he took his meals alone and practiced the few English phrases Sheila had taught him: "Hello. My name is Benyamin. What is your name?

On a day that boasted a glorious sunrise, the *Queen Mary* steamed into New York Harbor. Benyamin, along with the other passengers, crowded the deck to see the Lady of the Harbor, the Statue of Liberty. She was lifting her lamp beside the golden door for him, as the poem on her base said. Benyamin thought. America was perhaps, the doorway he was meant to pass through after all; until he could go to Argentina, at least.

First, however, he had to pass through Ellis Island

The *Queen Mary*'s passengers crowded into a line to pass through Customs. Benyamin, un-chaperoned, now, saw the Clark family a few yards ahead of him in the queue. He wanted to call out to them, but he doubted that they would respond. Then he thought of the money his uncle had given to them. They were going to pocket it, even though they were not going to see him safely to this new land! He felt his anger rising. He wanted to stomp up to them and demand whatever they hadn't spent; perhaps even summon a policeman to make them give all of the money back. But then, he didn't speak enough English to get his thoughts across well to a policeman, nor did he even know how to find one. At that moment, too, Sheila caught sight of him and buried her face in her father's coat. Dr. Clark looked up, saw him and curled his clean-shaven upper lip. Davida, on the other hand, smiled at him. Mrs. Clark did not see him; she was animatedly engaged in one-way conversation with the hapless woman in front of her.

Benyamin was now in fear. What if the Clarks told the immigration people what they thought he had tried to do to their daughter? They might declare him unfit and make him return to England, where his uncle was more than likely, Benyamin feared, to eject him from the shop or even send him back to Germany. Or the Americans might arrest him and place him in jail, where he could languish for years. Or they might send him back to Germany, without even allowing him to stop off in England.

When he reached the immigration window, however, the purser appeared with his travel documents and presented them to the officer there. His health and entry records were all in order, and he was waved through. Accompanied by the purser, he crowded onto the ferry to the mainland, where the steam line's office was. The purser took him by the hand to the office, handed him the envelopes for his patrons and the balance of the money Uncle Abner had provided for him, and deposited him on a bench, ordering him to stay right there and not to move until he was called for, as if he were a dog.

Passengers streamed by and into the purser's land office, gathering their documents, settling their accounts or sitting briefly until their relatives came. There were tearful greetings, Benyamin noted, and casual greetings; people jumping up and down and people coolly shaking hands. He saw the Clarks and started to go over to thank them for not having him arrested and to apologize to Sheila, but her father stood between them, glowering, and Benyamin quailed and went back to his seat. He was grateful when they piled their belongings into a couple of hansom cabs and left.

Toward evening, the crowd in the steamship office began to thin. Benyamin started to wonder if he might have been forgotten; if he might have to sit here with the money the purser had placed in the Cunard envelope for him and his sponsors; if he might have to go back to England and live with his Uncle Abner again, or worse, get sent back to his house in Cologne, now empty, to await the coming of the police and the faceless truncheon-bearing boys. He looked at the dollar bills and wondered about the people pictured there. He wondered if he had enough to get a room to stay in for the night, or to buy a meal, if no one came for him. He wondered if he had enough to take the *Queen Mary* back across the ocean to whatever fate might be waiting for him. His stomach was beginning to growl. He had had nothing since the hurried breakfast at the buffet on board, and he had eaten far too little then.

There was a tap at the window, and a uniformed Cunard man stuck his head in the doorway.

"You Rosenthaler?" he asked. Benyamin jumped off his seat and grabbed his bags.

The man walked him toward a car of a make he'd never seen before. Another man got out of the driver's seat and walked around to open the right rear door. Benyamin stared. The man's face was brown; a color he'd never seen, except in rotogravure magazine photos when Max Schmelling fought Joe Louis, the Negro boxer. He'd thought Joe Louis was jet-black, like a piece of charcoal, because that was the way newsprint made him look. He looked at the man's deep brown eyes and slender frame. He eyed his hair: finely strung wires, it appeared to be; a little like the hair that was at last growing thick and full in his own personal spaces.

Occupying the rear seat next to him was a man he decided must be his new caretaker, the person that was helping him to escape his miserable life in England. He appeared, from what Benyamin could see in the shadows, to be a man of about his grandmother's age, or perhaps a little older, with silver hair showing from beneath his bowler hat and long, thin fingers. The man made only a muted greeting; little more than a nod of his head, as Benyamin entered the seat next to him, and did not look at him as the car pulled off.

As they sped from the docks toward the city, he saw buildings – tall buildings – taller even than the Kolendom, against the skyline. So Sheila had been right; there really *were* such structures, and they were not unwieldly, as he had supposed them to be. They soared toward the heavens with grace and dignity. This was America, he thought. Limitless possibilities, Sheila had told him. There was going to be nothing ordinary about his life, he mused, as he caught a word or two of the men's brief dialogue in the car and realized he understood.

CHAPTER ELEVEN

The tall buildings streaked past the car window, and then the view grew black, with only a few intervening twinkles to indicate that there was anything at all except wide expanses of nothingness. Too late, he realized that he had not implemented his half-formed plan to leap from the vehicle and find LiLo and his Aunt Ayelet while he was in New York. He comforted himself for his thoughtlessness by noting that, with his dearth of words in this new language, it would take him months and months to locate his relatives in that mega-city. Perhaps where he was going, to this North Carolina, was the best thing for him to do. He would learn to speak, and then he would run away and find his people.

Contented with this plan, he turned his attention to the other occupants of the car. He could observe only the back third of the Negro driver's thick hair-covered head that protruded out from under his chauffeur's cap. As for the aging White man to his right, he could see little of his features in the dark of the car's interior. The man stared straight ahead and did not turn to even consider his seat companion.

Where were they going? How long was the ride going to be? What was the name of the towns they were passing through? Were there a lot of Negroes? Were there girl Negroes? Were they pretty, like White girls, just with brown skin? Was he going to live with the Negro man or with the White man? The Negro wore a uniform with braid on the shoulders and bright brass buttons. Was he some kind of military person? He drove the car. Was the car his, and the man beside him only his functionary? Or— and he thought it more likely—was the Negro a servant and the White man his master? He remembered something about black people and slavery. Was the Negro the White man's slave? Did the White man beat his driver? Would he be expected to beat the driver, too? Benyamin had so many questions, but apparently he was not going to receive an answer for any of them; not this night, anyway.

Nervously he turned to the White man and broke the silence. Extending his arm in the dark, he said in his very best English, "Hello. My name is Benyamin Rosenthaler. What is your name?"

"Aaronsohn," the stranger said, without looking up or taking his hand. He returned to his musings, his eyes fixed upon some distant and perhaps non-existent object beyond the windowpane. Too afraid to say any more, Benyamin closed his lips and made a quiet game of seeing how long he could keep them closed until they fused and required a bit of effort to open. Far away through the window he could see the occasional twinkle of other lights; he thought they must be other cities, since they seemed too close to be stars, and he wished it was light, so that he could see the landscape. He wished he had studied more about America. He tried to call back to his memory past history lessons at Gymnasium that he had daydreamed through. This country was, as he recalled, a huge, amorphous landmass that lay on the left side of the Atlantic in green, yellow and orange on the classroom map. Now that he was a microscopic dot on that map, he had the sense that he needed to make a great many changes in his life, from figuring out the American topography to riddling out the strange words; not just to escape, but also to survive.

It was still dark when Benyamin came to himself. He did not know how long he had been riding, and despite his efforts in English and German, there had been barely a handful of words between him and the tall silent Aaronsohn man in the opposite corner of the car. He thought that they should be chatting, or planning, or something. He wondered how he would get whatever he might need if he had to depend on this taciturn person. He thought of talking to the chauffeur, but it was too awkward; he would have to shout through the glass pane separating the driver from the passengers. Besides, he was sure that the Negro spoke no German, and maybe Negroes did not speak English, either. He wasn't sure; maybe they spoke some Hottentot language that would sound like gibberish to his ears. Maybe they didn't speak at all. Maybe they just leapt up and down and made monkey noises and scratched themselves. But no; that was probably just the propaganda that the Germans put out, like their ads that said all Jews had long tails and big noses, and that they killed Jesus and spread diseases. He bet this man-servant at least spoke English, but as Benyamin himself spoke almost none, it did not help.

They must have stopped during the night for gas, Benyamin figured; even a Bentley could not go on forever without refueling. He didn't remember stopping, though, and he figured he must have been asleep when they did. Now he felt as if his bladder was about to burst and he was ravenously hungry. He glanced over at the man who had identified himself to him as 'Aaronsohn'. He slumbered quietly, almost without sound, his bundled chest barely rising and falling.

Benyamin felt he could not hold his bladder much longer. "Clo", he said hopefully, tapping on the window. The Negro glanced up from the road and gave the most imperceptible nod. He pulled off the road and pointed to a clump of nearby shrubbery. Benyamin was too desperate to protest. He shivered in the early morning air as he relieved himself behind the scanty bushes. The Negro squatted not far away, behind another bush. Was this what Americans did? Benyamin was not a traveler. Before his trip to England, he had traveled only between his home and the lumberyard or to Temple or to Gymnasium. He never had to go to the

103

bathroom on the road, because his mother always made him go beforehand.

His mother! He wondered where she was and how she was doing. Was she managing on the Sabbath, now that she had to cook everything herself? Did her mother, Oma Rivkeh follow her to Argentina? Did his mother know where he was? Would he ever see her again? And Anya; did she get back to Poland all right? He felt the stinging behind his eyes and quickly tried to think of something else. But at this moment, in spite of all the possibility his brief glimpse of America had seemed to afford him, everything he could envision about his future seemed almost as depressing as his past.

The Negro straightened up and Benyamin heard the sound of his zipper as the man secured his linens. Benyamin wondered if a Negro's penis was the same color as his own; if he was the same brown color all the way through or if his underbelly was pink, and only his extremities and face were dark, like a panda bear's.

They headed back to the car. Benyamin began to feel uneasy about the White man, who only nodded to him as the Negro held the door open for him to return to the back seat. If the man did not like him—

Benyamin strained to see America in the rising light, just in case he had to flee; but his eyes would not cooperate, and he slept again.

He came to in a double bed. The linens smelled of the sunshine that streamed in through the lace-covered windows. The heavy purple drapes and the green flowery wallpaper, along with a wine-colored horsehair chair and several shelves overflowing with books gave the room an over-stuffed, but comfortable feeling. Benyamin tipped his head back and saw, above the heavily carved headboard, several paintings and sketches. The colorful quilts cascading from the bed onto the floor were warm and well filled. He saw the clothes he had been wearing neatly folded on the desk in the corner and his shoes laid out under the desk chair. Someone had not only put him into bed, but had also stripped him and placed him in a nightshirt. That same someone had unpacked his suitcase and put his things away. *There was a maidservant.*

He was hoping for an Anya: a pretty, round girl with golden hair, a soft smile and a very gentle touch. Perhaps she would like him; perhaps she would like him very much. And even if she spoke absolutely no German at all, well, Anya was always silent in bed: silent and secretive, and approaching him only from the back, so that there would be no 'accidents'.

He listened for her footfalls outside his door, and suddenly she was there. He fixed his eyes on the opening as it swung open, to reveal—

A Negress; forty-ish or even more. Her gray hair pouffed around her head like the parachute seeds around the head of an enormous dandelion. Her dark eyes were made huge by glasses with enormous lenses and her spindly arms and legs poked timidly out of her gray maid's uniform. She had no discernable breasts, and her breath whistled audibly in her chest with her every inhalation. Benyamin felt deflation below his belt. The woman brought in a bowl of steaming hot water and a towel, gave him a wan half-smile and closed the door again.

After a moment's disappointment, Benyamin almost laughed aloud. He would have plenty to tell Herschel about this new land! He washed his face quickly, threw on his clothes and combed his hair. He thought he smelled breakfast.

CHAPTER TWELVE

He found himself in an enormous paneled dining room with flocked wallpaper depicting pink, blue and yellow roses against a field of green. The overall effect was pleasing, though he missed his mother's pristine white-walled dining room. A long dining table covered with an elaborate lace cloth dominated the center of the room. The maid, whose name turned out to be Hattie, was bringing out from the kitchen various dishes from which the most incredibly delightful scents emanated.

Aaronsohn sat at the head of the table. To his right sat a woman that Benyamin would have assumed was his wife, had she not looked so much like him. To his left was a place setting, with a photograph set before it of a woman who appeared younger than the two at the table. Benyamin wondered who she was, and why her presence merited a place at the table, since she obviously was not expected to appear in the flesh.

Both of the people at table looked up, but neither smiled or greeted him when he entered the room; they appeared to be very depressed, and preoccupied to the point that they seemed hardly concerned about their new charge. He gave a slight bow, presented the envelope containing the money Oma Bina had sent for his sponsors, and sat across from the lady, one seat down, so as not to disturb the extra setting.

Hattie brought out the breakfast dishes: sliced fruit on a tray, a kind of corn porridge, eggs, ham and biscuits. "We don't keep a kosher kitchen here," the lady Aaronsohn said in excellent German. "We tried to train the staff, but they just wouldn't learn, so now we eat what they eat, cloven hooves and all. We *assume* that won't be a problem for you." Thank goodness, Benyamin thought. They spoke German! Perhaps he would not have to learn English after all. With a grateful smile, he ripped into the breakfast with a will.

After he cleaned his plate twice, though, Benyamin wasn't sure what to do. He would have liked to go outside, but for some not entirely unnamed fear. He did not speak very much English. Where was he? Were there wild animals? What if he got lost? What if he took a wrong turn and never—

"Here is your schedule," Miss Aaronsohn, who was at least sixty, Benyamin thought, but had never married even once, said. "You need show up only for meals today. Starting tomorrow, however, you will come for breakfast at eight, and study English with the tutor we hired for you from ten a.m. to noon. Then you will have lunch. At one, you will begin your regular academic studies with a tutor; we assume you are behind. At four, you will go to the factory with Mr. Aaronsohn. At six, you will have your supper, with us. After dinner, you may roam about the grounds, but do not go into the community until your English is sufficient. We have a sizeable library here, which you are free to use, and if you need anything, you may ask Hattie or Ezra; though, being Negroes, they don't speak German, so you will have to try to communicate in English. The cook, Mary, will fix your meals if we happen to be out or if you get hungry at odd hours. Knock at the kitchen door."

Benyamin rose to go, but Miss Aaronsohn stopped him: *"One other thing,"* she said. "We expect you to follow our rules here, or there will be trouble for you. Your grandmother, to whom we owe a debt, tells us that you are a good child, if a bit lazy. There are no children your age here, so you will have to amuse yourself most of the time. Do not make your idleness a workshop for bad actions. If we cannot keep you, we must send you away, and I can assure you: that would not be so good for you, as you are not an American citizen. We have a good standing in the community, and we do not want to be thought of otherwise because of a kindness gone wrong."

Angst now filled Benyamin's mind. So he *could* be sent away; probably not to his parents in Argentina, but back to Germany, where he was slowly becoming aware of the bad things that were happening. He determined to do his best to make the Aaronsohns happy with their choice to provide a place for him.

Back in his room, he contemplated his money. Perhaps he had enough to buy flowers for Miss Aaronsohn? He reasoned that flowers would soften her heart and let her know his intentions not to make her worry about him. He took some of the bills, etched with their images of men he did not know, and wandered about the place until he found Ezra working on one of the two cars in the garage. He was able to pantomime flowers, and held out the money, saying, "Fraulein Aaronsohn?" The man looked at the bills, selected two, put them in his pocket and poked his head back under the hood. Benyamin was not sure he had understood, and even wondered if the man might think the money was for his own use and run off with it. But an hour or so later, Ezra came up the road bearing a long white box wrapped with a red bow, which he presented, along with some change, to Benyamin. Delighted, Benyamin took the box and ran with it to Miss Aaronsohn's door.

She sat at a small writing desk, her quilled pen and paper at the ready. He looked past her into her room. The same style of flocked wallpaper from the dining room adorned her walls. Her bed, a large four-poster, was covered in a white chenille counterpane. There were lacy pillows and velvet curtains and chintz upholstered chairs. The heavy smell of patchouli hung over everything. There were also photographs, of people, some of whom looked vaguely like his father and grandmother and some that appeared to be from even earlier times. One of them was laid flat on the mantel. He wondered why it was not upright with the rest.

What most captured Benyamin's attention, however, were the oil paintings on the wall. They were as full of life as the rest of the room was not, with their brilliant reds and golds and greens. Some were like photographs of great works he had seen in his art history texts. He wondered if he might actually be looking at authentic works.

"What is it?" Miss Aaronsohn asked, laying the pen aside. Wordlessly, Benyamin held out the box. She lifted her eyebrows and something mildly akin to a smile crossed behind her eyes and bowed her lips. "Flowers," she said softly. "How long has it been, I wonder, since someone brought me flowers?" She smiled up at him.

"I'm sorry," Benyamin said, "not to have been able to get flowers to bring to you first thing. I hope you understand. I will do my best to make you happy you took me in. I will not do anything bad." She asked him to ask Hattie to fetch a vase for the flowers. At dinner, he saw a fresh bouquet of roses standing at attention on the dining room buffet. He hoped that, wherever his mother was, she would sense that he had followed her direction, hastily given as she left him on the hills above Cologne. For an instant, he felt pride, then a pang of sadness. He realized afresh how much he missed his mother.

CHAPTER THIRTEEN

Herschel walked slowly up the three flights of stairs on Sayavedra Street to the apartment that the Rosenthalers shared. His feet always moved more slowly on payday. Payday! He didn't know why he even thought of it as 'payday'. *He* wasn't the one getting paid for his labors.

For nearly a year, now, it had been the same: he labored at the machine shop. He fixed the machines, getting grime embedded so deeply into his skin that he sometimes felt he must look like a Blackamoor. He would go to the boss at the end of the week and receive his pay envelope. Then he would trudge home with his envelope intact and climb the forty-five steps to their flat. His father, who was usually out of his dressing gown and in his suit for the occasion, would hold out his hand and without a word between them, Herschel would hand over the envelope. Elie would inspect it to confirm that Herschel had taken nothing out of it, and then extract a few bills and hand them to his son. Some he would give to his wife for food shopping and household expenses. The rest—the lion's share—he would tuck into his waistcoat pocket and retire to his 'office'.

For Elie to have an office in this tiny two-bedroom space meant that Herschel slept on a grimy pull-out sofa in the living room. Elie, however, had gone out and purchased a new desk, filing cabinets, consultation chairs, art and even an expensive rug for his new space. Of course, he had said, he needed medical books; so even though he had not a clue what the thick tomes of Spanish actually *said*, he insisted that their existence in his space was essential to his appearing erudite and learned.

Herschel frowned. His father had not been 'right', he felt, since he appeared on the dock in Frankfurt, leaning heavily on his wife's arm.

Herschel was used to the masterful doctor; the man that saved life after life and brought baby after baby safely into the world. He recalled his father's office in its heyday, with ladies coming and going. He remembered how Elie's chest would swell when he discussed his part in the Great War and his medal, now lying beneath a mound of dirt in Germany. That man had disappeared. The man on the dock appeared to have shrunken. He had only 'harrumphed' when Herschel had run toward him, anticipating the same embrace he had received when he left for Frankfurt. Instead of hugging him and enquiring about his exploits, however, his father had just lit a cigar and turned away. On board the ship, he had spent most of his time in his cabin, and most of that time in his bed, puffing on his cigars and staring at the ceiling. Eliana sent Herschel and Ezra scurrying all over the ship to find the things she thought might cheer Elie up: his favorite cigars, different cigars, special foods, treats, magazines, extra blankets, pillows, newspapers—nothing pleased him. When they brought whatever bribe they might come bearing to rouse him from bed, he never engaged them, but waved them out of the room; most of the time with the very thing they had sought all over the ship for untouched. Ezra declared that Elie was depressed; broken-hearted over being cast out of his country; but Eliana always insisted that it was the ocean voyage, or some fault with a cook or a fellow passenger, or some mild illness he had contracted before embarkation that caused him to take to his bed.

Herschel had avoided contact with his father as much as he could. There was a ship to be explored; and while Ezra was years younger than he, they had a great time roaming the salons, swimming in the Olympic-sized pool and tasting foods they had only imagined, chiefly because all of them were not kosher. He tried not to notice his mother dozing in a lounge chair on deck even when it was windy or rainy or cold. Nor did he

112

ever hear her complain that sometimes Elie became so ill-tempered that he would make her get out of the room, no matter how tired she was or how late the time. His mother didn't have to tell Herschel that she feared his father might take his life, but he knew, and he feared, too.

Once off the ship, however, Elie had suddenly come to life, full of plans about how he would set up his new practice and achieve prosperity in Argentina in no time at all. He had gone from hospital to hospital, insisting that he would be accepted—no, *feted*, even though he spoke not even a smattering of Spanish; and then, having received no offers of a position, he had established a home office, ready to welcome a flood of colleagues and new clients that were never going to appear.

Well, his father could sham all he wished. The simple fact was that he could not secure a job, let alone practice as a gynecologist, in Argentina. He could not pass the Spanish language tests, he would not study the language and, he quickly discovered, there were other highly regarded German-speaking doctors in the immediate neighborhood that were not willing to share their clientele with him no matter how well known he had been in Cologne. Ezra, who resided temporarily in the cramped space, owed the Rosenthalers no debt, other than that of kinship; so as soon as he began to make money, he had given the family (meaning Elie) a modest sum for having allowed him to stay with them, and had found his own flat. Herschel would gladly have joined him, but his father would not hear of it.

"What son abandons his father?" he asked imperiously. "And how are your mother and I to live, if our only son does not support us? It is your *duty* as our child to assist us."

"Papa," Herschel would counter, "it would be so much easier for us all if you would just get a job. There are many things that you could do, even outside the medical field. You could work in the factory—"

"What!" his father had exploded. "And ruin my hands? What happens, if a woman goes into labor and I cannot even help her, because there are so many calluses on my fingers that my sense of touch is gone?"

Herschel found it best to mollify his father at such times. Elie would become enraged; almost violent, if he did not.

"I'm sorry," Herschel would say. "I'm a fool. I don't know what I was thinking."

"You were not thinking at all," Elie would shout at him. "That's been your problem since the beginning. You've always been stupid!"

And Herschel would swallow his impulse to shout back, "I'm *not* stupid! I've *never* been stupid! The stupidest thing I've ever done was to agree to give you my hard-earned money and live off the pittance you dole out to me while you waste everything on outrageously expensive office furniture and new suits and spicy foods that I hope give you gout, and Cuban cigars that I hope give you cancer!" Instead, he would stare at the floor and hope his father's tirade would end soon.

"May I buy something at the store for you?" he would ask, though he knew his father would not want him to. "I can't trust you with money," the older man would say. "How do I know you'll recognize if the clerk short-changes you? And how do I know you won't pocket the change and not give me back all I deserve? Get out of here; I'll get your mother to go out." Herschel would skulk away from him as if he were a whipped dog.

Nor could Herschel speak with his mother about his father's attitude. "He misses Germany so much, and would like nothing better than to go back", she would say. "I believe he is saving your money for the day when we can return. Naturally he is a little irritable sometimes."

Herschel knew his father yelled at his mother almost as much as he yelled at him, even though the voyage was behind him and any illness he might have brought from Germany was long over. He worried that someday his father's anger would take him beyond yelling at her. On that terrible day, he told himself, he would spirit his mother away and leave his father to die or adapt to life alone in this new country.

Herschel liked Argentina. He liked the warm weather and the wide plazas and the pretty, pretty girls that passed him on the streets. He thought he would like to introduce himself to one of them and perhaps become her beau, but his Spanish was still very bad. Whores were beneath him, and besides, he had no money to pay them. He looked at the bills in his hand: barely enough to travel from home to work and back again, and perhaps buy a coffee on the street for a couple of days. His socks he had darned over and over again; so much that they eventually were too lumpy for him to walk on and he had to throw them away. His clothing was stained with the grease and soot from the machines he crawled under and over, looking for their trouble spots. There were slashes and ripped pockets on every pair of his pants from his tools and his narrow escapes from grasping machine parts. He realized he looked shabby; and, while he did not need special clothing for work, he certainly needed to look nice if he would go courting.

He wondered how he would do in the dating pool. Because of his abrupt exit from Gymnasium and his premature retirement from his probationary position in Frankfurt, he did not really have an education. Women, he knew, wanted men who could not only support them with a nice lodging, but who also could take them places: to the beach, or out to a restaurant, or even on vacations. He could hardly take himself out for a coffee. Cinema was out of the question. He could feel every stone in the pavement through the soles of his shoes, but he didn't have the money to repair, let alone replace them.

And his ability to romance a woman, if he got one? He was still a virgin. It had taken him a bit to realize it, given Anya's attentions to him, and he had learned of his actual status only because of his discussions with the men in the factory in Frankfurt. Anya had done such a good job of pleasing him that he had no need to reciprocate, nor would she have permitted it. What was he supposed to – *do* – with a woman, he wondered. Anyway, under his bondage with his father, the point of even thinking about upgrading his sexual status was moot.

His mother's situation, he realized, was little better than his. Gentle and compliant to a fault, she had lived a charmed life in Cologne, with her servants and the support of her mother and mother-in-law. With them left behind, however, she had been frantic, trying to normalize the changes her husband was going through in her mind. On board, she had scurried around the ship from deck to deck; fetching food and cigars and wine and German magazines and whatever else he required or she thought he wanted. She had endured his tirades when she suggested that he come to dinner or even his explosion when she attempted to have a psychiatrist examine him, on the pretext of a collegial visitation.

She had served him hand and foot, at great personal cost. In the new land, she had not purchased so much as a handkerchief for herself. There was no question that there would be no household help, even though the natives would probably have worked very cheaply. Elie would not allow the money for that. He would not allow the money for anything but whatever he wanted. As a result, they ate very poorly. Meat was a rarity and vegetables rarer still. They ate mostly beans and white rice and drank coffee or *mate*, as the natives did. Occasionally there would be sliced tomatoes and lettuce. It hardly mattered, though, because she was certainly not the best of cooks. No one lingered over Eliana's meals.

Herschel suspected that his father spent most of his money at the local coffee shops, with a class of ex-patriate men much lower than he ever would have befriended in Cologne. It did not matter; it was an audience; sycophants that would listen to almost anyone who had a mouthful of words and a pocketful of pesos. Elie would don a freshly pressed shirt, his string tie, his favorite suit, his shiny leather shoes, and his gold watch and chain, and load his vest pocket with the finest of cigars, which were usually all gone by the time he reached home. Herschel dared not complain to his father, whose tirades were growing more and more frequent and intense. At times he would bellow so loudly that the neighbors would open their doors to make certain there was no immediate danger, then shut them quickly to keep out the noise. Herschel stayed close to home, when he was not working, to make certain that his father's anger did not boil over.

He missed Benyamin. If his brother were living with them, perhaps between the two of them they could control Elie's rages – and maybe Benyamin could work, too, and then Herschel could have a little more money in his pocket and *maybe* he could find a girl who would like him. With Benyamin there, Herschel could even move in with Ezra and live the life he wanted. He was, after all, nearly twenty. When was *his* time, *his* life, supposed to begin? It was he, as the breadwinner of the family, that should determine what happened to the money. His mother should receive a more generous budget, so that they could eat better. His father should receive no more than it made sense for him to spend. He did not need to be in the coffee shops *every* evening. Perhaps if he spent some of his time with his wife, listening to the radio or walking on the beach that was only a few blocks from their home, if he even tried to look at some of the books Eliana had insisted on packing from his old office, if he learned to chatter in Spanish, then he could have the life he wanted, and then he would not have to depend on Herschel at all.

Herschel made the factory his world. There was practically no written work to be done; and when there was, he would imperiously send the requestor to Ezra, who worked under him. Herschel's skills had not gone unnoticed by the factory owners. His prowess led to his being raised up higher and higher to increasingly responsible tasks, until he became foreman over the shop, just under the owners themselves. Unable to purchase lunch despite his new position, he spent his afternoon siesta times poring over Spanish children's books, struggling to learn the language so that he could be a better supervisor. 'Better', however, did not mean 'kinder'. He used the supervisory skills he had learned from the two central men in his life – his father and the German instructor at the Frankfurt school – as his guide for managing people. Some would call him a relentless taskmaster and some would call him far worse names, but never to his face. Most of the workers feared Herschel for what they perceived as his obsessive nit-picking over trivial details and his failure to socialize. He never seemed to find funny the witticisms they dared to make in his presence, and he tended to wear a brow-wrinkling scowl, even when there was no cause for it, as if life itself was a bad joke. Not one of those under him, however, would have criticized him for turning out a bad product; and when a repaired machine left his shop—well, it was not likely to turn up there again any time in the immediate future.

He never spoke at home of how others accepted his skills. He knew his father was still deeply disappointed at the 'simpleton' he thought Herschel was; and there was no reason, Herschel thought, to try convincing him to believe anything else. He was more likely to tell Herschel that he was lying or exaggerating, at least, which would most likely lead to an argument.

CHAPTER FOURTEEN

It was a great occasion for Benyamin when his mentors at last allowed him to go out unescorted during the daylight hours, and an even greater one when he finally could go to the public school. Despite the stringent placement tests, Benyamin actually scored a grade ahead of where he would have been had he stayed at Gymnasium.

He walked through the halls of the George Washington High School, looking at everything. The school had won trophies; there were tall trophies adorned with tiny football players or basketballs or tennis rackets. Photos, some weathered behind their dusty glass frames, depicted various groupings of robed students, obviously those who had graduated long ago. Newer pictures showed cheerleaders and choir members: all smiling, all happy.

Benyamin hoped he would be happy in this new setting. Although he knew no one, he felt he would make friends easily. There were no Brown Shirts here—at least he hoped not—that would threaten to beat his brains out. And Hitler, though he had been elected *Time* Magazine's Man of the Year earlier, an occurrence that had elicited the only shred of emotion Benyamin ever saw from Mr. Aaronsohn, continued to dominate Germany. Many people said all-out war between the United States and Germany was imminent.

War! It would mean the dropping of bombs and soldiers marching through the streets, people starving and being shot and dying. He hoped no bombs would fall on his house in Cologne, and nobody he knew would die. For the first time, he thought about his friends: the Jewish boys that he had not seen since the last time each of them packed up their rucksacks to go into hiding. Where were they now, he wondered.

The day quickly absorbed his thoughts. Dressed in his crisp white shirt, his grey wool pants, maroon tie and blue blazer with gold buttons, he could not help but consider how much handsomer he had grown, even in the year since he had come to America. He had managed to escape the acne that had so ravaged Herschel's face, and his bronzed skin all but glowed. He liked looking into his own eyes, so radiantly brown were they. And he was at least four centimeters taller than he had been when he first measured himself against the doorjamb to his room in America. Again a small pang of nostalgia touched him. There was a set of marks on a doorway in Cologne: one set denoting his ascent toward the stars and one denoting Herschel's. Again he pushed the sad thought from his mind.

There was, however, no forgetting that no one had celebrated his sixteenth birthday. The Aaronsohns had not even asked about it, and when he bounded into breakfast, expecting the usual confections and pile of presents, there had been nothing. Indeed, the Aaronsohns had not even looked up – their usual behavior—from their newspapers and business folders. 'Surely,' he had thought, 'they will have something for me at dinner!' But again, nothing. He had put on a brave face, but that night he had lay sobbing in his bed. He was sixteen; *sixteen!* Just two years from becoming a legal American man, but abandoned in this cold new world! "Shut up, Benyamin!" he had hissed to himself. "At least you are not in Germany!"

And yet—and yet—

In the moment, he could recall only good associations with Germany: the Gymnasium before the Brown Shirts came, the Kolendom, Anya, his mother humming contentedly in the parlor, his relatives gathered around the dining room table on Shabbas. How he missed the soft white walls and the deep dark buffet, the sturdy ebony table with its lace cover and delicate dishes, each holding a wonderful treat! The memories made him weep again. After manfully trying to stop his tears, he gave up and sobbed like the child he still was, wishing that there was an Anya to stroke away his sadness. But there was not. And there would not be. He, Benyamin Rosenthaler, was a sixteen-year-old boy and not a man, no matter what Rabbi Hirschfeld said or his faith professed. He was a child; he felt abandoned by his family, all alone in a world poised on the very precipice of war.

CHAPTER FIFTTEEN

Herschel patrolled the streets of Buenos Aires like a madman, possessed by a desire for a woman of his own. He could not help but stare at them as they passed by. The pretty senoritas sometimes looked back at him through their thick lashes, and every now and then one would raise an eyebrow or indicate with the slightest upturning of her lips that there might be some interest somewhere within her, which set his blood aflame.

He thought about the men he had been around in the machinery school in Frankfurt. Though half of them were probably raging Nazis by now and he was not allowed to be privy to their conversations as an equal, he remembered the few discussions he had overheard among the workers in Frankfurt. They often said that if a man did not discharge himself in a woman he would go insane. As he battled his urges, Herschel began to believe it.

He worried his member occasionally, when the house was quiet save for his father's sonorous snoring. But it was dawning on him that satisfaction of the need he had lay not in the mere stimulation of his organ. It was the *nearness*; the closeness, the affection, the sense of haven and belonging to someone that he desired.

Herschel didn't want a woman; he wanted a wife.

But where did one find a suitable wife; a Jewish girl of his age, in this pseudo-Italian city? Everyone professed to be Catholic; even some people that he knew were not. Catholicism was the religion to be, it seemed. And, he learned, it was best to be quiet about being a Jew.

Or about following no religion at all. The intellectuals that hung out in the coffee shops, where he sometimes went and sat without funds to imbibe, bandied about any number of –isms. 'Intellectual masturbation', Ezra called it. Ezra was more comfortable believing in God but declaring no specific religion. Herschel wished he could do that.

He knew his father would never let him marry any of the Spanish girls; not, the man would insist, because of race, but because of religion. "Who will keep your home kosher?" he would ask his son. "Who will train your children in the ways of the Faith? When it is time for them to be bar mitzvah'ed, she will want them christened instead, or baptized, or whatever it is that they do." It would have done no good to remind his father that, in Cologne, he had allowed them to attend the Kolendom and that adherence to his own faith was rare and seemed more like a by-product of his wife's.

He did broach the subject with his mother once, but only once. "In these uncertain times," she had said, "one does not really want to make a family or bring children into the world. Look at us. We live hand-to-mouth in a country that is not our own. Your brother lives in North America. Your grandmother lives in Switzerland. My mother—my mother is still in Germany. That Hitler that everybody thought was so wonderful has invaded Poland and is threatening everybody else. It is getting worse and worse for us Jews. You watch: the pogroms will return."

It was several minutes later that Herschel realized she had not addressed his issue about his wanting a wife except as a codicil to her belief that Hitler made it a bad time to marry. He turned back to her.

"Mama," he said, "Hitler or no, I need a wife. Life has to go on; should we stop everything until this Hitler says it is okay for us to resume? Does he control our every breath?

"It may come to that, Son," she said. "Even my sister in England says there are rumors—oh, I don't want to talk about it; it worries me too much."

So he continued to look at the young girls in the marketplace, the young girls in the factory, the young girls in the coffee shops. And he continued to study Spanish and to fix his machines, to oppress his subordinates and to hand over his paycheck every Friday to his father and receive his pittance: not enough to save, not enough to set aside or even to purchase necessities for himself. On Sundays when the factory was closed, Herschel would walk for exercise or just sit listlessly in the tiny parlor when it became too hot, wondering what had become of his childhood and all its promise, wondering how it was that Benyamin got to go to the United States and he did not, wondering about more things than he could fit in his head all at once.

"Herschel!" his father's voice would shake him awake as he drooped on the sofa. "Get up and go somewhere! Why are you such a lazy lout?"

CHAPTER SIXTEEN

From the moment he set foot into the classroom, Benyamin knew he would do well; not only because the Aaronsohns provided him with a tutor, but also because he was afraid. He feared that if he fell into his old habits—daydreaming and failing to do assignments—he would be sent back to England, or worse, to Germany.

That fear pervaded his every moment. His dilemma was never whether he should study or do something else, but whether he would be able to do anything else after he studied. His tutor was a taskmaster; a man in his late forties who smelled of tobacco and garlic at all times. He would drill Benyamin again and again and again over the smallest topics, until he grasped them. In his severity, the man made Rabbi Hirschberg appear pleasant, even kindly. Benyamin chose not to rebel against him, lest he should give a bad report to the Aaronsohns and they should withdraw their sponsorship and he should find himself back on a ship, headed east across the Atlantic and into the hell that Europe was rapidly becoming for any Jew that wasn't somewhere else by now.

Nor did he take an interest in the girls populating fully half the seats in every class he took. Many of them caught his eye, with their soft hair and softer smiles. He would just blush and look away. As much as he might miss Anya, as much as he might desire to be touched and cuddled, he could not forget Sheila Clark and what she had screamed at him on the ship.

As the days flowed into months, the reports from newly arriving Jews grew grimmer. People were disappearing every day. Soldiers were showing up with guns and marching Jews off to work; even professors and lawyers were shoveling snow and scrubbing the streets. Old people were getting pushed up against buildings, and if they didn't move fast enough, they were getting gunned down, right in front of everyone. Jews were being moved from place to place, and anything they had of value was being stripped away from them: jewelry, furs, silverware, even money, out of their frozen bank accounts. Germans appeared in formerly lucrative Jewish-owned businesses and formerly luxurious Jewish homes. Anybody Jewish who could was getting out of Germany; out of Europe, because everybody knew, by now, what was coming; indeed, what had already arrived.

A new girl turned up in his classroom one day. Her name was Lara Hecht, and she lived with the Appletons, acquaintances of the Aaronsohns. Lara spoke virtually no English, and the teachers had no idea how even to pretend to educate her.

Benyamin was the person designated to integrate her into her new environment. His heart had leapt when he first saw her. She was dark— almost olive in complexion—and had long, cascading black hair that waved only slightly and hung nearly to her waist. Her eyes flashed bright and brown with that soft sadness that only eyes that came from eyes that had looked on four hundred years of slavery and Mount Sinai and the building of the Temple and the Babylon abduction and countless inquisitions and pogroms could look. He felt almost as if he should bow to her or cover her hands with kisses and tears to comfort her for her suffering and the pain of all those that lived on in her genes.

But he did none of those things. Instead, he stepped quickly to the front of the room when summoned to be Lara's translator and woodenly performed the task. He hardly looked at her through all the days of helping her to decipher the hieroglyphics in her texts until they began to sharpen into meaning, as the language and its iterations in written and spoken words came out of the mists and spoke to her.

There came the afternoon, both feared and desired by Benyamin, when Lara approached him in her somewhat timid way. "My host family would like to have you come for a visit," she said. "They are very grateful for how you have helped me and would like to invite you and your family to a Shabbas meal."

His first impulse was to refuse. He did not know how the Aaronsohns would react to such an invitation; would they think he was now consorting with girls, and no longer controlling himself, despite their hospitality? This invitation could mean a one-way trip back to Germany. Nor did he wish to accept for a second very important reason: the Aaronsohns would have to reciprocate the invitation; and as they had just had a very succulent and tasty roast pig the night before, he did not think her host family, the Landaus, would be overly impressed with his mentors' brand of Judaism. He was about to refuse, when Lara added, "The Landaus do not observe Shabbas too closely. Will that be a problem for your people?" She gave him a little envelope addressed to the Aaronsohns.

Benyamin was surprised when the Aaronsohns not only accepted the invitation, but Miss Aaronsohn actually smiled. "I'm so happy that you are meeting young people in the community that you can play with," she said. Her words, however, made Mr. Aaronsohn furious.

"Play!" he said. "He's sixteen; a man. Men don't 'play' with girls. They seduce them and get them pregnant and then there are fees that must be paid out and shames that must be covered up when the 'playmate' goes off to war and does not return!" Benyamin became uneasy. He could almost hear the ship's deep bellowing horn steaming into the nearest harbor to snatch him from safety.

"Oh, but Benyamin is not *that* kind of boy!" Miss Aaronsohn said. "He is a *good* boy!"

Mr. Aaronsohn glowered. "As if *you* would know!" he said with vehemence. Miss Aaronsohn dropped her eyes and stared at her plate, tension pursing her lips. Benyamin pondered the two, wondering if there was some story he did not know about Miss Aaronsohn, or maybe about them both. He would, however, never be apprised of it, and he was too polite, or perhaps too frightened, to even intimate a timid interest. If he offended them, he might find himself headed back to Cologne.

Indeed, as reports grew of Germany's deterioration as a place any Jew wanted to be, he became more aware of his good fortune in being in America. He had begun having dreams: a sky; inky jet, with furious gray clouds boiling like slate-colored flames within it, back-lit by white-hot bolts of lightning streaking across the water's surface, with claps of thunder screaming after them. The ocean mirrored the spectacle in the sky, and spewed as much as it could of its total black contents across the bow of the ship where he alone stood, grasping the railing and screaming aloud, *"Mutti! Mutti!"* The ship would sail into the middle of Cologne, and the gangplank would fall on the very steps of the Kolendom, where a mob of shrieking Brown Shirts brandishing truncheons would cry out, "Kill the Jew! Kill the Jew! The Jew—the Jew—"

He would scream himself awake; his nightclothes clammy with sweat, his bedding flung about the room, his pillow pummeled into submission. So in disarray would he render his surroundings that he sometimes needed several seconds to realize he had only had a very bad dream.

No one ever came to him at such times. The servants had their own quarters, far away on the other side of the house, and he imagined that they would have little concern about the terrors of a young Jewish boy. Miss Aaronsohn's room was in another wing of the house as well. As for Mr. Aaronsohn—well, Benyamin thought, he was just a little less terrifying than Hitler. Benyamin vested in him the power to make that awful nightmare come true. He was, Benyamin considered, a man that must *never* be crossed.

He thought often of Anya in those days. He wondered if she had ever married and if he would ever see her again. He thought of her softness and her goodness and her kindness. And then he would have another dream: he was back on Ringstrasse and a parade was passing. The storm troopers tromped by, high-stepping in those shiny black boots that Benyamin had so recently coveted but now could not abide the thought of. When he looked closer, he saw that the soldiers were trampling Jews instead of cobblestones. He could see their faces: Avi Greenbaum and Mendel Blatt, Yacob Eisen and Moises Berg. He saw Herr Zitomer the tailor and his fat wife squirming under the crunching boots, trying in vain to avoid being crushed beneath the stomping soles. Even Herr Brecht came back from being Disappeared to take his place among those squirming, moaning Jews, whose blood spurted out of them and clogged the gutters. He saw, too, the faces of their persecutors—the German boys from his school, and Herr Knacht, and Anya's boyfriend Hans that had spoiled her, and thousands and thousands of people he did not know. Most were chanting slogans he could not understand. Others were strafing the crowd with their eyes, pulling out the Jews hiding among them and hurling them under the stomping Nazis' feet. Benyamin turned to flee, but the throng was there, pressing him to the front of the crowd.

Then someone would seize his neck, and he would swivel just in time to see that it was—

Anya! Anya, with a changed face, so angelic, so beautiful; but hideous with rage. "Here you are, my little Jew-*kind*!" she would whisper into his ear as she propelled him closer to the danger. "And who will offer up her virginity to save your ass *this* time?" Then, still gripping him, she would shriek, "Here is the one you are looking for, Mr. Hitler!" She would jerk Benyamin's head upward and he would find himself staring into the smouldering black eyes of Adolf Hitler. *Der Fuehrer* would lock onto Benyamin's face and suck his body up into those eyes, until—

No matter what, he thought, he must not pursue a girl. He must deny the gnawing thoughts in his head that led to gnawing feelings in his groin. He must wait, until the Aaronsohns gave him leave to marry, or until his parents—wherever they were in South America—afforded him a bride, or until some miracle happened and the right girl came to him.

Perhaps Lara Hecht *was* the girl for him, he thought. But then, he had mistakenly thought that Sheila Clark was the one for him, and earlier that Anya was to be his. So he could be wrong about Lara.

Besides—besides, closer proximity to her and scrutiny of her lovely face had revealed that Lara had just the faintest fuzz on her upper lip. The downy raven-colored hairs were just thick enough upon her golden skin to appear to Benyamin like a man's mustache. He imagined that they would tickle if one kissed them, and that it would feel almost the same as kissing a boy. Whatever her other charms—soft, round breasts that she could not hide beneath her thick sweaters, a sleek and slender frame, and her oh, so compelling eyes—that mustache was just too *present*. He imagined it to be flapping in the breeze when she spoke or becoming milk-stained when she ate her lunch. Surely, if he were ever to kiss her, he would feel that fuzz and it would kill all ardor and passion. He quailed at the thought that she might be the one chosen for him; that he might lift the veil on his wedding day and discover her with her handlebar mustache grinning up at him. He decided that she could be a nice friend to him, but that he must never show so much interest as to delude her family or his mentors into thinking that he wanted to marry her; oh no, not with that mustache!

So he went with the Aaronsohns to the Landaus' home, and he ate their Shabbas meal, which, for all its non-kosher touches, was far tastier than anything the Aaronsohns' cook had ever prepared. And when the Aaronsohns sent a return invitation by mail, he gallantly handed it to Lara to deliver. But he pointedly avoided Lara after that, and eventually she stopped seeking him out. He saw her at times, looking through lowered eyes at him, sitting alone in the crowded lunchroom at her table while he sat alone at his. Still, he didn't want himself linked to her in any way. Any thoughts he might have about other parts of her invariably returned to the hairs on her upper lip. "NO!" he would say to the mental image of her as his wife, standing next to him at the bathroom sink shaving off that walrus mustache with his razor. Once he even relegated her to his other nightmares; to the water-soaked deck or the broken throng beneath the Brown Shirts' beating feet. But he knew she would not go away until she actually went away, and when the semester ended and she did, he never saw her again.

When she went to her new sponsors, or to her parents, or her new school, he missed her a bit. Perhaps, he thought, the mustache was not so bad. It was her only flaw. It was noticeable only under serious scrutiny. That was certainly much better than how Herschel had fared.

CHAPTER SEVENTEEN

It had all started out so well, and Herschel had been so hopeful. Was love going to come to him at last?

Solange was a beauty. Her hair glistened soft and thick and long, from her crown to her waist. She had to keep it pinned up in a ball at the nape of her slender neck because of the machines, but he could tell by the imagined heft of it in his hand that it was lush. Her eyes were emerald green and flecked with gold. Her body, beneath her plain peasant's dress, undulated like the ocean when she moved.

She and her family sold beef, tomato, cucumber and cheese sandwiches on rolled tortillas, as well as empanadas containing meat or fruit to the workers. They were inexpensive, and she and her family were allowed in chiefly because the factory owners figured the employees would spend less time away from the factory if they purchased from Solange and then took their siestas in the park, rather than wandering off to the coffeeshops or their homes.

Solange noticed that Herschel sat alone on the grass, reading, or gnawing on whatever half-spoiled tidbit he had found in the family's icebox. She brought him a sandwich and an empanada on the first day she sat with him.

"I've been watching you," she said. "You never buy from me. I think you believe my food is not all that tasty. You don't know my cooking, It is much better than anything I've seen you eat."

Herschel blushed. "I don't have the money to pay you," he said.

"Oh, the first one is free," she said. "Then you pay. But for now, you enjoy." She plopped down on the grass next to him and watched as he bit into an empanada.

It was the tastiest meal Herschel had enjoyed since his voyage to this country. He licked his fingers and rolled the last taste over and over in his mouth. The combination of the wonderful flavor and the beautiful woman in front of him, her eyes and the fragrance of her almost overpowering him, left him feeling pleasantly weak. He smiled, musing that it was the first time he had done so in what seemed like an eternity.

"Solange!" a tall man called to her in a rough voice. "You are not done here!" She threw back her head and laughed. "I am done for today! I am all out of sandwiches and I deserve a siesta!"

Then her eyes had grown serious. "Do you think you can find a job for me in the factory?" she asked. "I will go crazy if I just make sandwiches all day and sell them to these factory men that paw at me and make their insolent remarks."

Herschel considered. He did not know if her experience would be much different in the factory, but he thought he might be able to protect her.

"Can you do anything secretarial?" he asked. "We always need people to help with inventory and letter writing and such."

She clapped her hands, her expression changing from angst to delight.

So began a new career for Solange. She was at the factory early, following Herschel around and writing down whatever he directed her to. He explained his difficulty with writing and reading to her and she understood, never mocking him about it. She would disappear from the factory floor around ten, and then reappear with the sandwich crew

138

around noon, flitting among the workers with her baskets full of sandwiches and empanadas. At three, when the workers returned to the factory floor, she was right back at his side or with the other secretaries, typing furiously to get his correspondence and invoices out.

He did not know what to make of Solange. When she was near him, she always managed to be touching him; not in an overtly sexual way, but in a far more subtle manner; brushing an arm or leg against some part of him or being in a space where he could inadvertently bump into her. It finally dawned on him that she liked him.

He was sufficiently adept to know that he needed to show interest, or she would chalk his confusion up to indifference and be off with someone else, He chose the date on which to speak with her carefully

"Solange," he said, letting his tongue glide over the 'n-g-e' part. "I wonder if I might speak with you?" She followed him into his little cubicle area and took her familiar secretary's seat, poising her pad and pen expectantly.

"No-no—this isn't about work," he said. "I – I –" He ran a nervous hand through his shaggy head of hair and lowered his eyes.

"Are you going to tell me that you like me?" she asked, with a mischievous smile. "I know it already. I like you, too," she added.

From that point they were inseparable. She would only let him kiss her, but kissing her sent such a vibration through his body that he could not imagine what more would do to him. She promised him more—in their marriage bed. Herschel determined that he would indeed share that bed with her.

"Ah," she said. "But you cannot marry me." Herschel blanched, waiting for her revelation about some husband or jealous suitor. But she said, "You are Jewish."

The words came out of his mouth without his volition: "I can convert," he said.
I will become Catholic." Solange burst into tears. "You would do that for me!" she said, embracing him and pressing her body far closer to him than she had ever done before. Herschel had to rip himself away from her to avoid losing his head entirely.

He hurried home, frantic as to how he would tell his parents about Solange and how he would seal his love to her. His father slumbered in his 'office' and his mother was out shopping. He thought of the money he had given his father every payday. Surely the man had not spent it all. He, Herschel, had made the money with his own sweat and rough, grease-stained hands; was it not his? If his father might have it stashed away in some hiding place—Stealthily he crept into their room.

His father had nothing useful. Short of a few articles of clothing and many, many tomes that had spilled over into the bedroom, he had nothing. His mother, also, had nothing of value.

But wait—what was *this?*

His mother's engagement ring twinkled at him from its half-hidden place in her linen drawer. He let his mind go blank as he drew the ring out. How it sparkled and winked at him! How brightly the gold shone, and how radiantly the rainbows danced upon the diamond facets! He pocketed it before he could feel a single pang of remorse for robbing his own mother. Why hadn't she hidden it with the rest of his family's wealth, which even now reposed in a place he could not hope to locate, by the sketchy directions he had received? He took no time to reflect. He wrapped the ring in a handkerchief and waited for the moment that he could present it to Solange.

The next several weeks were outstanding. Sporting his mother's ring proudly upon her finger, she allowed Herschel incredible liberties. "We are nearly married," she would say, as they peeled their bodies apart. They studied the Catechism and other Catholic books of instruction together, and though Herschel cared little for the doctrine itself, he embraced it wholeheartedly, knowing that embracing it would allow him to embrace Solange. He visited her parents several times, and finally went to the church and allowed himself to be sprinkled and 'Christianized'. They both swore that if he was to receive her as a virgin on their wedding night, they must not meet in private anymore.

"So now," Solange said, as she snuggled against his chest, "all that remains is for us to post our banns in the Church for three weeks, and then we will marry. But I have one question: when will I ever meet your parents?"

Herschel's contented mood broke. Of course, she and her family would want to meet his family! It was too late to lie to her; to tell her that they were both dead and that he was all alone in the world. He had shared too much of his disappointments and complaints about them with her. What a fool he had been, he realized now. He should have taken the ring to one of the local pawnshops and received the money for it. Then he should have bought a cheaper ring, which she would have appreciated just as much, and used the rest of the money to take her far away; even to North America.

How could his parents accept Solange? She was not Jewish. She was a Catholic girl—and he had converted; whatever went on in his heart, he was now a Catholic boy. Besides, Solange would walk in, proudly wearing his mother's ring, which his mother did not even know he had given her.

It would be a terrible disaster.

Still, it was one he must go through with.

They posted their banns the very next morning, and Herschel announced to his parents that he would be bringing her and her family to visit the very next evening. Elie scoffed at him. "What kind of a woman could possibly want you?" he asked. "What is she, some street woman from Telmo?" His mother had just looked sad. "Where will you live with her, Herschel? We have only this small space. Well, bring her, and I will make the house nice."

There was no way to stop the evening from coming, and so it came. Dressed in their finest clothing, Solange, her father, her mother, two brothers, a pregnant sister and her husband, and a couple of relatives that Herschel could not identify trudged up the three flights of steps to the Rosenthalers' apartment. He could read on all of their faces their disappointment that this was the life he was going to offer Solange.

Eliana had tried to make something, but she had burned it, and the scent lingered in the air. When Herschel opened the door, his father did not rise, but sat puffing angrily on a Cuban cigar and glowering at the party. Eliana rushed out of the kitchen beaming, but her face fell almost instantly.

"But—but Herschel, they are Argentines. Are they Jewish? They are not Jewish!" she whined. "How can you marry someone who is not *Jewish*?"

"Which one is it?" Elie growled. "The pregnant one? I can take care of this forced marriage in short order, if that is why you are marrying her!"

Solange's entire family stood frozen in the doorway. They could not understand Elie and Eliana's words, but some things carry over in tone and mannerism and require no translation. Solange raised her hand to speak, and her ring caught the light.

"That's my ring!" Eliana cried out. "That's my ring—*my* ring—" She rushed toward Solange and tried to seize her hand in an effort to tear it off her finger. "How did you get my ring? How did you find it?"

Herschel's head was buzzing. He could still rush out of the apartment with Solange and her coterie. He could still hock the ring, or continue at the factory and just never come back here again. He could even send money, which he supposed his parents would never acknowledge, but would have no trouble spending. He purposed to turn on his heels and guide the group out of the apartment, but his feet would not move. Nor would his mouth open, though he saw the fear and surprise in Solange's eyes, turned up to him for consolation and explanation.

Solange's mother wrapped an arm about her daughter's shoulders and whispered something in her ear, to which Solange responded by shaking her head 'no'. Then her mother gently led her daughter out of the apartment and down the stairs, the rest of the party following silently.

Herschel wanted to dash out of the apartment after them; to seize Solange in the street and, right there, in front of her whole family and his, declare his love for her and his desire to stay with her as her lawfully wedded husband for the rest of their days. But he could not. His legs were like rubber.

"You get my ring back!" his mother shrieked at him. "You get my ring off that harlot's finger and you give it back to me!"

Herschel heard himself say in his head to his mother that she and his father owed him something for living off him all of these days, and that he was his own man. He heard himself say he would move away, that all of his money was his—even that he was now Catholic, and could marry a Catholic and not a Jew if he wanted to, and he wanted to. He heard himself say all of those words, but they were not the words that came out of his mouth. His lips muttered only, "Es tut mir leid; es tut mir von tiefsten herzen leid" "—I'm sorry; I'm sorry from the deepest place in my heart."

The next day, Solange was waiting by the gate when he arrived. He had never seen her looking so lovely as she did today. She peered questioningly at his face for a moment, but he could not look at her. Without words, she took his head in her hands and placed a soft kiss on his lips. Then she slipped the engagement ring off her finger, placed it in his palm, closed his fingers around it, and walked away, not looking back. He could only watch her walk out of his life. He found her little clipboard and pen on his desk.

In subsequent weeks he heard her voice in the park, bantering with the factory workers, serving sandwiches and empanadas. He would not allow himself to look out. He would not leave his desk at lunchtime anymore. It was a long time before he wanted to look at another woman, and by then it was too late anyway.

CHAPTER EIGHTEEN

Benyamin figured that eventually he would go into the Aaronsohn factory. Now that he had graduated high school, surely his mentors would seek to recoup their sponsorship money by making him pay with free labor. He was therefore not surprised when, at breakfast the very next day, Mr. Aaronsohn announced that Benyamin would be accompanying him to the factory.

This particular factory made men's fedoras. As he passed through the cutting machines and piecing areas at Mr. Aaronsohn's side, Benyamin felt a rising fear. What if he wound up doing this work forever? What if he found himself stuck in one of these steamy, lint-strewn areas, bringing his lunch to work in a little black metal lunchbox and eating it furtively at his station as that man over there was doing, or getting yelled at for doing shoddy work, as appeared to be happening to that woman shaking with fear next to the sewing machine in the far corner?

They reached Mr. Aaronsohn's office, a claustrophobic's nightmare. Little more than a wooden crate just big enough to accommodate a man and his desk, it was built high above the factory floor and littered with papers and boxes, pattern pieces and faded notices, spread-sheets and calendars pinioned to the wall with thumbtacks. Mr. Aaronsohn lifted a large flap that covered a mammoth window. From this perch, Benyamin imagined, Mr. Aaronsohn could peer down from the mostly glass front wall of his aerial shack and see whoever was shirking work, then pick up the telephone on his desk and tell his subordinates whom to fire.

"Sit down, Benyamin," Mr. Aaronsohn said. He placed several pieces of decorated construction paper on the wooden desk, which was much like those in the factory. "This is a hatbox pattern. I'd like to see you assemble it so that—" he shoved some papers aside to make space for a large hatbox—"it looks like this."

Benyamin looked at the flat construction paper pieces and then at the fully constructed hatbox. Thoughts shot through his brain like lightning bolts. If he put the box together quickly, he could be chained to this building for most of the daylight hours of the rest of his life. If he flubbed the test, as he was inclined to do, Mr. Aaronsohn could well find him unsuitable to continue to support, and then it would be off to the Cunard Line office with him. *Choose, Benyamin; choose!*

His fingers fairly flew over the construction board as his brain fired instructions to them. The assembled piece stood before them in a matter of moments. Benyamin looked up at Mr. Aaronsohn, who was frowning. The older man stared at the two identical boxes for a moment. He lifted the lid of the new one and surveyed its perfect interior. With only a grunt to show that he approved, he laid out several pieces of felt.

"Let's see you put *that* together," he said. "That sewing machine over there works; every now and then I like to put a few hats together myself; just for fun, of course."

Again, Benyamin's fingers flew over the construction. In only a few minutes the machine was whirring, and in a few more minutes he came back with the hat. Mr. Aaronsohn hoisted it on his left palm and spun it round and round, inspecting it. Frowning again, he placed it in the newly constructed hatbox, and then handed the box to Benyamin.

"A gift," he said. "Chaya was right, for once. You're too smart to work here. All right; so it's college for you. Have Ezra work with you about learning to drive one of the cars. I'll not have him chauffeuring you all over Durham and waiting for you to come out of classes, while I sit at home needful of his services."

Benyamin could not believe his ears. *College!*

CHAPTER NINETEEN

Eliana was frantic. The entire contents of her linen drawer lay strewn about the bedroom. She had gone through everything—*everything!* It was not here; it was simply not here.

There was only one explanation that she could think of: Herschel had taken it again. He had found himself some other strumpet out there and placed his own mother's precious ring on her finger. How she wished she had just chucked the thing into that hole outside Cologne; it was clear to her now that she should have. She would wait until Herschel came home and she would confront him and ask—no; *demand*—her ring back. What right did he have to take it?

She remembered how amazed she had been; how very, very pleased she had been, when Elie had placed it on her finger. It was beautiful; more beautiful than anything her farm girl eyes had ever fallen upon, and the loveliness of it went far to take away her disappointment with the man that was giving it to her. She had stopped using the pumice stone and Castile soap she scrubbed with and begun soaking her hands in rosewater, which softened them and made them a much better backdrop for the ring. Even in cold weather, she eschewed gloves, as they obstructed others' view of her marvelous ring.

How dare he—how *dare* he!

She realized she would have to wait up very late to challenge him. Herschel was spending more and more time at the factory—or so he claimed—and some nights not coming home at all. He would show up in a day or maybe two, looking haggard and broken. He was still moping, she supposed, over the departure of that Spanish girl.

Sometimes she felt bad for Herschel; after all, she knew what it was like to have love taken away. There had been a boy; a young itinerant Gypsy farmhand that helped her father during the haying season. He would sit beneath a tree when the sun was too hot to labor under, and she would see him every day when she and her sisters brought water out to the men. He had deep black hair and bronzed smooth skin and laugh lines around his toffee-colored eyes that made them appear kind. He played a concertina, and loved to regale whoever was listening with his songs. The one he directed specifically to her was, 'Any Little Girl who's a Nice Little Girl is the Right Little Girl for Me', which he sang in what he told her was English. Nights she dreamed of being his Right Little Girl. Her father had happened upon them one day; she with her water bucket and gourd forgotten, he serenading her beneath the tree that the others had wandered away from. He had just put down his concertina and touched her cheek, leaning toward her in a way that made her heart hammer, when—

The gypsy lad had been run off and warned never to return. Her engagement to Elie had followed almost instantaneously. Though their farms were almost adjoining, Eliana had never seen this boy, known to her only as 'the studious one'. His father had deigned him to be too smart to work on the farm, and so he had been sent off to Leipzig, where, although he was plain-featured, somewhat short of stature and tended toward pudginess, he had apparently gained access to many of the salons and boudoirs in that city, for reasons that were mostly non-professional. Despite his extracurricular dalliances, however, he had obtained the necessary education and experience as a top-rate gynecologist, and was now deemed ready to take a wife. But at that juncture, when a yenta should have found him a fine young Jewish girl of his social standing, Elie had made an error. He had practiced his extracurricular arts with only a veneer of gynecological pretense on a non-Jewish girl from a questionable family, and had retreated in haste from Leipzig, just ahead of the pitchforks and pistols of her father and brothers. He would be coming home from a rather sudden trip to Italy in a few weeks, and he was to be married to her as soon as arrangements could be made. Eliana had been hustled to the city for clothing, and then pampered and brushed and educated as quickly as possible in the requisite kitchen and bedroom skills, neither of which had taken very well.

Eliezar Rosenthaler was indeed short—shorter by almost half a head than she. His features were not unpleasant, but certainly not remarkable, and he was already taking on a figure that promised only to become more portly as he aged. Eliana was pretty, for a farm girl. She was not fat, but blessed with an agreeable amount of flesh her gypsy would-be-lover called 'saftig'. Her auburn hair was full and thick, her skin almost white, despite the sun that beat relentlessly down on the farm in summer, and her gray eyes the color of the summer sky just before rain. Still, she always felt that she was not handsome enough for Elie, who had seen the world and according to her mother was very experienced, both in culinary and in sexual tastes. "When we consider candidates for marriage," her mother had told her, "we do not require of men the same level of virginity that we do of women. Men have different appetites. They live their lives as they are driven to do by God and nature. Women, on the other hand, settle in and turn their heads so that they do not see their husbands' indiscretions." Eliana had wondered if she spoke from experience. She was not going to share her man with any other woman, she determined. Whatever he had done in the past was his own business, but anything he did now would be *her* business. He would be true or he would be alone. She was not above returning to the farm and working there for the rest of her life, if things did not go well with this Eliezar fellow.

But things had gone well—at least until they left for South America. He had finished his studies in Leipzig, and shortly thereafter he had begun his gynecological work. She was uneasy that he made money by spending his time groping around in other women's vaginas. It made her wonder how clinical their own intimate moments were. She did not like the thought that, when he stroked her most personal parts he just might be looking for irregularities indicating disease, or that when he fondled her breasts he might actually be palpating them for tumors. He had become eminently successful, and even before Benyamin was born, he had moved her family from their farm to an apartment on the outskirts of the city. Her mother had been quite delighted, and there was not a word Eliana could say against Herr Doktor that Rivkeh would not rebuke. As for Eliana, although she was the model of faithfulness, she could not help but daydream, at times in their most intimate moments, that the man she was with was the one that thought her to be 'the right little girl'.

She came to herself. Goodness, what had she done to the bedroom? She began folding her clothing and straightening the soft projectiles she had disordered from her underwear drawer. Elie would not tolerate this kind of chaos.

Elie came home first. Eliana said nothing to him about the missing ring. He seemed to have too much on his mind these days. He would go out, sometimes for hours, and hang around the coffee shops; or so Ezra told her on his visits. "I don't know why he goes there," Ezra had insisted. "There are no women—not that he would visit them on a non-professional basis if there were—and the music is pretty bad." But Elie seemed so pensive. The old days pressed on him, she supposed; or perhaps it was the dreadful news from Germany that seemed to get worse every day. No, she would save her wrath for Herschel, who surely was the culprit.

Finally Herschel dragged himself home. He looked gaunt and frail; not at all the twenty-two-year old man that he was. Eliana's mother-heart panged for him, but she gritted her teeth and kept her resolve.

"And where is the ring you took from me again?" she cried out, with no preamble. Herschel looked stunned, as if she had slapped him across the face. He regarded his mother with his dark-circled eyes. "Your ring! I've no idea!"

Her voice crescendoed to a shriek that brought neighbors to their doors. "You lie!" she screamed at him. "You lie! What have you done with it? What harlot's finger have you placed it on *this* time? Bring her back here, so I can chop it off her hand! Get me my ring and get it *NOW*!"

Herschel stared at her. "But Mama, I don't have your ring. I put it in your hand and you did whatever you did with it and I never entered your room again. And there is no woman. I've been working these nights, trying to put extra money into Papa's hands."

"More lies!" she yelled. "There's no more money in this house than there has ever been since you began working! Is the food any better? Is there better furniture? Am I wearing a dress, even one, that I bought in this New World? No! You are seeing that girl, or some other girl, and wasting your money in the streets, or you're drinking, or you're doing something else that you shouldn't be doing. You took my ring and you know you did! Now where is it? Go and get it! Tell whomever you gave it to that you have to give it back. I need that ring! I *need* it! It is *mine*! Now you go and get it *right now*, or you'll be no son of mine! Thief! Robber! I should call the police on you!"

Herschel's head was abuzz. He had brought the ring home and slipped it into his mother's hand. She had, he presumed, returned it to its hiding place, or found a new one for it. Now she really didn't have it? He was trying to be patient and rational, but he had no clue as to where the ring might be.

"Think, Mama," he said. "Has there been anyone in the house? Any tradesmen? Any salesmen? Any repairmen?"

His mother's face was purple. "What are you implying?" she asked. "Why would any other man but your father be in my bedroom? Why would anybody else go through my underwear drawer?"

Herschel had a bemused moment. Though he had meant no accusation, clearly his mother was beyond the point that any man would find her attractive enough to venture into her bedroom for amorous reasons. She had let herself go. Her once curly auburn hair was now mottled gray, and not always bound up in its topknot, but more often than not, straggling loosely down the side of her head. She had become more rotund than she would like to think of herself. And her garments were becoming threadbare. He could see where the seams pulled and there were frayed spots at her cuffs and elbows. This ring, he realized, was her link to the old world; to her old life. It was all she had to mark her former days of prosperous matronhood. Her husband had no clients, Jewish or Christian, to provide her with the little treats and pleasures she had grown accustomed to, and he heard their bedsprings creaking only when one of them got into or out of bed.

Then Herschel looked at his father, who stood in the doorway looking at them both. He wore a new suit, and his shoes still had the scent of the cows that had sacrificed their lives for his feet. His shirt was starched and his tie crisp and unspotted. His hair was freshly cut and his whiskers trimmed. Two new Cuban cigars peeked from his breast pocket. Through the open door of his office Herschel saw books still in their wrappings. He had an idea of what he made and how much money his father gave him back. Would he really have--?

"I need that ring!" His mother was weeping now, and there was just the slightest hint of hysteria in her voice. "I *need* it!"

"Mama," Herschel said in his most soothing voice. "I never took it again. You remember, I gave it back to you and I promised I would never touch it again." He laid a hand on her shivering shoulder. "But look, Mama. I get paid tomorrow, and –"

"You will bring your money home to *me*," his father said, his face creased with anger. "I must have it! What does your mother need money for? Look at her; she doesn't go out unless she is food shopping. She doesn't socialize. She has no one to impress. *I*—" he swelled his chest pompously "—have people I have to deal with. I must be seen in the most important places and with the influential folks here. I need to lay out a little money among officials here."

Herschel felt his gorge rising. "You are gambling!" he said. "You are throwing your money around and having fun with riff-raff, while we starve and go around in rags! When was the last time you had a patient? When was the last time you brought home even a peso that you earned yourself?"

Elie's face grew so purple that for an instant Herschel feared the man would have a stroke and fall down dead at his feet.

"You do not know my needs!" he bellowed. "You do not know what I left—what I gave up—"

Herschel interrupted. "And you do not even look at your wife anymore. Look at her now; take a good look! Look at her dress; she wore it on the boat coming here, and it was old then! Look at her face and her hair and her hands; this is not a woman accustomed to working, but she looks like a drudge!"

Elie shot back, "And look how fat she has become! What work does she do around this place? She doesn't turn her hand to clean, and her cooking is impossible; I would rather take my meals raw! Some wife; some helpmeet! She drags around here, depressed all the time; I can't bear to look at her. I can smell her, though. Don't you even bathe anymore?" he asked Eliana, who looked almost beyond conversation.

"If she had a reason to look good," Herschel said, "I am sure that she would. But who would want to dress up in the rags she has to put on? You're a doctor; you know she is depressed almost out of her mind! What are you hoping; that she throws herself out a window one day, and then you will be free to marry again? Or is it even about marrying? I hear about town that you visit the whoop-de-doo houses sometimes and sing and dance with the Spanish beauties while I, who am making the money, stomp around town with empty pockets and holes in my shoes! Have you forgotten yourself? You are a *doctor*; have a little dignity!"

Elie's face was vermillion. "It is *you* who have forgotten yourself!" he roared at his son. "*You!* You scream at me as if I were one of your minions on the factory floor, dependent on you for every morsel of bread that goes into my mouth! You don't make enough to run this household, and you want me to get by on the chickenfeed you bring home? Who can live on that? I have to scrimp and scratch to get your little pesos to cover our needs!"

"To cover *your wants*, you mean!" Herschel shouted back. "Look at you! How can you stand in front of us in your finery, when we are both in rags? What kind of man lets his wife go around looking like a beggar? Who snatches every cent from his son with so little gratitude and gives only a few pennies, as if it were *he*, and not his son, who puts in two days' work for every day? It's a surprise when I find us not yet tossed to the streets, with your extravagance!"

He stopped. Eliana had sunk to her knees and was wailing and keening and ripping at her hair.

"Your mother has written!" she moaned between sobs. "Her money is frozen and she has very little left. She needs money to buy passports, and I've got to sell that ring and send her as much as I can. She and Reuven are safe in Finland—for now. But *my* mother—my mother cannot get out of the Reich! She waited too long—she waited too long, and now the soldiers are hunting Jews from house to house and sending them off to God knows where—"

"Settlements," Elie said. "Settlements in the East. She will be fine if she goes. The Jews work and manufacture goods there. They probably farm some, too. She grew up on a farm and she married a farmer, so she knows plenty about farm life."

"No—no," Eliana said. "That is *not* what Bina says, and she knows. She says—she says the Jews are being rounded up and sent away—and they are not coming back. She says they are being *murdered!*"

CHAPTER TWENTY

The revelation that it was Elie that had stolen the ring this time, and worse, that he had used it as partial payment for his mounting gambling debts did not surprise Herschel as much as it did his mother. Herschel had suspected that his father was not only using the money he made chiefly to aggrandize himself, but also to feather a nest somewhere for a lovely senorita or to bolster up his credit at the gaming tables prolific around the city. Elie never admitted to it, but Herschel was pretty sure. All he could do was to tell his father in no uncertain terms that, unless he produced the ring very soon, Herschel would give his next pay envelope and every one after directly into his mother's hands until the ring reappeared, and that there would be no argument.

"But I cannot make such a promise!" Elie said, and his voice was genuinely fearful. "These are powerful men; they do not like being crossed! Can you expect me just to get it back, without repercussions?"

Herschel shrugged. "Do what you have to. You see how upset it makes your wife. Have you no pity?"

Elie shuddered. "You don't understand," he said. "These are the kinds of men that would take what they are owed out of my hide!" He ran a hand through his thinning gray hair. "They won't take kindly to my request. I have to give them *something* in the ring's place!"

Herschel looked impassively at his father. "You find something," he said. "You find something to give them that will replace that ring, or you will not get another cent from me. I'll not see my mother like this again!"

It was only a matter of a few days that Elie met Herschel on the stairs to receive his pay envelope as usual. Herschel held out his hand for the ring. "What is this?" Elie asked, an injured tone in his voice.

"If you have no ring, you will get no money!" Herschel said through clenched teeth and keeping his hand extended.

He was surprised when he felt the weight of the ring in his hand.

"You've got the ring!" Herschel said, a smile spreading across his face. His father did not return the smile.

"Yes," he said. "I got the ring."

"So they gave you the ring back?" Herschel asked. "You were so worried about getting your legs broken or worse. But I see you've still got your watch and chain. So you didn't have to be afraid. Surely they understood about it." He leaned closer to his father. "I'll help you raise the money you owe," he said. "You'll see. I'll work Sundays, too, and you can make up the money faster. But you must stop gambling, so that you don't build up the debt again! How much do I have to raise?"

His father regarded him glumly. "Nothing," he said. "I'm square with them."

Herschel was incredulous. What good fortune! A moment later, however, he was not so sure.

"I made a barter," his father said. "My creditor will forgive the debt, but I must provide a service for him." He drew a deep breath, and then added,

"You must marry his niece."

CHAPTER TWENTY-ONE

Benyamin was determined to get far better grades even than he had made over the last three years in America. He had not, however, counted on the affairs of the world to impinge on his concentration.

First he heard that Poland had been annexed, if that was the word for it. Thousands of Poles had died before the country had surrendered. Hitler had said that the Poles, despite their Aryan visages, were inferiors that would never equal the Germans. He wondered about Anya: was she safe? Had she fallen victim to all the bombing and the shooting? Was she working on some farm far from danger? Did she ever think of him, and when he did cross her mind, were hers kindly thoughts or murderous ones? He wondered if Anya had found a husband, or if she was wasting away, running from place to place from the Germans.

Then he heard that the Jews were being more harassed than ever. From her new vantage point in Finland, his Oma Bina seemed to be aware of much that was going on throughout Europe. She wrote a short letter whenever she had a moment, perhaps once every other month; but her letters were so full of information that he felt as if he had read a newspaper. She wrote about families he had known: the Greenbaums had managed to get to Chicago; the Metzes had gone to Spain. The Schwartzes had vanished, and no one seemed to know if they were Disappeared or in hiding. The streets of Cologne were all in rubble now, she said. She had learned from her sources that heavy bombing had destroyed pretty much everything. "I suspect we will not recognize our familiar places," she said. "Let us hope that this war does not spread all over the world."

Worse was the news about his maternal grandmother, Oma Rivkeh. She was missing. Convinced that she was above being arrested, she had wandered off to Hamburg, and no one was sure if she had been detained, if she had escaped to Poland, or if she was rotting beneath some pile of debris somewhere. "I can locate no trace of her," his grandmother concluded. "We must suspect the worst, but we must hope for the best; it is all we can do."

America had been in the war for some time; since the bombs had fallen over a year ago on Pearl Harbor. The Japanese had turned perfidious, his grandmother said, and there had been little choice for America but to join the war, now, though Oma Bina insisted that the huge nation of America could hardly be in danger. She asked Benyamin if he had seen any evidence of war.

He had to admit that he had not traveled away from the borders of North Carolina, and not very far within the state. It had occurred to him, from his long drive coming into New York and from the textbooks he read in class, that this country must be huge. "All of Germany would probably fit inside it," he had said to her once in a letter. He had enquired after his uncle Reuven's health, but his grandmother had said only that he was 'fine'. It did not occur to him until after he had posted the letter that he had not asked for his aunt or cousin's address in New York.

To say that he was lonely would be an understatement. He saw his sponsors every morning at breakfast, though he was frequently still on campus long after dinner. Hattie would leave a plate of food out for him, which he usually ate alone in the deserted kitchen, hardly noticing what it was that he put in his mouth as he pored over some book or another.

Now and then he received a letter from his mother, but these were becoming more rare and said less and less that he could understand. He did not want to think it, but it seemed that her thoughts were somewhat muddled at times. She mentioned once her mother had written to her for money, but that she had nothing to send, since her ring had disappeared, and Herschel had no money to lend her above their basic daily needs. Besides, anything she sent would probably be opened by the German officials and confiscated before it ever got to her mother. She supposed that her mother was on her own. No, his father was not practicing medicine, and no, the only one of them that spoke Spanish at all was Herschel, so she felt rather alone in her new country.

One thing was clear, however:

His brother was getting married.

CHAPTER TWENTY-TWO

Herschel did not expect Geula to be a beauty, and he was not disappointed. In fact, he could not believe such an ugly woman could possibly exist. Her reddish brown hair spewed lankly and untidily down across her pale, pockmarked face as if attempting to shield others from the unsightliness of her. One eye was cast, and both eyes were blue and bleary, and cowering behind the biggest and thickest pair of glasses Herschel had ever seen. Her nose was without distinction. Her mouth was a thin, chapped gash in her face, and he could see the little bits of skin that hung from her cracked lips. Her feet, like her hands, were huge and man-like. Her shoulders were stooped forward, which pushed her head into the space between the blades as if she were a turtle. Her breasts, under her yellowed white wash-dress were tiny; barely a child's chest, he thought. She was, below them, all angles, without a single curve. Lying with her, he thought, would be like embracing a bare trellis or a sack of butcher bones.

She did not look up at him, nor did she consider him with any sense of ownership. She knew well that he was standing next to her only because his father owed her uncle a huge gambling debt. Herschel was his father's payment. Throughout their ceremony she kept her eyes fixed steadfastly on the ground. She knew she was not a good catch for a man; not even passable. Her only hope was that he would not mistreat her; she had made a silent oath to herself that if he beat her, she would take her own life.

Herschel, in the meantime, wondered if, with her watery eyes and bent over figure, she just might be an imbecile. In Germany, they were taking the imbeciles away to workhouses and sanitariums from which, new immigrants were saying, they were not returning. He was sure that, with her looks, the authorities would assume that something was wrong with her even if there wasn't. If they were a couple about to be married in that land, he thought, he would be in trouble for being a Jew, but for her, every moment he would have to expect the approach of booted feet and the rap of clenched fists, a rough command and grasping hands dragging her away to some infirmary for the dull-witted. His father had insisted that she was a bright girl, with no end of housewifely skills, and that she was a certified virgin, whose pristine authenticity he could guarantee, because he had examined her privates himself, in the presence of her uncle. Looking at Geula, her virginity was the one truth that Herschel did not doubt.

"She can cook," his father had told him with pleading eyes. "She can cook and she can bake and she cleans well. She will keep your house clean and give you children and do whatever you want her to in bed."

"She is as ugly as the back-end of a cow!" Herschel had protested.

"So you turn the lights out," his father had retorted. "When you're having sex, what's there to see? It's what you feel. Oh, yes, you got all tangled up with that Spanish tart, didn't you? Well, this is your woman now, and if she isn't as pretty as you wanted, you will just have to live with that!"

Herschel spat out the words before he could bite his tongue. "I am doing this to save your skin! I haven't decided if you are worth it!"

Instantly contrite, his father said, "Oh, son, I know. I've gotten you into so much trouble. I know this girl is not your ideal. I would have wanted so much more for you. But she is clean and she is a virgin. She will work hard for you and never ask you for a peso. She will be so happy to be wed that she won't trouble you for anything. Besides—" and here he drew close to his son's ear—"marriage doesn't mean monogamy, you

166

know. If you don't find her to your liking, she will not complain if you take on a woman or two on the side."

"Oh, no!" Herschel said mockingly. "*She* won't complain. But one of her relatives might ask her someday, and if she tells him I have dalliances here and there, it will be *my* legs that get broken, not yours!"

There was no honeymoon. Herschel had no money to go anywhere but home. He and Geula set up housekeeping in the living room. Geula had said nothing; she had just lifted one bushy eyebrow, then let out a soft sigh and put down her small suitcase. Eliana had prepared one of her meals: potatoes and carrots and beans and rice. Geula had said nothing still; she had just ladled the tasteless concoction into her mouth, her eyes fixed upon her plate, while Elie again and again toasted the couple with glasses filled to the brim with tap water, extolling both of their virtues.

Finally he had said to his wife, "Eliana, we must go to bed and let the young couple do their lovemaking." Geula rose instantly, and began scrubbing pots in the kitchen, while Herschel sat on the sofa, not sure what to do next. His parents puttered around the rooms, in and out of the bath and the parlor. Elie was like a naughty schoolboy waiting to glimpse something above his years. Finally he gave up and strolled into the bedroom. Geula just continued to clean

Herschel washed up first. He didn't have special bedclothes for a wedding night. He wrapped himself in a bath towel, since all of his underwear was worn and threadbare, and slid into the makeshift bed that Geula had arranged on the floor while he was washing. She dried her hands as he flipped the towel off beneath the covers. Then she disappeared into the bathroom. Herschel found himself wondering what her naked body would look like in the shower, covered with steam and soap. His mind traveled back over the years to Anya. He wondered what had become of his little Polish princess, and how it would be, now, to touch this angular creature when he had felt perfection against him. The sound of the shower and the sound of his parents' snoring lulled him to sleep.

CHAPTER TWENTY-THREE

Many, many miles away, Oma Rivkeh stood in another shower room, naked and shivering, clasping a sliver of soap. She was waiting for the water to come on. Every muscle in her body seemed to be aching. She imagined how good the warm spray would feel on her skin, after the long journey, with people piled on people. She ran a hand over her newly-shaven scalp. It felt prickly, as if every hair was standing on its own. She was not satisfied with the explanation the matron had given her for having to shave her head. *She* didn't have lice. Even when she had fled France to Poland, she had been very careful where she went; where she slept. She stayed apart from the others, that might have diseases, and when they went one way she went the other.

That, unfortunately, was how she had been caught.

She had actually been relieved. The idea of being re-settled in the East had its appeal. She had some skills; she could sew and she could spin, and she was no stranger to farm life. At this 'relocation center', someone on the crowded train had told her, she would be able to explain her skills and serve the German war cause, perhaps growing vegetables or taking care of cattle. But she had been exposed, the matron said, to head lice, and now she had to shower, along with the other women from the train.

She had known almost the moment she had told Bina that she would *not* go abroad—that she preferred to travel first class or to wait to see if Germany got better—that her decision was a mistake. But then, she had so much to stay in Germany for. She had, after all, the apartment in town to look after, now that the farm was gone. She had watched with amusement as her neighbors moved away. Fools! They would never be able to get such good prices on their apartments when they got back as they paid now! And many were leaving their home goods behind. Over the next month or so the neighborhood had changed from mostly Jews to almost all Aryans. She would nod to them, but they rarely looked up as they passed, and when they did, their looks were not pleasant.

Bina had contacted her only once more. She had begged her to get out of Germany—to come to her in Switzerland or to go to America. Now Rivkeh began to reconsider. She had reported to register as a Jew and to receive her *magen david* star, that she must never take off. That she had not liked at all. So she had secured a visa to the West and bundled her most precious articles—her silver, a few of the jewels that she had spared from that big hole outside Cologne—and she had gone to the steamer office.

There was a ship, the *St. Louis,* headed imminently for Cuba, and she had convinced herself to board it, once she found there was a first-class cabin available. She had enjoyed her crossing, largely because of the presence of foods long ago rationed in Germany, the ambiance of the accommodations and a flowering relationship with a Polish and Jewish family she met on board. They seemed to know all there was to know about traveling by sea, and they provided company for her all the way to the Americas.

But at Havana, she had not been allowed to disembark; nor had anybody else Jewish. Apparently, some law had been passed just before the ship left harbor that limited Cuba's quota of Jews. So the ship had sailed on to Florida. She had packed up her bags to disembark, when she heard a shot over the bow from the coastline, and everything changed. As the ship pulled away from the harbor, she had gone to her friends' stateroom, only to find the Polish woman sobbing. Her husband, two teenaged sons and ten-year-old daughter were nowhere to be seen.

"They went overboard," the woman said. "They went overboard and they took everything I had!" Her husband, she said, had suddenly come to her when it became clear they would not disembark. He had begged her to come with him, but she had been afraid: she could not swim, and she did not know what the Americans might do to them if they were arrested. So he had sent her to her stateroom and slipped overboard with the children. They were all excellent swimmers and the water was quite calm, so she was certain that they survived, but now she was all alone.

The voyage had gotten longer and longer, and that meant the quality of services, from food to quality of staff response to requests, had waned exponentially. The captain, a non-Jewish German, was apparently trying again and again to put off as many people as he could on foreign shores, determined that he would save them all from a terrible fate in Germany.

Rivkeh and the Polish lady were granted asylum in France, and Rivkeh would have stayed there, albeit in impoverished conditions, had it not been for her companion. She begged Rivkeh not to leave her, and when the two reached France, the woman had insisted they had a better chance of survival and livelihood in her home country, where she still had family. They had made their way to Poland and the apartment where the woman had lived before. Rivkeh sold her silver service and then, piece by precious piece, her jewels. She dared not go out anymore, so she gave everything to the Polish woman, hoping that they would soon have enough to try to leave again; perhaps if they could flee to Denmark, they could somehow get to Canada. Finally, she was down to her fur stole; one of her husband's last presents to her before he died. The Polish woman had asked for it along with Rivkeh's plain wedding band; she said she was sure she could get another voyage with a fine stateroom; but Rivkeh had insisted on keeping the coat; what if they needed money?

They needed something to barter for food until they could get money, she had insisted. The Polish woman had only shrugged, pocketed the ring and left.

Rivkeh had waited for a long time for the woman to return with her ticket out, but when the knock on the door came, it was not the Polish woman, but the Gestapo. They had hustled her down the stairs, across the plaza and toward the train station.

She still had her fur stole when she was put on the train, and she did not like the way the matrons eyed it. "I *will* get it back, won't I?" she had asked. "Oh, yes," one of them had said, stroking it. "But don't you need to mark it somehow?" Rivkeh had asked, when she saw the woman set it carefully aside. "I will remember you," the woman had replied.

As they passed through the gates, Rivkeh had seen piles of things: shoes and jackets and slacks. "Inefficiency!" she thought, and began planning her letter to the Center's head, just in case her stole disappeared.

There was an overpoweringly miserable smell everywhere. Rivkeh's nose told her that it was animal fat; this was some kind of rendering plant, or else this factory made candles. She could see the huge smokestacks, belching malodorous black smoke She had never seen any so big. It must be a very big factory. But then the candles must smell horrible, she thought. No, it must be that the fat was used for something else. And what kind of animal could smell that bad when it was burned?

The matrons were bringing in more women: more and more and more. Old women, women with small children, women with babies, women with bulging bellies. They were cramming against each other, their clammy bodies touching, and then crushing together as the next group of women crowded in. The matrons' voices had become strident and abusive, and there was the sound of scuttling at the door. Women were crying, now, and the babies were screaming. Someone was singing the *Sh'ma* in a sobbing, cracked voice. Uneasiness began to grow in the back of Rivkeh's mind. There was something she had heard; something so awful that her mind had spun away from believing it—

Somewhere behind the last woman forced in, a door slammed and bolted. The lights flickered and then died. The showerheads began to hiss, but it was not water that billowed out of them. Rivkeh wanted to scream, but could only choke and fall with the others as the death cloud drove the breath from her body and strangled her into lifelessness.

CHAPTER TWENTY-FOUR

Architecture had offered the greatest attraction for Benyamin, but both of the Aaronsohns had pooh-poohed his choice of careers. "Don't be silly," Chaya Aaronsohn had told him. "You'd have to be super-great; a veritable Frank Lloyd Wright, my boy, to sell your designs. You don't just start sketching houses and think people will buy them. Now, engineering—that's a field that will pay for many years to come! Pursue that."

So fearful still was Benyamin that he could be sent back to Germany that he dared not contradict her. He went quietly to his classes, studying voraciously. His grade point average climbed.

In Benyamin's third year, Ezra and Hattie's boy graduated high school and went to Johnson C. Smith University. Ezra picked him up every evening, because he said there was too much trouble a Colored man could have in the city, even if he was underweight, studious-looking and just traveling by himself or perhaps because of that very fact. Benyamin still didn't know much about Colored people. Ezra and Hattie went off grounds on their days off, and Benyamin had no reason to go with them. Occasionally in town he saw Coloreds, but they were menials, and therefore invisible, as most menials were to him. Other than Ezra, Hattie and Mary the cook, brown people had no faces.

Hattie and Ezra's boy lived somewhere in town with his grandparents, so that he could go to the Colored schools near his house, and he came to the Aaronsohns only on the holidays, such as Christmas, which the Aaronsohns celebrated with their management-level employees, to help with the serving and cleaning up. There came a day when Ezra was ill with influenza, and could not drive the boy home from school. Benyamin said he could do it, but Ezra hesitated for a long time. Finally it was Hattie that chastised her husband for being so 'silly' and told Benyamin where to find him.

The boy came out with several of his friends, laughing and talking. He ambled over to the familiar car and swung his books into the back seat. It was only when he opened the door to climb in front and realized that it was not his father behind the wheel, but the stranger from Germany that he hesitated.

Benyamin smiled his broadest smile, though he felt their uneasiness. Except for those five German lads on that street in Cologne, he had never been a threat to anyone in his life, but what he saw in these boys' faces was fear.

"Hi, Lester," he said to the boy he had come to pick up. "Your father is not feeling well. Your mother asked me to pick you up and drive you home."

The other boys backed away slowly. Lester sat silent and still next to him, opening his mouth only to tell him to turn left or right. Benyamin watched as, the further they drove from the campus, the more the lot sizes that the houses sat on shrank and the more the houses themselves became broken-down. Finally the boy told him to pull up in front of a dilapidated shack.

"Let me out here," Lester said shortly, and got out of the car, not looking back. Benyamin reached over and rolled down the window.

"What time should I pick you up tomorrow?" he called out to Lester's retreating back.

Lester turned for a moment to face him. "I'll be staying home until my Daddy feels better," he said.

"No, it's no trouble at all," Benyamin insisted. "I can pick you up and drop you off any time you like; just tell me when."

Lester looked exasperated. "*No* time," he said. "I don't *want* you picking me up! Word'll get back to Mister Aaronsohn, and next thing you know my momma and daddy will be out of a job. Thanks all the same, Mister Benyamin, but I'll get myself to school tomorrow, or maybe I won't go. Bye, now!" The boy scurried up the stairs and slammed the door behind him.

Benyamin's impulse was to get out and follow the boy up the stairs. He wanted Lester to know that he didn't mind at all taking him to school. It was no inconvenience. His own classes started late. But he began to realize, as people on the streets looked curiously at him, that perhaps there would be no convincing Lester that he was anything other than another white-skinned Jew living in the big house with the Aaronsohns. He served Benyamin eggnog and hot cider, cookies and those little sandwiches with the toothpicks sticking out of them on holidays. How could Benyamin even expect Lester to welcome his help? He drove away from the house, perplexed about Colored people.

CHAPTER TWENTY-FIVE

The sign called it a Jewish mixer. Benyamin wondered if it might be some kind of trap; a plan by the University to ferret out Jews and maybe deport them all. Miss Aaronsohn, however, said he was being ridiculous, and he should go.

"When was the last time you had some fun, Benyamin?" she asked him. "You don't go out. You don't have friends. You don't have a sweetheart. All you do is study, study, study. Go to this thing, and meet some young people like yourself."

Benyamin chose his outfit carefully. He thought of what he might need if he had to cross the ocean, just in case the Jew-catchers were there on the pier, waiting for the ship to dock. He still had the knife Fischer had given him, and he slipped it into his pocket, even though he thought it would be virtually useless against their truncheons and guns.

He also thought, however, of what articles of clothing might be most attractive to a young woman, just in case the mixer really was just a mixer. It had been some time since he had to dress well, and he knew his wardrobe was not as attractive as it might be, since he went nowhere except to college. He found a pair of slacks that did not bind his body too tightly and he had Hattie press his best shirt and freshen his jacket—just in case. Apprehensive and yet a little hopeful, he climbed behind the wheel and started the car.

He had paid very little attention to the gym, having gone there only for the obligatory physical education classes. Still, he could appreciate the decorations: the balloons, the streamers, the banners. The music blared, and Benyamin felt his spirits rising. Even the hovering presence of the chaperones could not combat his escalating exuberance. Somewhere in his mind the thought was growing: this was no ordinary event. Something was about to happen: something momentous; something life changing.

Still he had the lingering fear that all might not be as well as it seemed He couldn't shake his feeling that the Gestapo, festooned with guns and bludgeons, was going to sweep in, or that the college security was going to round up everybody Jewish and send them back across the ocean to Germany. It was a nightmare of his that would not go away, no mater how much he tried to reassure himself that Hitler could not reach him here. He sat in the corner, next to the punch bowl. It afforded a view of the exits as well as access to the hors d'oeuvres.

The room was full of Jews—Jewish men and Jewish girls. The men wore costumes much like his: yarmulkes, for the most part, though some, like Benyamin, went without. Their white shirts were crisp and their rainbow-colored ties added a note of festivity to their otherwise lugubrious garb. The more adventurous wore letter sweaters or pullovers in various colors, but all wore crisp white shirts and black, navy or gray pants and wingtip shoes.

The girls, on the other hand, were plenty festive in their sweaters: pink, yellow, blue and green, all with their twin young breasts struggling against the cashmere like prisoners plotting their escape. Benyamin dared not look at them for some time. He turned to the refreshment table, hoping a little food would temper his emotions.

Nothing seemed out of the ordinary; the feeling of destiny, good or bad, was all inside his head, he concluded. He had little ability to read people, he admitted to himself. Adults bored him, for the most part; and while he was by now one himself, he could hardly say that he understood them. He had never developed the skills to relate to females; he had known only two, and both attempts at relationship had ended badly. He had not had much better relationship with boys his age; his last interaction with his male peers had resulted in his precipitous flight to this strange new world. Perhaps he was, he thought, destined to be a loner. Or, maybe one day his father would find a woman for him, as he had for Herschel. Maybe that was his destiny. That was how it was in the old days, he thought. A mother or father would go to the local matchmaker—usually a woman from the community: a yenta, a meddler, a busybody. She would gather intelligence about eligible people; and no matter how competent the goyim and some more modern Jews he had read about might think they were to choose their own mates, the matches seemed to last until one of the people died. Benyamin felt that perhaps the old way was better. After all, how could anyone know enough about another person without an expert to tell what that person did not wish to reveal?

There was food: not quite kosher food, but food, nonetheless. He wandered over to the dessert table, where several girls doled out cookies and bottles of pop. They were a penny a pound, these girls, with their perfect hair and their crisp white blouses and their circle skirts and colorful knit cardigan sweaters that covered their breasts, which poked out like twin B-52 bombers under cashmere tarps, just waiting to go to war. Benyamin tried not to stare, but there was so much pulchritude! They totally distracted his mind from its assigned task of surveying the doors for Jew-catchers. This honey-blonde beauty with her long dark lashes and soft red lips, that raven-haired siren with black flashing eyes, that one with her body that screamed perfection even under its carefully donned wrappings—

"You want some punch?" a voice said. He looked toward it, and into a pair of gray eyes, set in an alabaster face framed by chestnut hair.

And there she was: the girl that sent a thrill through him. She was ladling out punch with a trembling hand, a forced, anxious smile prying her lips apart to reveal perfect teeth. He looked into her timid eyes and suddenly Anya and Sheila and Lara and all the other females in the room were no more. He felt his heart hammering: for him it was the sound of the knock of Destiny. In handing him the drink, her hand inadvertently brushed against his palm.

Fire.

PART TWO:

BERYL

CHAPTER ONE

It would take years for anyone to understand how Beryl got so messed up, because she didn't start out that way. Of all of Papa Gershom's children, she was the flower; the preferred one. When he came home from his job on the road—a phenomenon that became rarer as the years went by—it was not for his wife that he called at the front door, but for his 'Berlie'. She was tow-headed as a baby; quite a phenomenon for a Jewish child, which initially led to some vague rumors in the community that were squelched only by the fact that his wife was plain as a post and, he said frequently when nestled in the arms of some other woman, just as dumb.

Oh, Malka nestled in his arms plenty, at least in the beginning; at least he took her in his arms and she didn't squirm away. That was why there were so many little Kesslers about the place. She gave him his heir, she gave him his spare, and then she just kept on bearing, any time he came near her. And as pleasant as all of the children were, well, it took only a certain number of little heads stretching the cervix and points below out of shape to make his member look for tighter quarters.

Besides, she wasn't the woman he wanted. He wanted someone that had fire in her veins: who laughed loudly and loved with violence. Malka just—*lay* there. There were women who allowed themselves to be serviced—they made the blood rush faster in his head and he would wear himself out trying to please them. But Malka—well, it was kind of as if as soon as he climbed into bed with her, she died. He contented himself as a young man with taking from her inert and silent body such pleasures as round curves, soft skin and a normal body temperature might afford, but he was at all times acutely aware that he was really in bed alone.

And it was not just in bed that she displayed her lackluster nature. She was a *gray* woman. Her face was gray. Her hair, while actually reddish, was gray. The food she cooked was gray. Her conversations—well, there were few of those, and mostly about gray topics: "The children need shoes," she would say, with a verbal economy that was amazing to him. "The garbage needs dumping." He thought she would be just as bland if she were telling him that his hair was on fire or that the Meschiach had come and was waiting for them in the next room.

His parents had felt that he needed just such a boring woman to make his life successful. "You don't need a firecracker," they said. "You need someone who will keep the home fires burning." He had gone to his father just after the wedding. "So she's not burning up your sheets," the man had said. "Forget it; she's a woman, and what is a woman but just a *fickloch?* If she cleans your house, mends your clothes, cooks your food and gives you children, feel blessed."

But Gershom had not felt blessed; he had felt cheated, cursed and lonely. Therefore, he did what he felt was the only solution to his problem: he turned to other women.

Other women, he discovered, did not just lie there. They peeled off their clothes in front of him while he was still talking in their vestibules, and they seized his tie and pulled him as if he were a wild stallion into their bedrooms. They pushed him onto their beds and they tore into his linens and they gave their undivided attention to what they found there. They put their butts up to be smacked and they allowed him whatever liberties came into his fertile mind, and afterward they kissed him deeply and told him, with two-handed squeezes of his sacred parts, that he had better hurry back, because how could they do without him?

He had to *have* one of these women; no, he had to have *two*. There was the woman in Raleigh and the one in Durham. Neither knew about the other, and if Malka knew about either of them, she never said a word, though she grew bitter and nasty over time. She would glare at him with baleful eyes. She was colder in bed, if that were possible, and he could not remember the last time they touched lips; maybe there *was* no 'last time'.

His children, on the other hand, were the light of his life; especially the second girl, with her towhead and her dimples and her gray eyes that twinkled when she said the word, 'Papa'. He would ride her on his leg and hold her two hands: "Boogedy, boogedy, boogedy, BOO!" he would chant, while she screamed with joy. He gave the other six children attention, too, but only Beryl got the cream. Often he wondered to whom he would release her when the time came. Indeed, who was good enough to be a husband for her? She was smart, she was fun, and as she grew older and her long, thick hair began to take on a russet color, he began to realize how much she reminded him of the woman in Raleigh. He could only hope that she would keep that high spirit into adulthood and make some man as happy as he was, not withstanding his wife.

But it was not to be. It was as if some *dybbuk* was listening; some demon that saw to it that Beryl was dancing as he left for Durham, but by the time he returned home three weeks later, she was—well, *gray*.

CHAPTER TWO

Malka did have one passion: her religion. Many women might complain about the severity of the Faith; not Malka. The singular place that she came alive was at Temple. She went early and she left late. She served on every committee the Temple had. And when she looked at the dashing Rabbi Feuerstein, she felt something akin to what she knew she ought to feel for her husband, but didn't. She was in no danger, she knew; he would certainly have no interest in *her*. She already felt like an old woman, even though she was just in her mid-thirties. But when she heard about the next life, she salivated internally. Yes, there must be a better world for a woman like her, whose husband did not even like her and whose children, while physically beautiful and surely *mitzvahs*, were still children, that could annoy her unendingly.

She felt the most resentment toward her second daughter, whom her husband had chosen to favor. She often spoke harshly to the child about things that, had her other two daughters done them, would not have aggravated her at all. Beryl was the last one that Malka gave permission to do whatever came up: the last to get a new dress, the last to get money for an egg cream soda at the drugstore. She knew she was being mean to the child, and further, realized that Beryl knew she was being treated differently. But what could Beryl do about it? The very sight of the girl, with her face that mirrored Gershom's right down to the color of her eyes, was enough to make Malka feel a touch of the rage smouldering in her toward the child's father.

Rabbi Feuerstein mentioned to her one day that her daughters were becoming of an age to be bas mitzvahed. As the eldest, Peshella must go first. Peshella, whom she called Shelly, was a studious child, and more known for her bookishness than for her beauty. The eldest boys, David and Allan, now officially men, helped Shelly with her studies; and Malka, who felt an affinity for the child as well as a desire to be physically closer to the Rabbi, sat in at her every session. She drilled Shelly before and after her classes, making sure that the Hebrew letters and their mystical meanings stayed in the child's mind. "You should be able to wake up at dawn reciting your passages," Malka told her, and the obedient child complied. Her bas mitzvah was perfectly executed.

Beryl was next; but she had none of the preparation Peshella had. Her brothers were older and frequently not around. Peshella was tied up with her studies, and Malka did not like the girl enough to invest herself as she had with her first daughter and her two sons. Beryl went to her first study session feeling far from well prepared, and Malka anticipated her humiliation. As expected, the neophyte blundered her way through the alphabet; that was more than enough for Malka. There was too much that she had to do at home; no time for her to listen to the odious girl stumble through the passages that were so precious to her. She felt Beryl's awkwardness with her training would only reflect badly on her mother, but she certainly was not going to take her time helping her to look good. Malka begged Rabbi Feuerstein to let Beryl come on her own; after all, she was twelve, and could find her way to the Temple alone. Rabbi shrugged, and said it would be fine. But now Malka was confounded. Beryl had come home in tears; not over the lessons, but over what she swore Rabbi Feuerstein had done.

"He was adjusting the curtains," she said. "He said I wasn't paying attention; that I was getting distracted, so he drew them closed, so that I couldn't see out and no one could see in. He made me stand on my chair and read the text. He told me to keep my mind on what I was reading and to read at the top of my voice. Then—" she said, and by now her tears were streaming, "he raised up my dress and he—he touched me *there*, and when I told him to stop, he told me '*nothing* should distract you from the text! You see how distracted you are! I am trying to help you concentrate!' and he kept right on doing what he was doing until he didn't want to anymore, then he opened the curtains and told me to go home and don't say anything."

The further Beryl got into her story the more flummoxed Malka became. Had her precious Rabbi Feuerstein really molested her daughter? She had never heard tell of such things from other people. Whatever would possess Beryl to say such a thing about him? Could it be true?

Oh, but he was such a *nice* man; *such* a good soul; a *Tzaddik* of a man. And he knew the scriptures so well and interpreted them so wisely, yet so simply, so that even the simplest people could understand. Besides, he was married and had children of his own. He would, surely, never do anything to hurt a child. How many girls had he bas mitzvahed? Not a single one had said anything like this; at least no one that Malka knew of. Why would Beryl be his choice anyway? Malka did not consider her to be a *pretty* girl. Surely the child was lying; trying to get the precious Rabbi in trouble.

But how could her story be so graphic? Malka remembered a dirty, smelly old man back in the town where she grew up. He had snatched her one day as she passed him, and dragged her into a barn. She had gotten away from him, but only barely. Her brothers had run the man out of town, and far too soon after that she had been betrothed and wed to Gershom. She had lay in bed that first night, feeling Gershom's filthiness and man-stink come closer and closer. Her precious Rabbi was not like the man in the town; not like Gershom. And Beryl was a nasty, dirty little liar, to say those things about the Rabbi; to bring those evil thoughts back to her mother's mind.

She slapped Beryl across the face and screamed at her. "How *dare* you, you little liar! You will go back there, and you will prostrate yourself before Rabbi, and you will tell him the terrible thing you told me, and you will beg his forgiveness, and then you will go back to your texts, and you will keep at them until you complete your studies for your bas mitzvah. To make sure you follow my directions I will go with you to make certain that you do what I say!"

Indeed, Rabbi looked startled and a flash of concern crossed his face when first he saw Malka with Beryl at the door of his study; but when the woman pushed Beryl to the floor at his feet and forced the confession out of her, he smiled faintly. That accomplished, Malka grasped her purse, stood imperiously over her daughter and warned her: "I am not to hear *another word* about this holy man, this—this *Tzaddik* of a man. And don't think you can go running to your father with this vicious little tale, because I will see to it that he beats you to within an inch of your existence if you do!" With those words she slammed out of the door. Rabbi's smile had metamorphosed into a smirk. He strolled casually over to the window and drew the curtains, and then he bolted the study door. Rubbing his hands, he sauntered toward her. "Stand on the chair," he said.

Somehow Beryl struggled through to her bas mitzvah. She kept her lips sealed tight about what happened when the curtains swished shut and the study doors closed, locking out the safe world. From her precarious perch on the wooden chair, she shrieked out the fire letters and their emerging meaning at the top of her lungs, hoping in vain that the pain in her throat would distract her from feeling the profanity this vile man brought to her body under cover of her skirts. She learned, yes; but she learned far more than the texts taught. She learned to avert her eyes when she walked through the door, so that she did not have to look into the Rabbi's hot eyes or see his wet lips. She learned to stop feeling *anything* when his fingers went where they went; the numbness continued even when she didn't need it anymore. And she learned to avoid males; males of all kinds. That included her brothers and her father.

If she shivered when her father rumpled her hair or playfully swatted her rear end, he attributed her new reaction to her sensitivity about her developing body, and just stopped playing with her. He still brought her special little things, but he noticed that she took little delight in them. Even at her bas mitzvah, which should have been the high point of her life, she had been an automaton in her recitation of the scriptures, had prayed without emotion and performed woodenly at the reception. When the Rabbi had come and offered her an uncharacteristic hug in congratulations for her accomplishment, she had become an icicle; refusing to look at the man or even to acknowledge his presence. Finally, Gershom just figured that some latent gray gene from her mother had fired, and this was the way she too would be from now on. Maybe, he thought, his own long-term and chance encounters over the years, as he went from house to house with his cases to establish an ever-widening territory in the South for his company's brushes and household goods, were the aberrations and this behavior Beryl was manifesting was the way of women. He dropped the woman in Durham, settled in with the woman in Raleigh, and rotated home twice a year for a week or two. Malka didn't seem to notice.

Theirs had been a shoddily pasted together marriage. How could he love a Malka? He had not seen her face until he had lifted her veil at the betrothal. She had not raised her eyes to his, even out of curiosity. He had seen there only grayness; a grayness that had not passed from her: not as she circled him seven times under the canopy, not as she danced through the seven days of celebration as prescribed for their nuptials, not as he applied such tendernesses as he had been instructed in by his father and recommended by his rabbi to her body. She had lain there like a dead thing: eyes tightly pressed shut, lips pursed and resistant to his kisses. When he reached her sacred place he had felt only a shroud of grayness that caused him to linger in dread at the portal of what was supposed to be the palace of ultimate joy. The requisite blood had come forth when he finally penetrated her; but other than a grimace of pain, she had lain quiet as a gravestone, remote as the polar ice caps. He had attempted to snuggle with her afterward, as his father had directed him, but she had gone so rigid that he feared she had had a stroke. Ultimately his father had directed him just to satisfy himself and forget about trying to arouse her feelings, as long as he impregnated her.

That accomplished, he had come to ignore her altogether, except for the obligatory few minutes it took when he needed to relieve his pent-up passion and there was no other suitable object around. He gave her money and he did the little things that men do about the house. He played with the children when they came to him. Otherwise, he spent most of his visit in his remote study, pretending that he was so busy with his out of town clients that he had no time for anyone else, but in actuality he was most likely to be on long distance calls with Raleigh or Durham. One of the children usually brought his meals to his office. He was always hoping it would be Beryl. But Beryl never came these days. It was as if he didn't exist for her anymore.

In fact, for Beryl he *didn't* exist anymore. She wanted so to tell him what had happened with Rabbi Feuerstein, but her lips would seal themselves whenever the opportunity presented itself. She supposed she feared what would happen if she told him and he, too, did not believe her. She thought she would die; no, literally. If he didn't believe her, she really would die.

And so she didn't tell him. She preferred to think of what he *might* have done to Rabbi Feuerstein, *had* she told him. In her mind, she saw him striding up to the podium as the Rabbi, his hands sullied still from touching her, reached for the sacred Scroll. She saw her father seizing the man by the throat and ripping away all of his holy trappings—his tallis and his tsitsit—and trampling them underfoot as he strangled the man. She saw him standing above the fallen Rabbi, arms upraised like the Wrath of God, giving just enough pause for the recognition of his sin against her to come to Feuerstein's mind, but not enough to allow him time to repent and thus escape the fiery pit of hell. If he could do that, even in her dreams, then her other dreams might become less terrifying and she might sleep in peace.

In fact, one day she actually decided that she *must* tell him. The house was empty: her mother had taken the other girls to the city and the boys were wherever boys went on a Sunday afternoon. She crept to his study door and placed her hand gingerly on the knob. He was on the telephone, and for an instant she thought to step away until he was quiet. Then certain words began to catch her attention; words, and then phrases, and then whole sentences. He was speaking with a woman; and this was no client.

It was not that she sympathized with her mother. She despised the woman, and knew Malka felt the same way about her, though she did not understand why. But her father! Was this the way of men? Were they *all* like that? If her father, the god of her life, could so betray her mother, then how could he be her own hero and defender? He would not vindicate her with the Rabbi. He might even side with the man; in his own way, she thought, he was as criminal as the Rabbi.

Her father, the Rabbi; the two most important men in her life. Whom could she trust? And who might be next to take advantage of her; some male teacher in the public school that her mother insisted she had to go to? Some friend of her brothers?

Ultimately she had only God to trust. She went to her room, fell on her knees, and began to pray. But what should she tell God? He was, after all, a man, too. God, Who had created all, had also created both the Rabbi *and* her father. God was supposed to know everything; didn't He know what they were going to do? And if He did, then why did he create them anyway? And when He saw what they did—for surely, in His omniscience, He *knew*—why didn't He destroy them, as He had done to the Egyptians and the Hittites and the Perizzites?

And then, there was what was going on in Germany right now; the pogroms and that rising maniac Hitler. Jews were dying in Europe and people were saying it was going to get worse and God didn't seem to be doing a thing. Maybe God was just a hoax and religion was just what Marx said: the opiate of the people. Maybe there was no God, and maybe people just made up Him and all of the things He was supposed to have done for the Israelites and everybody else. Maybe *everything* was just by chance, and she chanced to be in the wrong place and with the wrong people at the wrong time.

Maybe the bas mitzvah had just been a waste of time; something that wasn't even necessary, even if the Rabbi had been somebody that didn't touch her. Maybe there was nothing to do but to live until she died and all of her feelings, even her good feelings, stopped.

But how did one spend the time until one's personal doomsday?

Boys were uninteresting to her, and food tasted like ashes in her mouth. She only tolerated school, and Malka ordered her home right after school, while even her baby sister was free to do whatever she pleased. She didn't draw or paint; didn't sing or listen to music. Everything she had loved before seemed empty since the first time the curtains in the Rabbi's study closed. She was too healthy to die and too disinterested to live. Life stretched ahead, bleak and never-ending.

Only one person offered surcease: Yael.

Yael lived in the big house on the corner. It was stuffed with real art and marble statuary and furniture that actually matched. Her mother, a robust, chesty woman, had a tinkly laugh and loved to bake. Because Yael was an only child, she had two rooms for her own: one a veritable parfait of pinks and whites that defined her bedroom. The other, a rainbow of bold colors, was her 'fun' room. She had a Victrola and even some records to go on it. The thick Empress Blue rug ensured that her jumping up and down and bopping to the beat disturbed no one. Her father loved her and gave her whatever she wanted; but to Beryl he was a non-entity, and she did everything she could to avoid him. At home, Beryl had no such luxuries. Her two sisters, one elder and one younger, shared her tiny bedroom, and they had to share a bathroom with her brothers, which led to far too many intrusions and unpleasant surprises.

Yael's family ate well, too. They didn't keep a kosher kitchen, as Beryl's mother did. Beryl developed a secret yen for the occasional bacon that Yael's mother served. The cuts of meat were thicker and more succulent, and the vegetables fresher. True, Yael believed in God; but Beryl forgave her that. She had, Beryl concluded, not been through what she herself had, which she thought would have convinced her of her error. Yael went to the big synagogue in Philadelphia—when her family went at all. Usually they went only on high holy days, Rosh Hashanah and Yom Kippur. The other holidays, her father felt, were not worth the drive, when they could celebrate them quietly at home. He did, however, give generous donations to the synagogue, which he said was "all they want anyway".

Yael was fun; being with her, for Beryl, was like breathing. She always had a scheme; a plan to 'ditch' school and run off to wherever: the movies, the shops downtown, and even to restaurants. Yael had secreted from her mother's makeup case mascara, powders and lipsticks, with which they slathered their faces before taking the bus that stopped around the corner from school. Beryl often wondered how they got away with so much hooky-playing. Finally, though, she figured that her teachers just didn't care. What was there to care about anyway? There was, after all, no God, no trust, and no love in the universe, except what she felt for Yael.

She *admired* Yael. She was amazed at the chutzpah of the girl. She could smile at a teacher and hand over a note that she knew good and well she had scripted herself, and never even look hesitant. She could stare down a movie proprietor who wanted to know why she wasn't in school and convince him of whatever tall tale she could invent on the spot. Life for her seemed to be one long caper. Beryl never told her about the Rabbi, or even about her loss of faith. She was fearful, when she reflected on it, that perhaps Yael would want no more to do with her if she told her. She preferred to sip what life she could from Yael's bright smile and incredible ideas. Yael became Beryl's temple; her faith. Beryl decided to model her life after Yael's, to the best of her ability. When Yael buckled down in her junior year of high school and began making straight A's, Beryl followed suit; and when Yael decided that North Carolina Women's College was where she would study homemaking, Beryl quickly applied.

But their relationship changed in college. Despite her machinations, Beryl could not get on the list to be Yael's dorm-mate, and, to her surprise, Yael did nothing to help her. Yael told Beryl they should meet other people, which would make their hanging out together that much more pleasurable. Then she joined a sorority without even mentioning her intention to Beryl, and soon she had friends that Beryl did not know. They went places to which Beryl was not invited. To Beryl, it seemed Yael did not seem to care for her one way or the other anymore, though she insisted to Beryl that she did. Beryl was crushed.

Beryl would see her idol in the cafeteria, surrounded by other girls, or in the library with a pile of books and study partners, or about the campus rushing from one class to another, elbow crooked and locked in that of one of her sorority sisters. Beryl discovered that they had no classes together. She tried switching into Yael's courses; but nothing was open. Yael would stop by occasionally and take her out for a soda; Beryl wanted more.

But Yael did not have time for more. She had discovered David, a fellow from North Carolina State, who was occupying most of her weekend hours. She and he spent most of their time at football games or doing sorority and fraternity things. Beryl felt betrayed. How could Yael grow away from her like this? Hadn't she patterned her life after Yael? Wasn't she *here* because of her?

In her heart of hearts, though, she knew Yael was not the only reason she had chosen this school so far away from her family. Her reasons went far beyond her dislike of her mother; she was closer to her father. Maybe she just wanted to keep an eye on him, but she rarely saw him at all, and she never did find out where he was living. She asked Yael to help her find him once; it was the kind of adventure that the Yael she knew in high school would have thrived upon. Back then, they would have drawn up plans to spy on him and follow him to wherever he was having his secret trysts. She went to Yael with much hope, but Yael told her she was too busy with 'things' to help her, and if she wanted to spy on her father, it would be best if she did so with someone else or by herself.

Yael was not a cruel person. She sympathized with Beryl, but made it clear that she was not going to change her new lifestyle, and certainly she was *not* going to drop David. Beryl was great companionship when they were in high school, but in college she was just a girlfriend among many girlfriends and she had to realize that Yael needed her own life.

"So, Ber," she said, "I've got an idea. You've never had a beau, and you don't seem to have any other friends here but me. There's a mixer for some of the Jewish kids on David's campus; why don't you tag along? I have an idea: David said they need somebody to help with serving the refreshments; giving out the punch and such. If you don't feel like talking to people, you don't have to; just offer them a cookie or a drink. But there'll be a lot of cute guys from NCU; who knows who you might meet there?"

A boy! Beryl did not want a boy. She avoided boys. When she gave them any consideration at all, a horror appeared in her mind: Rabbi Feuerstein, bigger than life, picking inside her underwear; picking at *her*. She would quickly turn away from any boy at that point, no matter how cute he might be, how charming his words. She knew what they were *really* like.

Still, she reflected at such times, she must steel herself for the fact that someday she must marry. It was her duty, she thought, to enter the household of a husband, so as not to become a burden to her parents in their old age. In return for his offering her room and board, food and clothing, it was her obligation to give him children, and there was only one way to do that: to endure the indignities of the marriage bed.

She did not relish the thought at all. Her elder sister had married only last summer. Her discussions with her mother of her awkwardness with her new spouse, albeit she had approved and even liked him before they wed, did not escape Beryl's ears. Perhaps she would be more fortunate, Beryl thought. Then Feuerstein's face would leer at her from the backdrop of her eyelids. Perhaps she would *not* be.

Beryl prepared herself for the dance, but without much enthusiasm. Still—who knew? Maybe there would be someone there that she could talk with; just talk. No matter what was going on in boys' minds, maybe they could just talk.

But no one had talked to her. She had stood, doling out punch and cookies to what seemed to be a million and one boys until her feet hurt. They had come to the punch bowl, all right, but with their girlfriends in tow, or requesting two drinks. One or two of them called her 'doll face' or 'cutie', but none of them actually addressed *her*.

The foreign-looking boy caught her eye. It was clear that he was alone, and he looked very uncomfortable. His hands kept wandering to his hair or his tie, which he adjusted frequently and without thought. He had obviously dressed with considerable care, and unlike the other boys, was pressed and combed with hair that was too short for someone his age. He was handsome, but didn't seem to realize it. Woodenly he accepted the drink and the cookies from her; then suddenly he turned and stared at her as if a fog had lifted and he had suddenly recognized an old friend.

CHAPTER THREE

She soon forgot about the punchbowl and the cookies. The two of them were engaged in conversation. Benyamin had, despite his many protestations of having little of consequence to talk about, a wealth of experiences that took Beryl far beyond the reaches of Camden or Raleigh, the only two places she had been besides Philadelphia, on her clandestine playdates with Yael. She detected almost immediately that he was inexperienced and unsure how to *be* around a woman. Something about him pleased her mightily, though she would not have dared put a finger on it, lest she should discover that she simply feared and disliked him less than other males. She wanted to believe that she felt attracted to him; that he could be *the one.*

Yael encouraged her to date some other boys before she settled in definitely on just one to devote her time to. On the other hand, she thought secretly and slyly, if her former best friend indeed had found *the one*, she would certainly spend less time stalking *her* on campus, and she'd have more time to spend with David.

As for Benyamin, he told himself immediately that he must *go slowly* with this girl. He could not allow his libido to leap ahead of his common sense, or he would risk disgusting her in some unknown way. He must keep conversation general and pleasant; he could talk about growing up in Cologne, but not about Anya. He could discuss his family and his flight from Germany, but he must not even think of bringing up Sheila. He could tell her that her dress was pretty, but he must not speak about how nice her breasts made her sweaters look, and he *certainly* must not touch her. He must talk about school and about his classes and about his ambitions.

What *were* his ambitions? He thought often of perhaps going to South America to be with his parents when he completed college, but Herschel's labored letters gave a most unflattering picture of his parents' situation and his own. He did not relish the idea of living with his parents, his brother, his sister-in-law and his bride-to-be, as he pictured Beryl to be, under the same roof, in a third-floor walk-up apartment with hardly enough room to maintain privacy. He felt (correctly) that Beryl would not abide such an arrangement, and as he had himself grown quite accustomed to the luxuries that the Aaronsohns offered, he thought that he must consider some alternative.

He knew his tenure at the Aaronsohns was nearing an end. As soon as he received his diploma, he could count on their serving him his eviction notice. He was sure of it; he was a very, very distant relative, and their obligation only through some unknown favor his family had done theirs, which his presence in their home had long ago repaid; and though his relationship with them was cordial, he was hardly going to be given a permanent space.

Although his command of English was by now that almost of a native, he certainly had no desire to go back to England, and there was no doubt in his mind that Germany was the worst place to be, right now. Everyone knew the war was happening there. Bombs were falling and people were dying. Far from wondering what might become of his aunt and uncle in Coventry, he just feared being caught up in the war and losing his own life. He knew returning to Germany was futile, but he wondered what was happening with his Oma Bina and his Uncle Reuven in Switzerland or Finland, if they were still there. He figured his grandmother to be a tough old bird that could survive anything, but he wasn't so sure about his uncle, whose heart threatened his life on the most pacific of days. He was in some sanitarium in Geneva the last time Benyamin had heard from them, which was he did not know how long before the letter arrived some months ago, now, and Benyamin wondered if perhaps he should try to go to Switzerland; maybe that was a safe place for Jews to be.

He thought about looking up LiLo and her mother; with more of a sense of America, he realized, now, that they could not be more than a day away by bus. His mother might know where they were. But it had been a long time since he had heard from her.

It had been a long time since he heard from anyone. Herschel's letters came only three or four times a year, and his mother scarcely wrote at all. His father never wrote; not even once. Benyamin supposed the *ganz grosse doktor* thought himself to be too important to write. He had, after all, not seen Benyamin since he was a child whose voice had not altered. But now Benyamin was a full five inches taller than his father had seen him last. His voice was deeper and his physique far more manly. He saw himself as the ideal male child for a doctor to have.

But was his father the ideal man for a son to have? Benyamin now saw everyone and everything in light of Beryl. How would she react to his family? He recalled his parents as quite respectable—even superior—in their presentation; but respectable for pre-war Cologne, not North Carolina. He blushed as he thought of his father in his very German bathrobe, eating his kosher food and driving his ancient car. And his mother—according to Herschel, she was wearing threadbare clothing and not combing her hair anymore. He couldn't imagine it; his mother had always been such a—*neat* person. Then there was Herschel. What would Beryl do when she met Herschel? He was pretty presentable, Benyamin recalled, but he couldn't *read*, after all. And his wife was a frowzy hunchback, for all of her extolled domestic virtues.

CHAPTER FOUR

Geula was a much better shopper and chef than Eliana ever could be. Eventually her mother-in-law learned to live with Geula's inability to grasp the concept of 'kosher'. The girl was frugal to a fault, and began making small changes about the place with the household money that made things much more comfortable. Herschel found himself valuing her abilities; if they weren't enough to make him want to come home to her sallow face, bag-of-bones body, and indifferent attitude, they did delight him when he chose to return to her. She mixed potatoes and carrots and broccoli and peppers and beef; seasoning them and rolling them in foil to bake everything, rather than boiling and serving each item separately. She scrubbed a chicken in salt to get the blood out, and then threw it in a pot with potatoes and celery and onions and spices, which she boiled until she could almost fish out the chicken's skeleton whole. She was a wizard with the occasional egg that they came across; mixing it with flour and lard and sugar and other spices to make incredibly elaborate and tasty confections and sold them to their neighbors. She put the pesos she earned into Herschel's pocket, or into decorating the sparse living room, or onto her mother-in-law's back. Herschel could not deny that she was a good woman, and his father continually reminded him of the necessity of being discreet with any improprieties because of her family.

Still—

She just didn't please him. He wanted beauty; he wanted sauciness; he wanted *saftig*ness.

He wanted Solange.

But Solange was gone. She belonged to someone else, now. Every now and again he saw her on the streets, her belly large and her arm linked through that of another man, her eyes twinkling up into his as they once had into Herschel's, her lips drawn up in a delighted bow, her delicate seashell-shaped ears listening to the stranger's every tenderly whispered word. Sometimes Herschel wanted to call out to her, to see if it might be possible to lure her back to his side. Sometimes he wanted to attack the suave, dark-eyed man she was with and lay him out flat, but he knew he was in no condition to do battle in the streets.

There were women in the streets that were far more casual with their loyalties; women whose skirts were shorter, whose lips were redder and whose smiles—and other personal attributes—were easier to elicit. They looked on his fair hair and whiter skin as strong indicators of what he might have in his pockets. At times, when he gathered enough from Geula's contributions, he visited their districts and took advantage of their charms.

It was all emptiness for him, though. He could not extend his soul to these women and he could not give to Geula what he did not feel for her. The feel of voluptuous flesh beneath his fingers did not compensate him for the void in his mind and the hollow place in his heart that he knew no one would ever fill. Yet, the bony body of a woman that was totally devoted to him provided him with no satisfaction.

He could feel only that life would be long; and, thanks to his father's foolishness, he would be yoked unequally to a woman he would never love for the rest of his life; forever, if Solange's religion was to be believed.

CHAPTER FIVE

Benyamin's world, however, was entirely different. He was head-over-ears with Beryl, even though he had never touched her in that man-woman way. He had met her the next afternoon and, per Chaya Aaronsohn's direction (though how she might be so knowledgeable he could not guess) he took her for a malted. The next day and the day after, he met her at the library and they studied for midterms. He kept the topics of their conversation strictly on course content and research methods, and he watched with satisfaction as the muscles of her shoulders slowly relaxed. He left her alone during Midterms Week, but he was at her dorm first thing that following Friday, and he spent nearly every day after that with her. The Aaronsohns began to tease him good-naturedly, and Beryl took Anya's place—the good Anya that he remembered from his boyhood—in his dreams.

Benyamin made a decision.

This was the woman he was going to marry.

CHAPTER SIX

Geula leaned her head against the toilet bowl rim. There was no doubt; she was indeed pregnant. Herr Doktor had insisted that she was, and followed up his diagnostic impression with insistence that she enter his sacred office and submit to an examination.

He had done it once before, when her uncle had brought her to the apartment for him to certify her virginity before he approved her for Herschel. She had had to strip completely naked before both of the men, and while Herr Doktor had probed her insides, her uncle had looked on disapprovingly. Only Mama Eliana's presence in the room had kept her from total panic.

She was not the kind of girl that would tempt a man; this she knew well, from the smirks and chortles of just about every male that had ever laid eyes on her since she had entered her teens. She had her mother's sallow skin and pale eyes, her mother's lank hair and gangly build, and, worst of all, she had her mother's bone disease. It would not happen this year or next year; but at some point, unless other events intervened, her days would end when her spine fused in an S-shape and her lungs so constricted that they would no longer inflate. Then she would suffocate and die. Until then, she would bend a little more each year. Until then, she would try to be as normal as possible.

From the third-floor window, she saw Herschel. He looked exhausted; his face was gray and he had dark circles under his eyes. He did not pay much attention to her these days, nor did she expect it. She was just grateful that she would no longer be an unwelcome burden in her uncle's house. His wife had made a drudge of her, and she knew that when the couple died they would leave her no inheritance. Herschel gave all of his money to his father, and she felt there would be nothing left for him either. Still, their apartment was small and she could clean it quickly. Eliana seemed happier with her there, and that comforted her somewhat.

She doubted that she brought Herschel any delight as his wife. He looked her directly in the face only when she happened into his visual field, and then, apparently shocked anew by what he saw, he turned his eyes quickly to some more pleasing sight in the room. They went nowhere together; she could not recall their even venturing out on the street as a couple. Although there was almost no money, there were things that the two of them could do without cost, such as go to the park or stroll through the marketplace together. She thought, sometimes, of suggesting a constitutional after dinner; just the two of them; but she did not dare. Perhaps, she thought, he might fear that someone from the factory would recognize her as belonging to him, and that would be more embarrassment than he could bear.

She knew the scent of other women's' bodies, and she smelled their musky perfume on him at times. That caused her gorge to rise against him, but she quickly swallowed her feelings. A woman with her many faults and deficiencies, she thought, should be content with whatever crumbs of affection he chose to give her, even if he was feasting elsewhere; that was what her uncle had told her. She tried to push whatever indiscretions, real or imagined, from her mind as she spread thin the few pesos she received every week from him, and tried as best she could to keep the household in order.

She did not spend every cent she received to run the household on groceries. She spent judiciously. A few pesos she gave to Herschel, for his daily use. The rest she secreted away each week. She now had a very tidy sum hidden in the pocket of one of her skirts. Periodically when no one was looking she would count out the money and put it in an even more secure place. She thought about having her uncle open an account for her, but she dared not; he might simply 'forget' it was not his money. As for Herschel, well, he did not require any more than he already received to spend on other women; oh, yes, she knew; but what more should she expect? She was not an attractive woman.

Herschel received the news of her conception with indifference; what did it matter? He might be the elder son, but he was not the most favored; Benyamin was. No matter that he had risen to a superior place in the factory; no matter that he now brought home a respectable amount of money. Benyamin had graduated college. He was going to a graduate school, and now, as soon as he secured a good job, he was going to marry.

His father was all excitement; he and Herschel's mother were going to America to see this son that they had not seen for almost ten years. But although it was Herschel that would be paying for the trip, he was not invited. His father had only laughed when Herschel, with uncharacteristic excitement, began speaking of his plans to book four tickets.

"And where would you be planning to take that wreck of a woman you're married to?" he demanded, mindless of Geula's presence in the room. "Do you want to humiliate your brother? How could Benyamin show her off to his friends as a member of his family? He works with doctors and engineers and college professors, and she would be an embarrassment. And *you*—" his father continued. "You with your work-worn hands and your ragged clothes; you look pathetic! Why, you'd need an entire new wardrobe to go. And do you even know how to act around that level of people? You don't speak English, and probably no one will understand a word that you say. Besides, we'll need a lot of money to travel first-class and to buy a wedding gift and to take people that we meet there out to restaurants. No; your mother and I will go and represent the family. I'll buy Eliana a nice dress for the occasion."

Herschel had shut his lips tight, so that words he might regret would not come spilling out and ruin the occasion for his mother, whose eyes were dancing at the prospect of seeing her other son again. But that night, when the house was still, he let fall hot tears on his thinly-stuffed pillow, and he did not resist when Geula, still wakeful, began rubbing his back and comforting him.

CHAPTER SEVEN

After much fussing, shopping and money gathering, Elie and Eliana had found themselves at Ezezia Airport, ready to board a plane to Miami and from there a bus to Durham. Benyamin drove to pick them up in the Aaronsohn's car.

Elie could hardly believe how Benyamin had grown. He was now several inches taller, broader through the chest, square of jaw and very handsome. He had gone from a dreamer of a child to a man of substance; a college graduate, a Master's candidate, a husband. Elie did wish that his son's German was a little more correct, but he had to acknowledge the great achievement it was that the boy had mastered English so well. He had not bothered to learn Spanish in his new country, and when he could not find someone to speak German, he relied on Herschel. If Herschel was not available, he just kept to himself, reading again and again from the gynecology tomes that had served him so well in Germany.

The wedding was simple; Benyamin and Beryl were there, of course, and her father and elder sister. The Aaronsohns came also, and Yael and David, who were also married now, found the time to attend the ceremony at the Hotel Carolina in downtown Raleigh, with a minister from the Unitarian Church officiating.

Elie liked Benyamin's new wife, even though she had patently refused his offer to give her a gynecological examination. He told her he wanted to ensure that she would be able to have children, but his real intention was to determine if she was a virgin; one did hear so many things about American girls, even Jewish ones. Her eyes had grown large and filled with tears; he concluded that marked her as innocent. But he did really want to know, and he just hoped his son would know what to do if she wasn't. He vaguely remembered his father telling him that somewhere in old-style Judaism was a law that a man could get a divorce if his wife did not conceive in ten years after consummation. Benyamin had refused even to entertain the idea of pressuring her, and assured his father that he would do everything in his power to help his wife-to-be conceive within the appointed time period.

In the United States, Elie had enjoyed a little of the flair of his old life. Thanks to Herschel, he had flown first-class, and his pockets were full when he got off the plane. Eliana had managed to rally. She looked almost as she had in Cologne, though her formerly *saftig* form had grown spare and her hair was mostly white. She smiled wanly and almost seemed interested in Miss Aaronsohn's conversations with her. Benyamin wondered, as he waved 'goodbye' to her at the airport, if he would ever see her again. He sighed. He loved his mother, but she had been out of his life for too long to feel like a mother or to measure up well to his idealization of her. Beryl would have to be his all, now; his Everywoman. She would be his mother and his Anya and herself, all in one. He would never say that to her, however, just in case she might disagree with him.

CHAPTER EIGHT

Elie looked with horror around the apartment. He had been gone for only three weeks—three of his son's pay periods—and he and his woman had done this!

"How could you spend the money on yourselves?" he demanded of Herschel. "Why don't you have money to put into my hands when I return from a long journey? What kind of son are you?"

"Geula is pregnant," Herschel said. "She needs things; we need space. We moved you and Mama into your 'office'—the biggest room in this miserable place. We are taking your bedroom and you may use the parlor for whatever you choose. Most people entertain there. We, of course, are not 'most people', because we've had to sleep like poor relations on the living room floor. No more! We are not slaves. We are not hired help, that you can treat as you will. We have spent the money as we pleased. We have made the place better. You will receive no money from our past weeks and you will receive only what I choose to give you after I pay the bills."

A mortified Elie stormed into his office and slammed the door, but not before shouting, "I should go back to America! I should go there, and live with Benyamin and Beryl! Benyamin put five hundred dollars American into my hands! He is a filial son! And—" here he turned his glare on Geula—"his wife is pretty and she has a straight back!"

Herschel turned toward his crestfallen wife. For the first time, he felt a sense of her humiliation; her shame at how she was formed and what her entry into this family had cost her. True, she had a husband; but one that did not love her, that used her like a toilet and then sullied himself in the streets with voluptuous painted whores that he loved about as much as he loved her.

It was she, not he, that had made the final objection to his servitude under his father's rule; she that had chided him. It was she that had watched him push the envelope with his pay under their father's office door. She had retrieved it and come to him in a fury. He had been convinced that she was right, and so they had shopped together and moved the furniture together and bought clothing for him, so that he would not be embarrassed at work.

It occurred to him that, no matter how attractive Benyamin's wife might be, she would never measure up to the fidelity and the resourcefulness and—and—dare he even think it? The *love* that Geula had for him.

CHAPTER NINE

Benyamin and Beryl had muddled their way through their consummation. She had been stiff and fearful in their bed; but having had no counsel or experience and being primarily interested in his own gratification, Benyamin had not noticed for some time. And so it came that Beryl found herself to be pregnant. She was a hardy girl; and bolstered by her relief at the reprieve from sex that her father-in-law recommended as well as from the download of mother-hormones into her system, she got on quite well.

As she neared term, the question inevitably arose: was there to be a *Brit Millah*: a circumcision for the firstborn child, provided the baby was a healthy boy? Despite her wariness of all things Jewish, Beryl did not see how she could avoid it. She had overheard his mother's comment, "At least she's Jewish", to Miss Aaronsohn. Her knowledge of her elder sister's fall from grace in her mother's eyes, because she produced only one child, a girl, led her to believe that if she was to matter at all, she must produce a son, and on the eighth day of his life, be ready to submit him to the ministrations of a *moyel*, so that he could enter the faith of his ancestors even if it was no longer her faith.

So it was that, barely two weeks before her lying-in was to begin, she and Benyamin made the trip to Camden. Her father was there for one of his rare visits, both of her brothers were there, Miriam, her younger sister, who had not yet finished college, still lived at home, and sat next to her. For a brief period Beryl felt some contentment; the ancient joys of the time before—

"—Oh, come *in!*" she heard her mother exclaim at the door, and her body grew rigid. Here stood Rabbi Feuerstein: older, now, but still with his long, filthy fingers. The specter in all of her dreams, the usurper of all of her happiness, the one that made her husband's touch feel clammy and dirty to her, had been invited in to haunt her dreams anew. She shivered. Benyamin, who had never heard the stories of suffering under this man, adjusted her wrap, thinking her merely chilled.

"I invited the Rabbi," her mother was saying, "to perform the circumcision. He is wonderful at it, and he has been our family Rabbi for such a long time. Why, it would be ridiculous to ask anyone else!" She beamed beatifically as she seated him directly across from Beryl, who suddenly had no appetite at all.

"So this is Benyamin," the Rabbi said jovially. "I have heard so much about you, and to think, you married our little Beryl. She has always been very—*special* to me." He then turned to Beryl. "I half expected that you would ask me to officiate at your wedding, my dear. Both of your brothers and Shelly did. I expect to see you under my canopy when your time comes, too, Miriam," he said to her younger sister. Miriam had chosen not to have a bas mitzvah with her father's approval, and her mother had reluctantly agreed.

Beryl could not answer; in the Rabbi's presence she felt choked. She was only now allowing her husband to put his hands on her, and this dybbuk's presence brought back her memories of ancient shames. She felt suddenly queasy. Excusing herself and praying that the man would not follow, she stumbled toward the bathroom. Fighting the nausea, she stared at her face in the mirror. She was twelve again, standing on that damnable wooden chair, with that horror of a man doing unmentionable things to her. It was several minutes before she could regain enough equilibrium to stagger back to the table and plop into a seat next to Benyamin. It took fully another minute before she realized the conversation had changed.

"…It doesn't matter anyway," Benyamin was saying. "We don't go to Temple; we both joined the Unitarian Church."

The room went deadly silent. Even Shelly's little girl stopped worrying her mother's necklace and stared at them.

Indeed, they had joined the Unitarian Church. Membership afforded them the acceptance of the larger community, without the burden of having to declare some level of belief. The Unitarians allowed their members to believe whatever they desired, and even nothing at all, but still to be a part of the congregation. Belonging to a spiritual community that most people assumed was Christian satisfied Benyamin's employers, and even gave him access to some of them. But how could Beryl ever convince these people gathered around the table that belonging to a church, no matter the denomination, did not mean abandonment of their beloved Judaism?

She needn't have worried about explaining anything. The Rabbi rose and muttered something to her mother. Without another word, he donned his coat and strode from the house. Her mother and father rose together—perhaps the first thing they had done in concert for some time—and stormed into their bedroom, slamming the door behind them. Shelly rushed up the stairs, almost dragging her little one behind her. Miriam rose, hugged Beryl, and then fled up the stairs, weeping. Her brothers had already retreated to the kitchen, where she could hear their raised voices, but could not make out their words. She and Benyamin were left alone at the table, still laid with the only partially consumed meal. Enquiringly, she turned to him.

He just spread his hands out before him. "I didn't want that man anywhere near our son's *pizzle*," he said. "Did you see his fingernails? Filthy! Who knows *where* his hands have been?"

Beryl waited. One month, two months, and the baby was born: a beautiful boy with a round and comely face. Beryl sent word to her mother, but there was no response. She thought perhaps she must be away; she sometimes went to the seashore for a week or more in spring, even though it was a bit early in the season and the temperatures were still brisk. She tried Shelly and each of her brothers, but there was no response. She sent a note to her mother, but the letter came back unopened. Finally, she called and her mother picked up the telephone. "Hello?" Malka said.

"Mama", Beryl said. "I called to say 'I'm sorry—'"

"Who is this?" her mother asked, a note of suspicion in her voice.

"It's Beryl."

"Beryl *who*", her mother asked.

"Your daughter, Beryl," Beryl replied, a little exasperated.

There was a long silence. Finally her mother spoke.

"I had a daughter Beryl, but she died," she said. Without another word, she hung up.

It was the last time Beryl would see or hear from her, and the first time Beryl heard that she herself was dead—dead! The Rabbi declared her dead and the family sat *Shivah* for her. They tore their clothing and put ashes on their heads and covered the mirrors and the windows. They fasted and squatted on the floor, chanted the requisite prayers and notified her acquaintances of her demise. Numerous visitors streamed through the house and commiserated with them. Malka sobbed openly and wailed aloud with more drama than was necessary; her 'beloved' Beryl was gone; dead to the faith she had betrayed. Oh, but she should not have been so shocked, she said. After all, hadn't the girl continually lied and been an embarrassment and a disappointment to her mother? She had even told hideous untruths about the Rabbi; she was spiteful and deserved to die young.

As for Gershom, the sorrow he showed was from his confusion as to where he should stand. He had loved Beryl; loved her with all his heart. But hadn't she changed over the years? She was no more of interest to him now than his wife was. True, he had returned to Malka after the woman in Raleigh had found him no longer appealing. He didn't have the energy to go looking for a new love, and decided that he would have to make do with Malka. He could no longer really care for himself. Malka— or perhaps Bernie, but it really didn't matter to him—saw to his linens and brushed him at the door, so that he did not appear linty and disheveled before his dwindling clientele as younger, more vigorous men took over his accounts. He might as well be dead, he often thought. Malka, after all, had money from her family, while he had little left. His out-of-town playmate had pretty much wrung out his account before she put him out. He had returned home in humiliation; and under his wife's satirical eye, he had dared not utter even a word that would dissuade her from killing Beryl spiritually. He reported where he was going, except when he wandered down to the river to stare vacantly at its tempting ripples and wonder what had become of his life.

CHAPTER TEN

The boy, Andy, never received circumcision from a moyel. Some *goyische* doctor snipped his foreskin with precision, but without ceremony, on his second day of life, not his eighth. Beryl quieted the boy as best she could until he healed, feeling acutely the absence of her family. Her husband's family was half a world away and her own had cut her off, so there was no acknowledgement of the man-child's arrival, except a small vase of roses from the Aaronsohns. Benyamin wore no black suit, no tfillin, no yarmulke. When he espied the gathering storm in her eyes, he said only, "Well, at least the doctor's nails were clean."

Beryl looked into the doughy face of her progeny. He stared back at her with a gassy little smile and mildly unfocused eyes of indeterminate color. She could not help but recall an old Russian man that had lived in the neighborhood: a toothless, good-natured old soul that doddered about collecting garbage from the streets every day but the Sabbath, and who regaled the children with coins and songs and sweets at Chanukah. Her mother had always made her throw away the sweets, even though they were wrapped; but she always kept his coins, and remembered him with prayers, when she still prayed.

The smile she would have given this little creature stuck in her throat. She remembered that it was over him that she had been cast out of her family; declared dead and apostate. And so it was that, as he grew, she withheld the caresses she might have given him, that might have softened her young girl broken heart; that might have made her a happier woman. As for Andy, he remained mild-mannered, but the serenity went out of him. He did not know that his mother bound her breasts so that he could not drink from them. He did not remember, as adults do not recall the specifics of their infancies, that he imbibed only evaporated milk, and that only when the clock chimed that he must: six and ten and two and six and ten, with no two a.m. feeding, no matter how much he flailed his little fists and screamed for relief.

She felt rage toward Benyamin, too. It was, after all, his blurted revelation that had resulted in her ejection from her family. If he hadn't opened his mouth, they could have lived however they wanted to, and her parents would never have been the wiser. She wanted to shout out her anger at him, but choked it down. She could not express it, because she felt she would go too far, and their marriage would become as full of misery as she perceived her parents' union to be. She could not and she would not live like that; she would leave before she would endure what her parents' marriage was.

But then where would she go? She had no legacy to fall back on, as her mother had had when Gershom cheated on her. Even with so many children, her mother could have locked her father out and lived quite well. Beryl, however, had no work experience; she had married right out of college and had not even waitressed or worked in a department store on her summer breaks. She supposed she could do something with her Home Economics degree, but its purpose, as she believed that of most of her classmates had been, had been chiefly to help her to gain an 'M-R-S.' degree. She did not feel motivated, nor did she have the means, to go back to graduate from a Master's program in another field. Instead, she put her homemaking degree into practice. She cooked economical meals consisting chiefly of organ meats, powdered milk, pasta and peas. Almost from the moment Benyamin left for his job until she heard his footfall on the apartment stairs, she scrubbed and cleaned, deaf to Andy wailing away for his next meal in the background. She scoured the second-hand stores for furnishings and clothing and decorative pieces. The rare visitors to their home—his friends, as she had none—remarked at how comfortable and homey and even *expensive* their place looked. No matter how much they complimented her, though, she felt only grayness inside.

Life went on, from day to dreary day for her. Benyamin watched her descent from the girl that was mostly sunny but had some dark clouds covering her full brilliance to one whose every moment was overcast. He tried such jokes and silliness as he recalled from his childhood, but her reaction ranged from annoyance to none at all. Finally he gave up altogether and threw himself into his work.

His work! He could work again, now that the war was over and he was out from under the curse of being German. His response to "Where is your accent from?" had led to many a rejection, and even one rather painful ousting from a prospective employer's office. His protests that he was actually Jewish went worse. That his people had been the victims of the enemy—that the maxim, "The enemy of my enemy is my friend" did not seem to count in America, and that poem on the base of the Statue of Liberty seemed so much bunk in the face of what he had experienced a lot more than once.

But now he was doing a great work. His engineering classes were behind him, and he worked with people that didn't seem to care that he was from, as one rejecting employer had said, "the Semitic races".

CHAPTER ELEVEN

Opportunity came knocking for Herschel: his supervisor had told him his company planned to open a new factory near the docks in Montevideo, and if he wished, the man would submit his name for the open foreman there for shorter hours and a lot more money.

Herschel very much wished it.

He told Geula first. She was ecstatic. Living in the tiny back room with a man and two children and two other people that occupied the rest of the apartment space was too taxing. Eliana was much better emotionally these days, and would play with the children, but her health was not as it had once been, and she never lent a hand at the cleaning. She took little interest in the cooking, but that was a relief. She had never had any real skill or art, and her lackluster spirit seemed to permeate anything she cooked.

Herschel hesitated to tell his mother about the move. She had not been quite right since the end of the war had brought the news that her mother was among those that had died in the gas chambers. She wondered about other relatives: her sister in England, her girlhood friends, her neighbors. She frequently became overwhelmed in this strange place with its rapid-fire speech. Rare were the days, now, that she set foot outside the apartment. She took even less interest in her appearance, and would be quite content to remain in bed most days, just sleeping—or pretending to, if Geula did not roust her up and groom her.

The worst one, though, Herschel realized, would be his father. Elie would, he supposed, want to cling to where he was. He steeled himself for the day that he would have to deliver the news that he had been offered a job at a substantially higher rate of pay ten hours away by bus and three hours away by boat. He would have to tell him that a move was in order, and offer him the option of going or staying in Buenos Aires with Eliana.

Elie, however, was ready for the move. He had heard, he said, that there was a German community in Uruguay, and he thought—no, he was *sure*—that a gynecologist and obstetrician with his skills would soon be overrun with patients. He began packing almost immediately.

Geula found the house, a three-bedroom place in a quiet section of town. Herschel had wanted a larger place, but their budget was not big enough. Still, there was enough for the five of them; or would have been, had Elie not once again demanded a bedroom for his 'office', meaning that the children had to sleep in their parents' room with them. They had so much more room, however, that Herschel did not mind too much. As was her way, Geula devised a little niche for Gil and their new daughter, Shoshana, to sleep in, while still leaving enough space for Herschel to feel as if he were lord of his bedroom, and therefore of his house. Geula found scraps of furniture at trash bins and constructed passable items from them—a dining table from a door and two-by-fours, a bed from an abandoned mattress that she re-stuffed and set on milk crates, which provided space for storage underneath as well, and other creative pieces that brightened their spare living space.

Herschel knew that his wife did not particularly care for his father. The man ordered her around all day, and she tended to avoid him. When they sat at table, he would compare her cooking (always negatively) with meals he vaguely recalled from his Polish maids in Germany. He berated her for failing to keep a kosher kitchen, though she was only half Jewish from a family that did not keep the dietary laws, and since traveling out of Germany he had not been able to keep kosher anyway. Her worst complaint against him, however, was about his constant jibes at her for her plain-ness and particularly her back, which he commented on almost daily. She begged him, at least once a day to smoke in his bedroom or outdoors when he was puffing on his smelly cigars. He, however, would not give up his spot in the big chair next to the radio in the parlor, even though he had little knowledge of what the announcers were saying. Herschel made excuses for the man, who still wanted a substantial cut of his salary, but Geula insisted that he was just being cantankerous.

It also occurred to Herschel that his wife's back was getting worse. The changes were almost imperceptible, and they did not yet hamper her being able to perform her duties, domestic and intimate. However, he knew that someday—probably when he most needed her—she would be not only unable to take care of him, but she would need someone to look after her as well. He tried not to think of her as a bent-over, crippled-up old lady, struggling for her every breath as her lungs found it more difficult to push her collapsing spinal cord away. But every passing day brought that reality nearer.

CHAPTER TWELVE

Married life was little better for Benyamin. Beryl had no scars; no bulges that promised to encroach upon his future. He had chosen her not only because he judged her to be beautiful, but also because she seemed so helpless and small; so unlikely to hurt or abandon him. She had seemed nice enough and friendly enough, though she was not as playful and coquettish as he would have liked. He had taken her reticence to allow him the little privileges his college friends whispered to him about or even to cuddle with him as signs of her virginal reserve. He had framed her shying away, when he moved to hold her close to him, as bait; to entice him to hold her closer when they reached the marriage bed.

But their wedding night had proved to be a disappointment. She had stayed forever in the bathroom; he told himself she was making herself ready for him. She had slid in woodenly beside him, drawing her lips into a tight line when he had tried to part them with his own, fixing her eyes on the ceiling as he explored her breasts and soft places. He had awakened in the middle of the night to find her drawn up almost into a closed circle. He knew she was not asleep; but not knowing what to say to her, he had left her alone. Over time she came to tolerate his need, but her forbearance chilled his passion. Somehow, he kept feeling, it must be his fault that he did not inflame in her the same feelings he had for her. After all, theirs was no arranged marriage; had she not agreed to marry him?

He was too ashamed of what he perceived to be his own error to consult with his colleagues, who all assumed he must be having an incredibly blissful time with this beautiful and well-formed woman. He thought of writing to his father about the matter, but his father, who had offered Beryl his skills, was probably so put off by her blatant refusal that he would give no advisement.

She had seemed happy enough when she had discovered that she had conceived. Perhaps, he thought later, her joy came from not having to submit to sex, since her doctor had recommended against it during the pregnancy. Afterward, however, had come that debacle about Andy's circumcision and her family cutting her off, and then she seemed to have no interest in the baby, other than to provide for his elemental needs without tenderness or feeling; much, it seemed to him, as if she blamed the little one himself for her ostracism.

It had been some relief when Danny had come along. He seemed to have been stamped with Benyamin's face; he was so like his father, and his temperament was sunny and happy. Even Beryl could not resist his smiles, and cuddled him regularly—particularly when she was in Andy's presence. It was as if, Benyamin thought at moments when he had not consciously guarded himself against such thoughts, she *wanted* the older boy to be jealous.

But surely that was not a mother's way, was it? His mother, who had possessed plenty of idle time to effect all sorts of devious plans, had never done anything like that. He could not remember a moment's quarrel with Herschel, except when he himself had been out of line. The only time he could remember any disagreement with him he recalled with some remorse: his failure to heed Herschel's warning about running to the Hitler parade. It was he that had dashed off, evading his brother's clutches, and found himself staring into the eyes of the monstrous man that invaded his waking thoughts even after the war ended and Hitler himself lay dead in his blood-spattered underground bunker. It was as if some transfer had occurred; as if some nameless fear had entered him; but

234

slowly, and over time. He thought often that every wretched thing that occurred to him in his life had happened after that moment: Anya's departure and subsequent rape on the train platform, his own ostracism and ultimate attack at Gymnasium, his separation from his parents, his flight to England and from there to America. Might his life have been different if he had just listened to his brother that one time?

Periodically, when he gave it thought, he did not know in which column he should place his choice of Beryl as his marital partner. Was she a plus, because she had given him two sons, because she kept her home as neat and as beautiful as a feature in *Ladies Home Journal*, because her meals, though unimaginative, were nourishing and always on time? Or was she a minus, because she created such inequity between his sons, was frosty between the sheets and might take to her bed without any preamble or provocation that he could see and not get up for days?

It occurred to him that she might be depressed; that he might have married a woman with mental problems. He remembered enough from his religious studies and his father's advisements to know that she could pass such a malady on to her children through her genes or her behavior. He should have been more careful! He should have *insisted* on meeting her parents, no matter what she said, before he was inextricably caught up in a marriage. But he had been so intent on winning her; so fixated on holding her close and caressing her. He had been so sure that marriage would unlock the portals of passion and affection that she had so carefully guarded. Now he realized that she was not wanting him to touch her, marriage withstanding; and when he partook of what she offered so reticently, he still felt unfulfilled, even after his release. It was not uncommon, after the experience was over and they lay side by side in what should have been the afterglow, for him to lie in the dark staring at the ceiling and listening to her even breathing, knowing that she was probably still awake herself and listening to his even breathing, hoping it indicated that he was asleep; that he was satisfied and would require nothing more of her for awhile.

Still—her beauty so tantalized him. From the sumptuous russet mane that hung long and thick almost to her waist, when she unbound it, to her steel gray eyes, to her supple mouth, to her velvety pale flesh, to her dainty feet, she was a wonder.

As well, she had so many skills. She knew how to hunt down quality clothes from church bazaars and thrift shops, and she knew how to fix up broken-down furniture that she found abandoned in storage rooms and, she was proud to admit, in back alleys after hours. By the time she sanded and painted and shellacked and reupholstered, their cheap rooms, compared to those of their peers, looked almost palatial. She scrimped on their meals to fund trips: first small day excursions, and then expeditions that were longer and longer and further away. On their journeys abroad, she would search for pieces by undiscovered artists from out-of-the-way places that promised to be worth a great deal more in the future; many were real investments.

Benyamin could not know, coming from his childhood in which he was indulged with practically everything he wanted, from his life with the Aaronsohns, who met his needs if he made them aware, or from his economic standard, what it was like for Beryl. He could not grasp her fear that one day he just might leave her or find someone that provided him with more love and affection than she could bring herself to. How could he grasp her fear that, if he tossed her aside and she found herself on her own, she would have nothing and no one to help her? Yes, she had many skills; but they were talents she developed so that when she found herself alone, she could still survive. She had knocked on her brothers' doors and appealed to her sisters in pleading letters with no response at all. Only he, who did not count her as dead, held hope for her ongoing existence; she feared his need of her, and she feared that he might wake up one day and find out that he did not need her anymore. So she continued in her efforts to make herself too smart, too helpful, too valuable for him to throw away.

She had an artist's eye, developed from years of wandering through art galleries and sitting in the cheap seats at theatre matinees when she was supposed to be in school and from poring over art books and listening to operas on the Victrola at Yael's house. She picked up a sense of style from reading *Ladies Home Journal* and *Good Housekeeping* and *Better Homes and Gardens* and picked up odd information about the world from *Reader's Digest*. She spent hours perusing newspapers and insisted to Benyamin that as a man of learning, he *must* read *The New York Times* faithfully to know what was going on around him. Though he rarely had time for leisure reading, she faithfully read it, from the front page to the Classifieds; and could spend an entire Sunday in that pursuit. Benyamin asked her once why she paid so much attention to her periodicals. She tossed her head, and said only, "Well, when I am with you and talking with people, I don't want to look ignorant!" He knew how hard she labored to entertain his colleagues. Hosting was a skill she excelled in; if not for her own fulfillment with their guests, then definitely for the forum to show off the effort she put into every decoration, every dish that she prepared for whatever the occasion might be.

She could entertain his students, telling stories of their travels, and he knew that in her journals she wrote flowery poems and even short stories. She could carry on lively conversations with his friends, and her looks, when he caught her looking at him, were affable. She was conversant; almost at times to the point of hysteria, when they were alone. But let him drop his eye to her body and she became little-girl frightened, and wordlessly stiffened and climbed into bed beside him with the greatest— resignation. Why? What had happened? What didn't he know?

Was it, he wondered, his blurt-out of their religion change? He did not *think* sometimes; to him whatever faith they chose to pursue was a minor thing. After all, they rarely went to the Unitarians; Beryl seemed more interested in dragging through the ragbags and shelves of toss-away things in the church's basement than listening to the sermons, which were, to him, so much droning. His Sunday mornings in the Kolendom were by now only a hazy blend of pleasant memories, and they had attended Temple in Cologne only for specific holy days or at his father's whim. The Aaronsohns never went to Temple; not once, while he was living with them. He had studied world religions in some kind of survey course in his second year of undergraduate school that had left him unappreciative of any benefits to being Jewish or anything else, for that matter, though it seemed being Jewish afforded him the least benefit of all. And so he abandoned Judaism, preferring to think of himself as a 'free thinker', a self-image quite compatible with Unitarianism.

After the war, when he was coming of age and looking for work, things had just been so *different*. He knew well, from incidents in employment offices and interviews that Jews were not popular, despite the transient sympathy afforded by Hitler's atrocities. Christians felt bad about the Holocaust—sickened by the horrific photos of living wraiths that used to be prosperous people, piles of shoes that ought to have children's feet in them—but whether it was survivor guilt or the persistent belief that the ancient Jews killed Jesus and these descendants of Abraham were still guilty more than nineteen hundred years later, too many doors had slammed shut in his face because of anti-Semitism. He worked on masking his accent and making sure he was turned out in true American style by encouraging Beryl's studying the magazine and newspaper articles and advertisements so that she could help him to mimic how successful American men dressed. He Anglicized their names, becoming Benjamin and Beryl Rose, and for good measure made all of the necessary legal name changes for the four of them.

Still, he supposed they could have linked up with a Temple, but Beryl had not wanted to. He finally decided anyway, that the most sensible thing to do to restore Beryl to her family would be to call her parents and tell them she was now affiliated with a Temple, after seeing their reaction, even though he was not happy about lying. He actually made the call, but Beryl's mother had hung up on him as soon as she realized who he was.

One evening he decided to broach the subject of his concern for the things between them that troubled him. Seven-year-old Andy and little Danny, who was nearly four, were already asleep. It seemed a good time.

She came into the den to watch the evening newscast, as she always did when the boys were asleep, with two glasses of wine. He couldn't help but notice how exceptionally beautiful she looked tonight, with her hair piled high on her head in a loose chignon, so that a few stray wisps hung down. He felt the rush of fluids in his body, the desire to take her in his arms and satisfy himself. He began gently, complimenting her on the way she kept the house and ran the finances, on the good work Andy was doing in school, under her extra tutelage, on the excellence of their food—

She perched on the edge of her chair like a sparrow waiting for the cat to pounce.

"What is it, Beryl?" he asked. "Why don't you enjoy it when I try to make love to you? Am I doing it wrong? Tell me what you like, so I can do what pleases you."

She put the wine glass down, stood up and left the room without a backward look. He waited for her to return. Five minutes, ten, thirty—

The bedroom door was closed, but not locked. Quietly he pushed the door open.

"Ber—" She lay there on her side, curled into a fetal position, her arms over her face. Listening to her breathing, at first he thought she was weeping, and he reached to comfort her. That was when he realized that she was unconscious and there was blood everywhere.

CHAPTER THIRTEEN

She spent six weeks away; first in hospital and then in a sanitarium, during which time Benjamin cared for the children. He told everyone, even his parents, that she had suffered a miscarriage, which was far more respectable than admitting that she had tried to take her own life.

Suicide!

How could any Jew that had been fortunate enough to out-live the Holocaust even consider such a thing, he wondered. And how could a mother of two small boys let leaving them alone and motherless even cross her mind? How could she leave him without an answer to his question of why she would do such a thing; of what he was doing wrong? He felt his confusion rising every time he went to the hospital. He wanted to shake her; to make her tell him what was going on; to make her stop persisting in whatever this silly game was that she was playing at everyone else's expense.

In the end, it was her psychiatrist that gave him the answers. At last Beryl had talked; she had revealed what the rabbi, the very man that had sat across from him at the table, had done to her so long ago. She had talked about being dead to her family and how it galled her; about feeling nothing for Andy—and far too much for little Danny.

Danny, it seemed, was her personal Meschiach; the man of her dreams in the body of a toddler. Except for Yael, she had never really loved another creature before in her life, not even Benjamin; but she loved this little boy. He was her hero. He was the light of her life. She would have loved to run away with him to some secret place in the south of France or the hills of Italy, or even some remote campsite in New York or

Colorado, and raise him up to fight her battles and slay her dragons. "That's a lot to put on a baby boy," the psychiatrist said. "Does he share some of that burden with his brother?"

Andy, she admitted, was a void to her. It was his fault, she told her psychiatrist, that she was at odds with her parents; after all, if he had been a girl, she would not have been thrown out. "They wouldn't have just— *killed* me had it not been for him," she said through tears. "I think of that every time I look at him." She said that she did little things to make him feel ashamed of himself. She accused him of things she knew he was not responsible for around the house, and she would never smile at him, let alone touch him unless it was absolutely necessary. The boy tended to avoid her, now; preferring to seek out his father when Benjamin was at home. She even admitted to once—just once—breaking one of Andy's toys and hinting to him that Danny had broken it, just so that Andy would hit Danny and Benjamin, all unawares, would punish him for it. Again, the psychiatrist said: "That's a lot to put on a little boy." Beryl did not respond.

Benjamin was quite the conundrum for her. She felt the pull of his warm, sad brown eyes and the friendliness of his smile. She liked his height and his hair, and she particularly valued his ambition. She had, indeed, wanted to marry him, because he was educated, talked about interesting things, had a minimum of family ties and doted on her. Knowing, as all women of modest means did, that she must prepare to marry a man that could support her well, she had made herself as knowledgeable as possible, and felt that he, as an engineer and professor seeking tenure, was well worth her diligence. She felt only chilliness, however, when it came to bedroom matters. Try as she might, she could not convince herself, when the lights were out and he reached for her, that she was not twelve years old and in the clutches of Feuerstein. She knew that, without the sexual piece, there would have been no reason for him or any man to marry her, and she had tried to brace herself for that. He didn't give any hints of being that interested in sex before they were married; he never pawed her or tried to force himself on her, so she hoped against hope that maybe—

Medicine helped. She was stable for twelve years, with only one, albeit almost fatal, relapse, almost at the end of Andy's teen years. The psychiatrist, the same one, upped her medication and she resumed stability after a while. But in all her years she never once told her boys she was sorry for a single thing she ever did. Somewhere inside herself she felt smug and untouchable; justified for any worry she gave anyone. How could she be responsible, she often asked herself, for her beloved Danny being the one that found her, naked and disheveled in her bed with six of the fifteen sleeping pills from the bottle still on the nightstand, screaming for the Rabbi to leave her alone? The boy's blood-drained face, the shock and horror in it barely masking his arousal at having unexpectedly discovered the first nude female he had ever seen, never left her memory.

She herself had felt at once ashamed and stimulated. Over time she became enraged at Danny for engendering in her for all time what should have been momentary emotions. Why had they not faded with the rest of her memories of that time? As for Andy, he had stood transfixed in the doorway; she remembered his being there, no matter how often he denied it. He turned up moments later at the Lindemann's house, three blocks away. He wandered into Mrs. Lindemann's kitchen, where she was regaling a Virginia ham with cloves and pineapple circles, and without a word he laid his head against her back, wrapped his arms around her and began to sob. The woman, who knew no psychology, having been pulled out of school at age fourteen to work in a factory where she met her supervisor husband, wordlessly pulled him into her arms and rocked him as if he were six months old, while his peer, Jeremy, stared, his tuna sandwich poised halfway to his mouth.

This time, Beryl had had to go away for a bit. The Lindemanns had kept both of the boys while Benjamin made preparations, even though Andy insisted he was old enough to care for himself and his brother. Andy had wanted to go back to high school, where he was a senior; but Benjamin would not allow it. "You can take the time out of school," he said. "Your mother is the most important thing now."

Andy didn't think so. Nor did he think much of his father. In fact, Benjamin had been more than a disappointment for him, since he was usually too absorbed in some tome or another or charting some engineering project or perusing student papers to attend to typical fatherly tasks, such as coming to Andy's baseball games.

At times his father had even terrified him. There was, for instance, the time his father had come into his room, one hand behind his back, concealing an object Andy first thought was a gift for him.

"I have been reading the sacred scriptures," Benjamin said, standing over him in a way that made Andy most uneasy. "I read the story of Abraham and Isaac. Do you know that story, Andrew?"

Andy's then-nine-year-old mind raced. He did not pay much attention at the Unitarian services; he was much more interested in looking at the people and playing pencil games with his friends. He vaguely remembered something about a man cutting up animals and traveling across the desert.

"No," he told his father.

"Well," Benjamin said, his face growing stormier, "Abraham had a son, Isaac, and he had to offer him up to God. Why, I don't know. But I figured that, since Abraham had only one son and I have two, one of you has to go. I decided it is you." Benjamin whipped out a gun and placed it against the boy's temple.

Andy said nothing. His mind was totally without thought. He could only squeeze his eyes tight, in anticipation of the projectile from the cold gun against his temple sending a fiery bullet shrieking through his brain and ending his little life. The next sound he heard, however, was not the sound of metal against bone and brain matter, but the chuckle of his father's laughter. Startled out of his *in extremis* rigidity, Andy turned to see his father's mocking smile—and his own orange toy squirt gun, its muzzle wrapped with black tape.

"Bang-Bang!" Benjamin yelled, hardly able to contain his laughter, and pulled the trigger, sending a stream of water spurting over Andy's face and spraying across his math book. The boy blanched and began shaking all over—not at all the reaction Benjamin expected. Then—even less anticipated—Andy bolted from the room, fled the house, and did not return until long after dinnertime. Benjamin tried to apologize, stumbling out sentence after convoluted sentence about wanting to study the boy's reaction to get some sense of his own feelings, but Andy clearly was not in the mood to forgive him; in fact, he never did. Nor did Andy forgive Danny, even though his brother had done nothing wrong but exist. Was he not the one Benjamin wanted to keep, the one he was willing to sacrifice Andy for? What made *him* so special?

Danny was always up to something fascinating: boldly sitting on the girl students' laps when they came over for tutorial visits with his father, now a Distinguished Professor at the local college, or sassing his parents in ways Andy never would have dared. Andy was nothing of the show-off that Danny was. If Andy resented his brother's attention-getting before, he despised him for it now.

Not to mention the fact that Danny was starting to interfere in Andy's own life. Always reticent and shy, Andy hung back when around new people. Danny would drag him up to people, especially girls, and announce in his loudest voice, "This is my brother, Andy. He's quiet and shy, but he would make a good friend." Even when they didn't laugh at Andy, even when they actually became his friends, he could not forget that it was his little brother that engineered the introduction. He hated being managed by the little twerp, as if he were some half-wit that couldn't take care of himself. Worse, Andy's friends liked Danny. At first, Andy would try to shoo the little brat out of the backyard or the living room or the den when other kids came over. He'd call out to whichever of the adults that was about to make him leave. To his horror, one or the other of his friends, usually a girl, would always pipe up: "Oh, Andy, let him stay; he's a lot of fun and so cute, not like *my* little brother." And Andy heard in his head, *"And not like you!"* He would never admit to anyone that he was jealous of the little jerk, but he knew that he was.

There was, in Andy's mind, only one way to get even, to stand shoulders above Danny with his parents and his friends, and to reclaim his own value: to discredit Danny. At every hand he must show him up: Yes, Danny was handsomer, friendlier and outgoing, but just look at his report cards! Were Danny's grades not based on his personality, whereas Andy's own A's and B's resulted strictly from his extra hours of studious application?

Still, Danny got good grades, even in subjects he hardly even paid attention to. If Benjamin scowled at occasional C's sprinkled throughout his report cards, Beryl seemed to gloat about them, and minimize Danny's need to achieve to Benjamin. "Danny will always come out on top, she said. "He is sunny and smart and beautiful."

"Better he should learn a skill," Benjamin grumbled. "Better he knows how to take care of himself when he becomes a man, instead of becoming a – a – *Bohemian.*"

The chance comment caught Andy's attention. His father had pointed out a significant thing that he disdained in his otherwise perfect second son. Slowly there grew in Andy's mind a plan of such perfidy that he couldn't believe he had come up with it on his own. Danny looked up to his older brother; he wanted to do everything Andy did, and targeted his big brother's behaviors to guide his own way. What Andy needed to do, he realized in what he could recognize only as a stroke of genius, was not to discredit Danny, but to let him disgrace himself.

What were the characteristics of a Bohemian that his father hated most? Andy knew well, because his father told him, almost at every hand. Benjamin remembered a different world: one in which children were respectful and war was always a threat. He did not like the Sixties in America. There were things that annoyed him—whether from resentment at not having experienced his teen years fully or a genuine disdain, he looked down on any family outside his nuclear one, of which he was absolute *paterfamilias.* And while he was a free thinker, he was not a part of the formal Free Thinkers movement. Religion had little meaning for him, particularly Judaism, for which he had the least use. If there was God, he reasoned, how could He have allowed a madman to rampage across Europe and even into Benjamin's own dreams, with such impunity even though he was far away; even though he was dead now (or so they claimed)? What had those six million Jews died *for?* He viewed their deaths to be as senseless as the martyrdom of the Christians at the hands of the gladiators and the lions in the Roman Coliseum; surely there was another way! Until it was found, Benjamin preferred to consider religion as the socialists did: as a mere opiate of the people, to distract them from the finality and inevitability of death. Drugs, free sex, and *ennui* enraged him even more. He preached constantly about the hold cigarettes had on him, the proliferation of mononucleosis and syphilis cases at the college, and the growing sense of purposelessness and dissolute behaviors he observed on campus and in the workplaces he visited on site visits. As his father did, Andy thought all of these vices (with the possible exception of free sex, maybe judiciously practiced) were reprehensible—but did his brother?

It was no great task for Andy to find someone that would load his pockets with as much weed as he could pay for. One night when Danny slept and his book bag lay enticingly open, Andy slipped six joints inside. The next day, when Danny took out his Social Studies book in his classroom, the joints slipped out and onto the classroom floor. Half an hour later, in the principal's office, Danny's mouth was still agape as a purple-faced Benjamin screamed his disapproval of him. His protest that he had no idea where the drugs had come from was met with derision, not only by his father, but also by his principal. He moved instantly from an interesting person to a person of interest. After all, he had enough on him to classify him as a dealer.

But Andy's plan went nothing like the way he expected it to. When the word leaked out, as it always did in schools despite the most stringent privacy precautions, that Danny had access to drugs, students began coming up to him after almost every class, requesting something from his stash for this party or that. They took his denial for superiority; which took him out of the mere 'friend' level and jettisoned him onto the 'super-cool' plane.

Sex, then.

But Danny was too cool, now, for the chicks. The girls saw him as some kind of god, after the weed thing. They wanted to be near him, but not totally in his power, though they imagined aloud that he must be "*something!*" to be with. They fancied him a "*real* bad boy". Without laying hands on a single girl, he acquired a reputation more expansive than those of many of the seniors and even some of their college freshman brothers. Tales of his supposed exploits, embellished and aggrandized, suffered limitation only because of the imaginative limitations of those re-telling what they'd 'heard'; most of the legends about him began with the words, "You, know, they *say*..."

Danny, as far as Andy knew, was a virgin and had not a single drug experience right up until he left for college. He had gone too far, Andy realized. There was no way he could bring Danny down.

It took Beryl to do that.

It took her wide-open stretched gray eyes and the tousled sprawl of her tresses like russet blood down the bed covers, the Thulian pink of the tips of the twin mounds on her bare torso and the alluring dark of her thick bush of vaginal hair against her ivory skin, the spill of deathly white pills on the deep ebony of the mahogany nightstand, the flash of rainbow mirrored in the cut crystal glass—to push him away from stability.

That and the discovery two days later, provided by his father's carelessness.

Andy had always known that both of his parents were Jewish by birth. He had been around during the controversial years when Beryl was still calling and trying to visit her sisters, her brothers, her father, her mother, her aunts, whoever; praying for one of them—just one—to flash her a smile of recognition, to return her calls, to answer her letters. With Benjamin at work and no one else to watch him, Beryl had dragged him from place to place. He had heard her plaintive pleading and the stories had been fixed in his mind. One day, before the Abraham incident, he had confronted his father.

"I know you're from Germany, Dad", he had said. "But I've gotta ask—are we Jewish?" Benjamin had answered in the affirmative. A few weeks later, Benjamin had gone down to the Bureau of Vital Statistics and shortened his and everyone else's surname by seven letters.

Danny, however, had no such memory. He had not even started kindergarten when the name change came, so he did not know any other name he might have had, and he knew nothing about religion of any kind, except from what he learned by proxy from his little buddies at school. Once—only once—he had asked his parents about praying, something a friend had told him about. "Oh, Danny," Benjamin told him, "Religion is for *poor* people." The answer had satisfied Danny for the time: the religious kids in his class were, after all, not as well off as his father. Benjamin was the head of his department now, and people looked up to him. Danny had been careful not to pray after that, and had even warned his friends that, if they continued to be religious, they were likely never to make any money when they got older, because only poor people prayed.

His father had been getting their travel documents together and they were spread out across his desk. Danny had just gone to his father's office to find a sheet of graph paper. He had not really meant to look at his father's papers; he was, after all, not allowed in his father's private room. But the documents were in plain sight, and he thought, with his father at work, a peek wouldn't hurt. There, plain as day, lay his father's birth certificate, and, fascinated by the curlicued border and the quaint, old-fashioned writing, he ventured to look at it.

He scanned the document, at first with interest—and then his eyes had been riveted to the lines of information. His father's name was <u>Benyamin (NMN) Rosenthaler</u>.

Rosenthaler!

Danny knew a much shorter name; he had learned to print it when he was five years old, and he wondered if, in fact, this was really his father's birth certificate. But here were his grandparents' names: Karl and Bina Rosenthaler. His father had been born in Cologne. He had an elder brother, David Herschel Rosenthaler, and his religion was—

<u>Jewish</u>??

How could he be Jewish? Danny had always imagined himself to be just a regular American, from German and New Jersey stock. His hair had curl, true; and he had his father's warm, soft brown eyes. But—how could this be? He knew kids at school that were Jewish. Some of them wore skullcaps and couldn't play sports on Saturdays. They muttered with each other in their own language that nobody else understood and they pretty much were the best scholars, because they were expected to take over their fathers' businesses when they grew up, and so they studied for hours and hours. When the cafeteria served cheeseburgers or hot dogs or ham sandwiches, they would just eat nothing at all or bring their lunches from home. Who didn't eat hot dogs, Danny had wondered. He distinctly remembered one Christmas pageant at school, complete with angels and Wise Men and the Star in the East. The Jewish kids had squirmed in their seats and some had even asked to be excused, because they didn't believe in Jesus. Danny didn't either, but then for him that was the beauty of not being trapped in some specific creed. He had gobbled up the candy canes and the deli sandwiches and the gingerbread men and not given a thought to having to give homage to Jesus or Santa Claus or the elves or Rudolph the Red-Nosed Reindeer or anything else.

Bud he was *one* of those people!

Frantically he scrambled through the papers. And here was his mother's passport. Surely his bright, beautiful, poised mother—

Danny flipped the pages anxiously. And there it was: RELIGION: Jewish.

He dropped the document to the floor and staggered out of the room.

Everyone noticed the change in him. The boy that was everybody's idol lost his vivaciousness. His made no pretense of studying. Days he spent staring out the classroom window and nights he spent in his room alone, music blaring through his Koss headphones. When people asked him what was happening, he said 'nothing'. Indeed, the accidental discovery that he was not just another American kid but a Jewish boy turned his internal world upside down. He felt as if the universe had just given him a kick in the solar plexus. There was some response he should be making, but he could not for the life of him figure out what it should be. It angered him that his parents had not told him who he really was, and he could not help but wonder what other information about himself they might be withholding. When Benjamin asked him why he was so moody and what he wanted to do with his life, he said he wanted to be in a rock and roll band; a proposed profession that so distressed his father that, though in keeping with his liberal stance he provided Danny with an electric guitar, he came to none of his son's band's performances at the high school and left the house when Danny's friends came over to rehearse. As graduation grew closer, Danny began growing his hair out, and the day ultimately came that he smoked his first marijuana cigarette.

He abandoned most of his White friends and found new acquaintances among the few minority students at his school. Hanging out with the Black kids between classes served multiple purposes. Let them fight for their rights to be equal to everyone else; he loved their disfranchisement, because it so mirrored his own feeling of being Outside: no longer a member of the White society he always thought he was a privileged scion of, and never initiated by ritual or acceptance into the Jewish community. He asked Andy if he realized they were Jewish. That was when Andy told him about Beryl's family's rejection. Danny became doubly upset. He was supposed to be Jewish; okay, but and he should have had rights as a Jew; but being born to a woman outside the faith—a 'dead' woman—how could he even be Jewish? So he declared himself to be Black, despite his recorded ancestry and his external appearance. He eschewed his father's affluence and the decadence his privileged circumstances allowed. He preferred the urban neighborhoods, with their uncollected trash and their noise, their throbbing night-life and occasional bursts of gunfire in the streets. Yes, there were affluents among the Colored: preachers' children and doctors' progenies; the cream of Black society that could float even among Whites, and aspiring affluents: overachievers that flat-ironed their hair and didn't drop the endings of their words. He avoided them; he was far more comfortable among the underclasses. Jews were rarely poor, even though their forced isolation had coined the word 'ghetto', where the majority of minority people now found themselves. If he lived and acted like the Negroes, how could he be Jewish? And if he dated Black women, wouldn't it keep the other girls, particularly the Jewish ones, at bay? He found his basic sense of beauty changing: latte and chocolate-colored skin was beautiful, whereas alabaster and pinkish skin repelled him. Kinky to gnarled locks were to be admired, while the silken curls of Clairol girls and the lank, chemically straightened tresses of their dusky imitators turned him off. The soft brown-to-black eyes were sufficiently like those of his father to make him feel closer to them.

It always irritated Danny that his mother seemed to push Andy toward Benjamin and hold him back for herself. Obediently, as a child, he had followed her to museums and art exhibitions, feeling himself superior to his brother for a long time. He had sat patiently by as she conferred with the other women in the anterooms or in their own home during some meeting his father felt called upon to officiate with their husbands that did not require feminine participation, other than the straightening and the cleaning up. He had listened to the women's complaints and laments against their men, and he found himself sympathizing. He got it: his father and his father's cronies were so far into their own lives and accomplishments and urges to excel that they never looked around to see what was going on in the lives of their wives and children. Certainly, it appeared to Danny, some big piece was missing in his father's ability, or perhaps even desire, to extricate himself from his all-important task of bringing his dreams of acquiring a doctorate to fruition long enough to look at what he could do to keep his own woman from self-murder. He resented his father's aloofness. He had seen emotion in his father only twice: once when he had thought Danny was indeed on drugs and then when he had sat gripping Beryl's hand in the emergency room, summoning her back to a life she had so thoughtlessly tried to abandon. Didn't the man realize, Danny wondered, that in so doing he would be forcing her to acknowledge yet another failure in her striving to achieve autonomy over her own existence? Couldn't he let her have the control over her own life and death? He did not want his mother to die; he loved her, after all. But it was all so confusing; so confusing—He told himself it was better to focus on things he did not like that she did, rather than the more central issue of her not loving him enough to stay alive.

Thus Danny decided to resent his mother's taste in art. Her preference for 'unique' pieces, no matter how avant-garde that sounded, usually led her to purchase carefully sculpted works that fit the *New York Times* taste, rather than the genuinely primitive or avant garde, which Danny admired, but his mother insisted was "not real art". Danny began to paint; he did most of his work in primary colors, depicting grinning ethnic faces with bold, snake-like plaits and bright, mischievous eyes, and he told her this was 'real art; what the people liked, not her pristine pastoral paintings in their pastels and neutral shades. Beryl looked at his compositions with a contempt that surprised even her. She did not like having her studied and hard fought-for tastes mocked; and love Danny as she might, she would not tolerate such a thing from him. She strongly advocated that he consider becoming a critic, rather than a creator; he would thus more closely reflect her, she thought.

At times, following her second attempt to die, he would find himself sitting in her walk-in closet, caressing her clothes, as if willing her to remain in them. They smelled of her perfume and her body musk as well as the silk or cotton or Martinized dry cleaner scent. He noted their classic nature: colors and cut that would pass the test of time. She always looked poised and perfect in her Coco Chanel suits and Oleg Cassini gowns, most of which she rescued from upscale resale shops. Danny hated her precision. Even more, he despised her efforts to be 'trendy'; her native-styled dashikis and caftans reeked of European-inspired bad taste. He recalled with disdain a particular item of her 'ethnic' clothing that actually was made of a tartan wool. What self-respecting Negro, he wondered, would be caught dead in a tartan wool caftan? After she wore it for the second time, he snatched it out of her closet and sneaked it out to the garage, where he painted it with gold flying fish and then took it back to the resale shop, in hopes that his mother would see it there. But even Goodwill wouldn't take it, so he had wound up putting it in a bin at one of the Negro churches. He never saw it on anyone, but he always imagined some super-stylish Black woman sporting it with a head wrap, red patent leather high heels and massive gold door-knocker earrings. After all, Black women, at least the type he was attracted to, or perhaps never met but imagined actually existed in some ideal parallel Black universe that he would discover someday, would love wild colors and anything experimental: uncooked spaghetti in their ratted-up hair, faces painted with bright tribal symbols, maybe even an exposed boob, festooned with beads and cowrie shells.

College came inevitably; and while he didn't know how to confront his parents with his wish not to go, he certainly could fail to perform well enough to make it clear that he was wasting his time and their money. He took cinema courses at his second school, and tried his hand at writing scripts and finding Black girls to act them out, then submitted his masterpieces to his mystified White cinema instructors; most of whom did not understand what they were seeing and therefore declared him to be an up-and-coming new voice in the genre.

Ultimately, among the student body at his third college, he encountered a Native American man, who invited him out to Montana for a powwow. Peyote was a part of the ceremonies, and the man warned him that he must be in perfect harmony with his spirit before he even considered the possibility of participation. Danny, who had removed himself out of any but necessary contacts with the White race, felt that he must be a part of all other cultures. He certainly felt kinship with the neglected earth and all minority peoples. He not only sympathized with, but also internalized their suffering: displaced American Negro and Native and other sub continental, lower hemispheric inhabitants were his brothers, and he was honored to be invited to participate in their rituals, which he felt could only bring him closer to them.

He may have been ready for peyote, but certainly he was, unfortunately, not steeled for the crazy mix some of his well-meaning friends made with the remnants of what he brought back from Montana. Someone called an ambulance, and he was rushed from the dorms to the hospital. The jangling phone cut through his parents' sleep and summoned them to his side.

Staring down at his broken brother, Andy prayed that his earlier efforts to pull his brother down were not responsible for what he saw as Danny's total alienation from reality. Despite whatever he had felt about him of late, Andy had been as charmed by his brother, almost, as anyone else. It was hard to recognize this Danny. His curly hair was clotted with sweat and vomit and clung wetly to his forehead. His pupils had shrunken to pinpoints. He had scratched up his face and his mouth was bloody. He was strapped to a gurney, on which he flailed his arms and legs about like a skewered centipede, and screamed obscenity-laced nonsequiturs at anybody that passed.

"Drugs," the psychiatrist told Benjamin. "Lots of kids coming in messed up recently. I guess Camels and Kools and a little purloined whiskey just aren't enough for them nowadays; looks as if everybody under thirty is intent of smoking up everything growing wild on the planet."

Benjamin failed to see the humor in the doctor's words. This was his son: his second–born. His fear, after Beryl's two breakdowns had been that her condition was hereditary. He dimly recalled something his father had told him, about mental illness passing down from generation to generation. "Women have all kinds of hysterias," his father had told him years before, in Germany: "When you marry, avoid any woman that has a crazy relative; you know, a nutty grandmother, a mother that's hyper-religious, even an odd uncle. We have to keep the lineage pure, or how can the Meschiach come?" He had been bemused by his father's statement when he heard it; but more interested in his comment about the Messiah than the advice itself. He had never supposed that Elie actually gave such matters serious attention, but now he wondered what his father's feelings were about spiritual things. He wrote to him, but it was his Oma Bina, ailing, now, and making her last visit to her surviving child, since Reuven had succumbed at the height of the war, that answered:

"You work with machines and figures," she said. "You do not do the kind of work your father did, with where life begins. Only the most blind of men can bring a child into the world without knowing that God *is*; and every new mother has seen His face smiling just behind her baby's eyes. So many things can go wrong in forming a human being. Every doctor worth anything believes in miracles, because they see how often things go right; how often, against all odds, a child arrives on earth perfect, how frequently a person given up for dead suddenly recovers and goes on to live an invigorated life."

Benjamin pondered his grandmother's words. Perhaps, as she said, it was his failure to have witnessed birth that made him such a non-believer. Maybe it was a mistake for hospitals to keep husbands out of delivery rooms, denying them the ability to see the moment of juncture between

258

body and spirit. Maybe some women had their eyes closed when the little human inside them experienced the birth-slap and began breathing fiery oxygen into their bodies. He thought Beryl must be such a woman.

Indeed, when Benjamin had asked his parents to accompany him to Germany with Beryl to see one of the practitioners that was a part of the burgeoning field of psychiatry, his father had said only, "I only allow myself to be kicked out of my country once." No amount of cajoling, of reminding him of the fortune they had buried in the ground so long ago, of old friends he might encounter again, of encouraging him to come and walk the streets of Cologne once more, would convince him. " I would guess somebody found all of our belongings years ago, or maybe some bomb fell there and blew it all to smithereens. As for my old friends and colleagues, they are probably all dead or gone," he said. "It's ghosts I would meet on the streets of Cologne now. Besides—" he had said, "I don't know exactly how my presence would help your woman. She isn't interested in having me around. Or your boys." He had hesitated before he went on. "Or you." Benjamin had raised his eyebrows, but said nothing, and Elie had fallen silent.

Benjamin had thought about his father the entire time he spent in Cologne. Although their house had been heavily damaged, the Kolendom stood intact. He wandered with Beryl into a diner and deli newly opened by a Jewish family on the very site of Herr Brecht's store. Within moments of the proprietor asking his name, a man came out of the kitchen. "Rosenthaler! Benyamin! Don't you remember me? It's Avi—Avi Greenbaum!"

Not many of them were left. Avi and his family had hidden out in places the man did not care to specify. Some of the other boys they knew, he understood, had escaped, or were hauled away to concentration camps or killed in the bombing of the city. Reichstetter was believed to have died in Russia. Word spread, though; and more than twenty years after the last bomb fell, over a quarter of a century since he had last strode these streets as a young not-quite-man, Benyamin Rosenthaler, known in America as Benjamin Rose, found himself again among friends: boys from the Gymnasium, boys from the Temple, a former patient or two of his father's, who, whatever their sentiments during the war, went to some old place inside themselves to remember the boy they would give a chocolate or a hard candy to just outside his father's office. They enquired after his parents and his brother, admired his wife, whose internal state they did not know, and wished him much success in America, with promises to visit him there 'someday'.

Benjamin even saw Fischer; an older man, now, who had been bombed out during the war, but who had managed to survive and was teaching again. His mother had finally died of old age; peacefully in her sleep, if that were true, as old people were apparently intended to die. Fischer sent his most cordial and respectful greetings to Herr Doktor. Benjamin took him to dinner and gave him his address, but did not expect to hear from him again.

Finally he had made his way to the place outside Cologne. With his digging tools and the help of a few friends, he managed to unearth the treasures left behind so long ago. The money was no good, now; but he gave such trinkets from his mother's bag of jewels as his friends were willing to accept as payment, and the rest of the items he shipped back to America. He divided them as he saw fit among his remaining relatives, but, he had to admit, he kept the lion's share for himself. The truncheon with the German blood on it he left buried behind in the ditch; he saw no reason to bring that kind of hatred back with him.

Beryl had gotten better, under the ministrations of the Swiss psychologists and the change of scenery. Benjamin had come home thinking he had left mental illness behind him. And now, this! They had hardly fallen exhausted into bed when the phone rang.

Far from feeling the eye-stinging sadness Benjamin felt when he looked at his beautiful son, reduced to a frothing, invective-shrieking lunatic tethered to an iron bed in a back ward because of something stupid he had done to himself, Beryl had glared at the boy with her upper lip curled. She was enraged at him. Why, Benjamin wondered. Did she see his illness as manifesting weakness? Was she infuriated that her little warrior had an Achilles heel? Was it possible that she was just—jealous?

Andy thought she envied Danny. He saw his mother as a shrewish, selfish virago that needed to be the center of everything, even madness. She made him feel sour about all women. Every girl he encountered on campus was his mother, and when he first arrived, he set out on a semi-conscious campaign to spoil and humiliate as many of them as he could. Deep within some shady corner of his mind, each time one of them stared at him, eyes wide open, tears streaming because of his betrayal, he juxtaposed his mother's face onto hers. Women were to be dominated, conquered and then forsaken; it was all they deserved. 'Fickloch', his grandfather had called them. Maybe he was right. Maybe 'use them and lose them' was a good maxim.

But then there was Jenny.

Her parents were Reformed. She was everything Andy thought would never interest him: religious, studious, quiet, considerate, gentle. She was attractive; probably few of his friends would consider her really pretty or 'stacked' in the way they talked about girls they lusted after. When he gave her his best line, his best explanation as to why she should fling aside her high-minded principles for a night she would never forget, she had given him a 'no'; not a shocked, slap-across-the-face 'no' that he usually got from rejecting females, but a "You're-better-than-that" 'no'. The next day she had greeted him as usual in her shy, friendly way. He had chalked her off his list of prospective conquests, avoiding her in the two classes they took together and evading her at the local eateries and shops along the strip. He had tried going out with a couple more girls "for kicks", but it wasn't the same. He found himself stumbling over his pick-up lines and miffed as to where to go next if he got someone's attention. He realized Jenny had gotten into him too deeply; he had to forget her.

But he could not; she was all he could think about.

Andy walked woodenly down the steps of the psychiatric center. He wandered over to the parking lot, climbed behind the wheel of his car, drove to a service station, gassed up and drove the six hundred and nineteen miles to campus, stopping only when he had to. He parked in front of her apartment just off the square.

Jenny and her roommate were studying hard for midterms when he pounded on the door. He walked past her roommate.

"Jenny—" he murmured, grasping both her shoulders, then pulling her close as tears streamed down his face. "Jenny—" He fell to his knees, wrapped his arms around her slender waist and opened the floodgates to his soul. Jenny stroked his head and let him weep, then fed him a bowl of vegetable soup, wrapped him in a warm blanket and rocked him in her arms all night, as if he were a sickly baby and she the only mother he had ever had.

CHAPTER FOURTEEN

Benjamin closed his eyes to the changes in Beryl's behavior since Danny's hospitalization. On the rare occasions that the boy came home on visits and remained under their roof, she berated and upbraided him: 'Con man', 'shyster', 'sicko', 'weirdo'. Those were the names that she bandied about ever since he had spat on her and called her unspeakable names at the hospital.

His younger son had come home gaunt and in need of additional nursing, no matter what the psychiatrists said. If he had looked bad when first he came home, he looked worse in the ensuing weeks. Often, Benjamin thought, the boy could have passed for one of the specter-survivors of the camps, if he had just had striped pajamas. Benjamin did not like to think about that too much: Danny, of their two boys, more closely favored him.

Danny recovered, with the help of medication and a space apart from hallucinogens, and returned to yet another school. His psychiatrists dubbed him 'cured', like a repaired ceramic vase or a broken bone; however, his fracture lines showed to the discerning, and sometimes to just anyone that was looking.

For instance, when Andy married Jenny. He asked Danny to be his Best Man, since he was his brother; but when Danny arrived ten minutes before the service, having painted grinning mask-like faces with canyon-size nostrils and enormous lips in gold and silver all over his rented tuxedo, Andy had quickly grabbed one of his less garishly regaled buddies to replace him and relegated Danny to the groom's side of the aisle, two rows back from his parents. Andy stood through the entire service with his anxious eyes more fixed on Danny than on his lovely Jenny.

Jenny's family had insisted that they wed under a canopy. They had made some assumptions about Andy that were incorrect: they assumed he had been ritually circumcised; that he knew more than a little about the faith; that he had been bar mitzvahed. He allowed them to labor in ignorance of the truth that only the first thing was true and that only partially; there had been no *moyel*.

Jenny also assumed some things about him that were not true. He was an ardent lover and a generous provider, and there everything she believed about him ended. He was not *cruel*; just highly opinionated and determined never to let a woman best him, ever. He recalled his mother decorating the house without consulting his father, and so he was the one that not only chose the house, but also decorated it right down to the dinnerware and the art on the walls. He remembered his mother sitting at the dining room table, surrounded by travel magazines and itineraries, planning every moment that they would spend abroad, and so he planned out everything, from where they would park their car to which hotel chains they would stay in to which sights they would and would not see. If Jenny brought up something he had not planned, he would work it in—or at least try, or maybe *not* try. Whatever his mother did, he determined he would do the opposite.

The first high holy day Jenny asked him to attend, he went; but found the text impossible to follow and the traditions foreign. The next holiday, he refused to go, without explanation. She brought home a menorah and wanted to put up a mezuzah, but he refused the latter, insisting that it would destroy the wood on the door. He watched her go through the motions of celebrating a holiday without his active participation, and forced himself to register no remorse when she complained.

His ultimate attempt at control, however, imperiled their marriage. One, two, three years had gone by, and he had insisted on putting off their having a child. He remembered his boyhood with sadness. He could not recall a happy moment, though surely there were some; more likely many, just none he could remember in his parents' house. Besides, he reasoned, there were so many wars. He thought of the pictures of the tiny rotting bodies of the innocents from the concentration camps, the tearful eyes of the Korean War orphans, the napalmed babies from Vietnam, the babies that died on the plane that was bringing them to America and safety. Safety! There was no place safe for a child in this world. No one with any conscience would have one in these times. He would have loved a baby; he loved children, but he could not fathom how he could be a good father. When he thought about his father and his absence, at least in spirit, or his mother and her coldness, at least toward him, he felt justified.

But he could not say that to Jenny. He thought it would make him sound like a wimp. Even with this woman that loved him so deeply and who wanted only to be at the center of his heart, he could not banish his fear of derision. "I don't have time or the patience," he had insisted, "to have to put up with some brat yowling all night. Kids are expensive and messy. They get sick, and who is going to take care of them? You want something to love besides me? Get a dog!"

For the first time, Jenny took a stand. This had never been a part of their discussion before. She had wanted to give him two children: the proverbial 'heir and spare'. "Who is going to carry on the family name?" she asked him. "If you don't have somebody to follow you, your family's name is going to disappear."

"Danny'll have kids," he said irritably. "Or my cousin Gil down in South America. Let them carry on the family name."

The family name! Theirs was not the family name. Their real name was in some dusty file in some Vital Statistics office, with the end part, the part that tagged them as Jewish, X-ed out.

Jenny was usually gentle with Andy. She loved him deeply, and she more than suspected, having spent time with Beryl, that his childhood had been none too easy, at least emotionally. While she maintained her belief in God and all things spiritual, she had given up actively practicing her religion and even managing her own home the way she wanted to in order to satisfy him. On this one point, however, she held her ground.

"You decide," she said. "Do you want children or do you want to live alone? I'll be at my parents' house; call me if you feel differently." She went into their bedroom and began packing. Andy thought it was a bluff until she began piling her luggage by the door.

CHAPTER FIFTEEN

Gil made only a pretense of working at the factory. He did not need to; his father was, after all, his boss, and he doted on the boy. As his father's adored son and the one that would be first to carry on the family name, since Benjamin's boys weren't reproducing, the day that Gil announced his desire to wed was a great one for his father.

It was hard, living up to the charm and mystique of his brother, even though he was so far away. Herschel needed to excel in *something* Benjamin could not best him at. He was a factory supervisor, but Benjamin was a college professor and head of his department. He was married, but Benjamin's wife, clear from her photos and his parents' report, was a beauty, and certainly no hunchback, as Geula was. Herschel had made only one long trip: from Frankfurt to Argentina. Benjamin had been to every corner of the earth, it seemed, and his parents had, lovingly preserved in a cigar box, the postcards and letters with their foreign stamps to prove it.

An elated Gil took his bride-to-be to his grandparents. Elie made his usual offer, but she politely and graciously refused. And in an unprecedented act of generosity, Eliana went to her bedroom and returned with her engagement ring; that precious ring that had been unable to save her own mother's life and that she had considered too fine for bent-over Geula. She placed it in Gil's palm, to put on his woman's finger when they were alone.

Gil closed his fingers over the diamond-encrusted band and hefted it in his palm. Dimly he remembered a story his father had told him, and decided to pawn the ring. He could tell by the pawnbroker's eyes that it was a good decision; that he would get a great deal for it; and in a display case he found a modest ring that would serve just as well to secure the woman of his dreams to him. The remainder of the money he put toward a long-desired honeymoon in the United States; he thought he would visit his uncle and his cousins and show off his beautiful bride.

That he managed to do. He had a wonderful time in North America, touring around by rail to see as many of the sights that he had heard of as possible and satisfying himself that his bride was far lovelier than Andy's wife, who appeared a bit annoyed at having to come out of exile at her parents' home for the sake of appearances. By the time they were ready to leave, though, he observed that Andy and Jenny were on much better terms, and as they were now talking about having a child, he assumed all was well with them.

Back home, the new couple elected to move in with the rest of the family while they shopped for a place of their own. Gil still had a little ring money, however, and he decided to spend it on a car. There was a Ford Falcon he had had his eye on for some time, and this seemed to be his opportunity. Above the objections of the entire family, he contracted for it and laid down the last of the ring money for the down-payment. He was driving it home on a rain-slicked road when he hydroplaned into an abutment.

Elie sat in the room he shared with his wife, first staring at the wall and then rising heavily from his chair and seating himself at his desk. He must, he thought, urge Benjamin to convince his boys to have children, or the line would die out, and then what good would their escape from Germany be?

Eliana wailed the whole night through and far into morning. She sat Shivah for Gil and then she took to her bed. Her health was never the same after that. She cursed herself for having ever kept back the ring—the dazzling engagement ring that she had held back from burial in Cologne. If it had been in the ground—if it had been in the ground, it would not have tempted Herschel to steal it and put it on that Spanish girl's finger. It would not have given her husband the collateral to gamble. It would never have resulted in Herschel having to marry that sway-back, broken, ugly girl, even if he did love her now; and Gil, the flower and future of her family in South America, might be with them still.

Geula mourned her son. She had been so happy with him; so proud that she had given Herschel an heir. A man regarded a wife that gave him sons as an asset. She was past bearing age, now, so there would be no more children, male or female. Anyway, her condition was making her more and more tired, as her collapsing spine placed more pressure on her internal organs. She resumed her service to her adopted family, after her period of grieving, but she felt tired; tired and drained. She had looked forward to seeing her grandchildren: sturdy boys and winsome girls that would scurry around her feet and call her Abuelita. Now she doubted if she would ever see that day. Gil's woman did not conceive during their short time together, and she knew the woman would eventually move on to another man. And even though there was still Shoshana, who was not quite of marriageable age, Herschel would not see her children as his successors, because they would not have the Rosenthaler name. He, too, Geula thought, would shut her out now that he could never become his father's favorite son.

Gil's death made Herschel all the more leery of allowing Shoshana out of his sight for even a moment. She was, everyone that met her concurred, a beauty; a girl that could turn the head of any man that saw her. Herschel saw their eyes and he was determined that, knowing the ways of men, he would take a very active part in determining whom she would marry.

A college boy came first; a callow fellow that was more brains than body. Shoshana seemed to like him; Herschel did not. He was not at all the kind of man he wanted his daughter to share her life with, no matter what she might think. How could such a skinny, un-muscular man defend her or even be strong enough to support her? Then came a pleasant fellow whose father was a butcher. Faugh! He would smell like cows and slaughtered pigs all day, and she would surely tire of his stink after a very few months, did she not think?

Shoshana did not tell him about the third man.

He told her he was a spy, who posed as a banker by day, but was hot on the trail of German war criminals that were rumored to be somewhere in South America and needed to be flushed out and brought to justice. Shoshana met him every afternoon when her school broke for siesta, and sat cuddled up with him in some corner or another of the library. As a spy, he told her, he could have any woman he wanted, but as he favored Shoshana, she should give serious consideration to moving their relationship along to consummation. Shoshana considered; and after several weeks of his gentle but insistent coercion, she decided she must slip out and fulfill herself with him or risk losing him.

All would have proceeded as planned, except for one chance encounter.

Shoshana knew her first sex should not occur until after a marriage, so though they were not having a ceremony before the consummation he was pressing her to fulfill, she chose to regale herself as a bride for their first night of love. It so happened that Ezra had stopped by the house when she came home with her bag from the modish lingerie and ladies' intimate wear shop. He knew the place: he had patronized it more than once to gift some lady-friend or another that he was romancing. Respectable women did not shop there.

"Ah, a parcel from *La Freca*, Shoshana?" he asked pleasantly. "Did you buy something for your mom there?" He did not really fathom that she might be buying something there for her mother in such a place. He just wondered: why would a virginal girl shop there?

While his question was innocent enough on its face, he recognized immediately that her answer was not. She flushed, and stammered out a few incomplete sentences. It did not take him long to extract the entire story from her. He felt his insides curling up: this was his first cousin's beloved daughter and that she could be so naïve as to believe—

"I will wait here with you," he said, "and, with me at your side, you will tell your father this fantastic tale. We will then investigate this young man and find out whether or not he tells the truth. In the meantime, you must tell him only that you are ill, you will be away from your school for at least three days, and you will call him when you feel better."

For the next two days, Shoshana sat at home with streaming eyes; anyone that saw her could easily have believed that she really had influenza, as she claimed. In the meantime, Herschel and Ezra stalked the alleged 'spy'.

He was not even a banker; he was a minor clerk at the bank, who sorted the mail and ran errands to the Panaderia for medialunas and other pastries. Ernst and Herschel followed him to his home the first day. On the second day, they rang his doorbell while he was at work. A very pregnant woman with two toddling children clinging to her skirts answered. She said the man was her husband. That evening, they waylaid the 'spy' as he turned into his street, and, with the assistance of a stout length of pipe, convinced him that Shoshana was not only off-limits to him, but if he tried even to communicate to her what had happened, the pipe would crease his skull and then would be jammed up his rectum.

Shoshana never saw him again. She did, however, hear from her father that, should she have any ideas of marrying anyone at all, she had better bring that person straight to her parents, or she would suffer for it. She was rushed off to her grandfather for the requisite examination to ensure that her hymen was still intact and then sent back to school to finish her studies.

CHAPTER SIXTEEN

Danny joined a New Age group and moved off the campus of College Number Four and into a commune with what must have been fifty other people. Beryl now felt as if she had lost him forever. Benjamin had read something about deprogrammers: people that could talk people out of just about anything; but Beryl pooh-poohed the idea of having their son dragged off somewhere to have his mind further messed up. As well, she said, they were liberals; and forcing him to give something up that he really wanted to do and that didn't seem to be hurting him just did not fit with their image.

He was here and there throughout the world, always calling, always sending postcards. When he found himself on the east coast, he stopped in for a few days. If he looked better, much more lucid than how Benjamin remembered him, Beryl's recent memory of him was largely shaped by his rage-reddened face shouting curse-words at her. So no matter how much Danny tried to emulate the work of Jesus and go about the world doing good to spread the good news of the imminence of the Kingdom of Heaven on earth, she could not bring herself to embrace him.

Danny, however, with his worldview supported by the consensus of people he valued, had the feeling that she, as well as his father, should be able to embrace all people. Almost every time he dropped by the house, he had a guest with him: usually a person Benjamin and Beryl would consider unfit to sit at anyone's table, but given their broadminded stance, they could not turn away. Danny brought prostitutes that he insisted he was helping, not sleeping with, and drug dealers he made it clear he was not among the clientele of. He brought homeless people and street musicians and people that made their living in ways it was better not to know about, underclass Chicanos between migratory seasons that he could hardly communicate with himself, Black people, dispossessed Asian people, down-and-out White people, and Native Americans fresh from the reservation. Despite his own casual attire and questionable circumstances, his invited guests respected him, and therefore they did nothing that might embarrass him. They stole nothing, despite Beryl's constant fears. They made offers (gently declined) to help with the cleaning up, and they never brought up even the notion of planning to overstay their time or loiter in the neighborhood. The stories they told and the rapt way in which they listened to their hosts intrigued the couple.

Benjamin and Beryl's friends were not that open and forthcoming; even those that had something to say. Some had endured concentration camps or flights far more perilous than Benjamin's, but they remained tight-lipped about their struggles, even when someone else might have learned something valuable from their trials. On the rare occasions that they did speak, Benjamin listened carefully; Hitler's dreams were not yet dead in the world, and he wanted to make certain he knew any trick the neo-Nazis might use against him. He did not like to think about the fact that, though the war was so long ago, he still waited for it to erupt anew. The way the war had gone for Germany's Hitlerized soldiers meant that the boys that had attacked him back in Cologne and the University student that turned out to be Anya's nemesis were, more than likely, just mounds of ruin in some German ditch or offal in some unmarked grave on the Russian front. But on odd nights, their resurrected essences arose to seek him out. They patrolled his office; and then, not finding him there, piled into their ghost-tanks, menacing every Jew on the streets. They slashed and tortured and raped and murdered and burned their way to his doorstep, then burst into his bedroom and stood at the foot of his bed, bayonetted rifles at the ready, and began strafing them. He would throw his body over Beryl's, to protect her; she would jerk awake and shove him off her, a look of utter panic on her face. The Stormtroopers would shrink away into the mists of his room and he would find himself unable to explain anything reasonable to her for his actions. She would roll into her accustomed coil to surrender herself to her own demons, leaving him staring at the door to the room, dreading the next onslaught.

CHAPTER SEVENTEEN

Andy, the son that swore that, with the world so dangerous and the future so perilous, he absolutely would never have a child, now had not one, but two daughters. Sophie and Lydia were both beautiful, lively and fiery in ways that made it likely that they would be sought out by every young man that encountered them.

Colorado was a long way from the east coast, where Benjamin and Beryl lived. Andy called his parents religiously on the first and fifteenth of every month, and Benjamin thought often that he should return his calls, but he rarely followed through. He missed his first son, but with everything from his elusive PhD to his job to Beryl's stability to the long-extinct Nazis crawling through every unoccupied corner of his thoughts, it was too easy to put Andy and his family out of mind. He left it up to Beryl to send out the cards and the gifts, and she did so; though often she just sent a check to mark whatever occasion appeared in her little address book. Benjamin thought checks were heartless; they showed, in his opinion, a lack of involvement; just an effort to discharge a duty. He tried to learn little things about everybody and often thought of things that his granddaughters or his daughter-in-law or even his son might like. Money always went into bank accounts that Andy had set up for the girls' futures, when what Benjamin wanted was for the girls to enjoy something right now. How else, he wondered, would they remember him as a 'cool' grandpa?

Benjamin wanted to be cool; no, not really; he wanted to be *there*. His father had worked at home when he was a child, but he still had not been *there*. His offices had been off-limits to his boys; they went there on pain of death or at least a severe chastisement, unless their situation was so desperate that, as Queen Esther approached the Persian King Ahashueras, somebody's life depended on it. Now his father was so far away that there was not even the comfort of an occasional glimpse of him. He had seen his father only once since he emigrated to England so many years ago. He read Herschel's chicken-scratched complaints about Elie and tried to sympathize, but somewhere he couldn't help thinking, "I would be willing to put up with anything—*anything*—if I could just live with my father!" Herschel once offered to let Elie go: to send him to America so that Benjamin could have his longed-for closeness, but Beryl had vetoed that plan as soon as she heard of it.

And Benjamin had wanted to be to his boys what his father had not been, but it just hadn't worked out that way. He couldn't have had the boys pulling through his papers. What a disaster it would have been to lose a student's paper or, worse, to have something disappear from his research for his doctorate! Therefore, he had barred them from his office, just as his father had done to him and Herschel, and he spent more hours there than he ever planned to, so that they were often asleep or out of the house by the time he emerged.

It seemed Andy had moved as far away as possible as quickly as he could after graduation from college. He said he had a better chance of getting work right away, but Benjamin had his doubts. He couldn't help but wonder if Andy just wanted to get away from his family.

Benjamin missed the girls. Over his sixty-day vacations each year, he made it a point to fly out with Beryl; and while she remained aloof in Andy's best bedroom, he made up for her detachment and *ennui* by being the prince of entertainment. What movie had they not seen? Where had they always wanted to go? Every night he took Andy and Jenny and the girls somewhere; *anywhere* that they might find cool. He had invested his money well, and now was able to afford whatever whims they might want fulfilled. Andy protested; he was able, he said, to provide the girls with what they needed, and he didn't want them to grow up as spoiled princesses, unless he was the one doing the spoiling. Benjamin just laughed at him; he wanted the girls to think of *him* as their hero; the irreplaceable one in their lives. Andy was too polite and too used to his father's ways to oppose him.

Benjamin wanted to be closer to Danny too, but he didn't trust him, particularly about issues of money and belongings. Danny gave everything away to the poor: druggies and harlots and homeless people. Many an item of value that Benjamin passed over to him languished in local pawnshops, while Danny used the money he got from the pawnbrokers to take a bunch of hungry teenagers or elderly people or immigrants to lunch in some restaurant they had never have had the resources to visit before and probably never would again. Benjamin was convinced that handouts promoted indolence, but nothing he said to Danny seemed to convince him.

Benjamin had always agreed to pay Danny's tuition and rent; but after Danny spent his security deposit on hosting a barbeque for the neighborhood, Benjamin decided to pay the fourth college and the landlord directly and give his son just enough for his own food. If he chose to starve to death, Benjamin told him, he could; but at least he would die with an education and a roof over his head.

Even if he wasn't big on taking Benjamin's advice about his future, Danny adored his father. It had become clear over the years to Benjamin, though he would have never dared say such a thing to Beryl. Danny was, after all, supposed to be 'her' child. But she had disowned him in her affections since he fell apart and wound up in the mental institution. No amount of cajoling on his part or apologies from Danny would convince her that her former hero was salvageable in any way. Once Danny had reminded her that she herself had been hospitalized twice, and maybe his illness was something he had inherited from her. She had strode from the room and not even spoken to him for weeks. Danny promised he would never criticize his mother again, but Beryl made no such pledge in return. Theirs was a spiderweb relationship, apparently: once broken, no machinations in the world seemed capable of mending it.

Danny called his father almost every day; not annoying, paranoid calls, as Beryl insisted they must be, but practical calls, requests for advisement and even suggestions for Benjamin's research that, applied, tended to work out well. Benjamin felt that he had failed him somehow; shouldn't he be at least as well-adjusted as Andy? Not that he felt Andy was happy with him. He saw how Andy never looked him in the eye; how he never argued about disagreements, even when he objected strongly. Andy seemed resigned to just allow him to do whatever he wanted, as if he realized all would be well once his father left. Danny, on the other hand, spent more time communicating than Benjamin thought was appropriate, given his need to study. He was, however, to his father's surprise and perhaps even to his own, doing well. Danny decided to go back to school at a fifth college. He was even talking about graduate school when he completed his course work. Benjamin did not know if he would actually do it, but he seemed more levelheaded, somehow. And then Danny told his father he was getting a job to supplement his income. That meant he would stop spending his time making cheap items for sale on the street or praying for America or Cambodia or Somalia or the polar ice caps with no thought of how he himself would survive. Maybe the Christian group was a good fit for him; or, though he could still do some pointless things, maybe he was just growing up.

Benjamin loved his boys; both of them. He wished, when he was with Danny, that Andy was there, too; that they could all just knock off and go somewhere and be—*men*—together. He wanted to take just them, just those two, and do something, even though he wasn't sure what that 'something' should be. Andy and Danny were still uneasy in each other's presence. They were not openly hostile, but he always felt that Andy looked down on Danny's religiosity and self-enforced poverty and Danny looked down on Andy's agnosticism and growing affluence. Benjamin did not want to find himself in the middle of some tiff between the two boys.

Besides, how could he go anywhere without taking Beryl? She had developed a new interest in travel since her journey to Europe, and now she came to life on cruise ships and airplanes, as long as they required crossing an ocean. For weeks before a trip, she would spend her time poring over maps and guidebooks, planning every mile, comparing accommodations, scheduling and re-scheduling, making arrangements for caretakers for the house. She would spend hours haunting thrift store racks and second-hand shop bins for 'new' wardrobe items and accessories, then spend even more hours packing and re-packing their well-traveled luggage. She would consult weather forecasts and almanacs and even make advance calls to the State Department to make certain they were not about to wander into some political hot-spot. She plotted the best route to the airport or dock, lined up a car service to deposit and return them to their launching place, and planned meals carefully, so that they would eat well up to the day they left, but would leave virtually no food to spoil while they were away.

On their trips, she would be almost frenetic. She had to visit every museum, see every flower garden and sample every restaurant the guidebooks recommended. She was at the front line of practically every tour and in and out of all of the local shops. She kept careful lists of people she felt should receive presents from abroad—Ayelet and LiLo with whom Benjamin had recently re-connected, Jenny and Andy's girls—though never Andy or Danny—and certain secretaries and important staff at the college. She would bound out of bed at first light and not crawl back between the sheets until after midnight. Benjamin found it harder and harder to keep up with her. Sometimes they stayed in the homes of foreign students he had taught. When they found themselves in some country from which he had no students, they might wind up anywhere from a hostel to the home of a local she met at a bistro on her last visit to that country or even just that afternoon. Bicycles, cars, Euro-passes; she arranged for them all.

There was only one thing she did not schedule in: sex. They were in such a whirlwind mode during her trips that he did not have the energy; nor did intimacy, other than with his pillow when the time for rest came at last, even enter his mind. Slowly it began to dawn in his consciousness an understanding of why Beryl enjoyed travel so much: she did not have to communicate disinterest. She could trek him over hill and dale and render him so exhausted that, enticing as she might look when viewed through a wineglass in the haze of a smoky European bar, he was happy to confine his ardor to a gentle cuddle that she stoically endured.

Something else was going on with Benjamin as well; something that was so insidious that he was only dimly aware of it until it was just moments from too late. Without a parent's guidance, he had lived his life pretty much by his own rules once he became an adult. Stringent to a fault in some areas, his sense of self-preservation did not rescue him from overindulgence. Whatever his doctor might tell him, he *was* going to chain-smoke; he *was* going to slather butter on whatever went into his mouth and he *was* going to make certain that whatever he ingested was *not* a vegetable. He might trot across campus if he became too involved in a conversation and found himself running late; but other than his jaunts trying to keep up with Beryl, he drove, rather than walked, everywhere. Beryl set aside an hour of every single day to exercise; she would lock herself in the back bedroom with a VHS tape of her latest workout guru and her yoga mat and not come out until she was wringing wet. Benjamin laughed at her, insisting that she had no one to please but him, and that she was thin enough. She always retorted, "Well, you are getting too fat; one day all of your bad habits are going to catch up to you."

That prophesied event happened in the campus cafeteria. He was debating a thoroughly-researched but still highly controversial point with an academic colleague when a white-hot pain shot up his left arm, pulsed with his heartbeat for a moment and then screamed down his superior vena cava and overran his terrified heart, which responded by retreating in spasmodic protest. One minute, he and his colleague were flailing their arms around with theatrical flair, not so surreptitiously aimed at attracting the attention of the graduate social science students populating the room, intent on drawing them into becoming an impromptu audience and forum for intellectual discussion; the next he felt himself propelled in horrific pain onto the concrete floor, fighting to draw a breath. His next sensation was of being lifted; roared in a semi-conscious state through the streets, swept along by a cacophony of screaming sirens and urgent voices. Then there came a blissful quiet in which everything stopped together. He woke up what seemed like an instant later, but proved to be half a week. He opened his eyes, and the pain returned immediately. Monitors flashed information from the most intimate reaches of his body onto various ticker tapes and monitor readouts. Tubes to measure and mete out protruded from his every orifice; only his eyes and ears were free. A half-full bottle of lactated Ringer's solution dripped what he hoped was something vital into the vein in his left arm. He was in a narrow white bed in a pea soup-green room. A flimsy clay-green curtain separated him from the rest of the world. Half-comprehending, he closed his eyes and slept again.

He awakened with a jolt, feeling not unlike Rip Van Winkle. He had no idea how many minutes, hours, days or years had passed. Most of the tubes had disappeared; only the IV and its pole remained. Beryl sat at the end of his bed, gazing mournfully at him. He had to wonder, for an instant, if her sadness derived from her fear that she would lose him or from her unhappiness that their scheduled trip to Zurich, which should have happened two weeks after his heart attack, had been indefinitely postponed. That glimpse into her mind, however brief, was more than enough to chill him. He knew he must never, ever let his mind go there again. When she recovered herself enough and came to his side, he let his eyelids flutter; as much to clear the tears as to give the impression that he was groggier than he actually was. She talked to him, but he did not hear the three words he craved so much. He more than suspected, from that moment, that the balance of his life with her would be a charade of goodwill overlaying feelings of deprivation, loss of vision and loneliness.

CHAPTER EIGHTEEN

Benjamin found out about it from Andy, who found out about it from Jenny, whose best friend Magda, whose dog Danny was sitting, told her: Danny had gotten himself engaged. He had gone to the elders of his Christian society and asked them to recommend a wife to him. Danny had not become engaged to a Jewish girl, or even a White girl. His woman, according to Magda, who had actually met her, was Black and she had a child.

Beryl was beside herself. If Danny didn't want to pick someone himself, if he wanted an arranged marriage, like some Bedouin or some back-village Chinese, why hadn't he at least spoken to his parents about it? They knew women—to be sure, troubled women—that she would have felt some pride in welcoming into the family. Did she not, by now, have her own little cadre of women, mostly mildly neurotic souls, that came to her house openly or surreptitiously, depending on their issues, and sat around her dining room table spilling their woes and soliciting her advice? True, some of them had received treatment from eminent Park Avenue professionals; but *she* had had therapy from a *European* psychiatrist, who was obviously superior to anything America had to offer, they all thought. She therefore qualified to be their personal guru; and, like a good guru, dispensed balm for their healing while keeping her own raw wounds safe under cover of her figurative regal garments. None of her crew knew the nameless fears and pains bubbling in her; nor would she reveal them to anyone else for love or money. She possessed a secret fear of dying and going to Gehenna; a dread of learning that her parents were dead; and her ancient bugaboo, that it might be Feuerstein at her door one day when she opened it.

There was something that she would tell no one, not even her pillow. She had been violated repeatedly by the grasping, grabbing Feuerstein, who did not deserve the title 'Rabbi'; his defilement of her besmirched the honorific so badly. Each time he released her and walked away, wiping his fingers on her underskirt and continuing the instruction as if nothing had occurred, she had felt filthy. She felt she must reek of her own nastiness, and so she scrubbed herself raw, but it was never enough; she could never get his foulness off her. But what shamed her most was that the man had picked the exact right time in her life to fondle her; the time when her own interest in her body was awakening and the nerves in what had hitherto been only a place for her body-water to exit were now evolving that site into a pleasure palace. Nerve endings were nerve endings; his touch, however unwanted, was skilled and not altogether unpleasant. The only way to escape wanting his hands to come near was to escape in her mind; to leave her thoughts remote and far from the reality of him and what he was doing while he profaned the holy words he quoted with his mouth. It was wrong; so wrong that the horror of it caused her stomach to quail and the fear that someone—Benjamin—might re-awaken some momentary flush of repulsive desire in her was almost more than she could bear. Her nerve endings in—that place—had found the experience of being touched electrifying, and had the man not been so furtive—well, she did not wish to go down that road. She had tried to tell her mother; tried to be rescued from him; and her efforts had gained her only rejection and derision, so she had had to endure what she knew was wrong and deny herself any association between loving touch and violation. And now she stood outside her family, and she would never allow herself the experience of feeling pleasure, no matter how legitimate it might be; not ever again.

Sex with Benjamin was an obligation. She had known it would be a part of marriage, and had steeled herself for it. A tiny part of her had hoped the experience would be cleansing for her, but it had not been; and when he came near, she felt only the fear and guilt of waiting for Feuerstein to strike and wanting and not wanting, desiring and repulsing. Surely there were other ways to make Benjamin happy; to repay him for rescuing her from the loneliness of having lost Yael's friendship and the isolation of college, the alienation from her mother and the abandonment by her father, the escape of her brothers into the world and her elder sister into marriage, and the clinginess of her younger sister, who just wanted to be like her, but who had escaped Feuerstein's groping fingers.

She thought about her younger sister sometimes. Beryl had told her, too. Had she believed what she heard? Was that why she elected to not have the bas mitzvah? And was that why Malka had not pushed her to do it? Had Malka believed her all along, but used her for the secondhand thrill of being close to Feuerstein? Was Beryl the sacrificial lamb for her mother's vicarious pleasure?

She had not expected, at first, that dealing with the local businessmen and faculty wives would be something she would enjoy. When Benjamin had suggested it, she had at first rejected the suggestion out of hand as something foolish; but it had been therapeutic for her. They had become the family she did not have; the family she wanted. She would never classify herself as having an 'interest' in women; but she did not particularly care for men and she certainly had her reasons. So when these women brought up their complaints about their husbands, she listened with genuine sympathy, and from her figurative perch on Mount Sinai she dispensed such wisdom as she had; wisdom that her little band of devotees treasured and lived by.

She cared for Jenny, but Jenny was so far away, and she found their infrequent telephone conversations unsatisfying; partly because talking on the telephone was talking to a piece of plastic and partly because she was always eyeing the clock and thinking of the cost as each minute ticked away. She rarely spoke to Andy, and claimed to be in a rush if Jenny offered to put him on the phone. She saw her elder son as a pusillanimous being, however much success he might have in the wide world, however much Jenny might adore him, however much he might make excellent decisions and emerge as a leader in his community. When Benjamin would praise something Andy had done or make her aware of some achievement he had gained, she would immediately bring up some event from his childhood that did not show him in the best light—his tears when he was bitten by a dog at age nine, his fear of thunder when he was six. If Benjamin asked her why she disliked the boy so, she would retort only, "Oh, don't be ridiculous. How could I dislike him? I'm his *mother*, after all.

Now, Danny was bringing this new creature into the family. How was she to relate to a Black woman as a daughter-in-law? There had been a colored maid that cleaned in her dorm at her college, and there had been Negro women working as orderlies in the hospital when Benjamin had his heart attack. Lessie the dorm maid managed to break or misplace or possibly steal everything, and the orderlies never seemed to show up when Benjamin rang the call button. The law had just changed to allow White and Colored to marry, and that law had still not been accepted everywhere. Apparently Danny's church elders were trying to challenge that law. All kinds of people were marrying all kinds of other people, and she supposed she should not be so shocked that Danny would go outside of his race for some exotic person. She wondered how Danny, formerly the love of her life, could feel about such a person, so alien from his own culture and upbringing; so alien from *her*. That thought brought her up short.

Danny's life had become so different. He had hung out in places she would never have thought he would and associated with people she had nothing in common with. He had told her, not once but many times how he despised being born White and well-to-do. He told his father in her presence that he had willfully given away the things of value that they had given to him, because he felt that poor people were more compassionate and *things* made rich people forget about God. Now, he had apparently attached himself to a woman he could feel compassion for, who was bringing along her own pickaninny. Images from her own childhood and youth flooded her mind: Prissy that told Scarlett O'Hara that she knew "all about birthin' babies", but when the moment of truth came, knew "nothin' 'bout birthin' no babies"; Buckwheat and Stymie from the 'Little Rascals'; the African chief with a bone in his nose from the Bosco cartoons; the Tar Baby in 'Songs of the South'.

Oh, those weren't *her* stereotypes. She did not believe she had a racist bone in her body. After all, the Jews, her own people from whom she had been estranged, had been in slavery for four hundred years; that was nearly twice as long as the Negro had suffered in America. Jews had also been used as slave labor under Hitler in Europe within this century. There were plenty of people that still didn't like Jews. But Jews had made academic and financial strides that the Colored had not. Jewish kids with their heads screwed on straight went for achievement and accomplishment, while the Colored went more and more for comfort and numbness, through drugs and sex and indolence. Jewish kids did too; but they generally knew when to give up the solace those feel-good things provided. When they didn't, they usually had their parents and their tradition to pull them out when they got in too deep. There were twelve tribes in Judaism, and a person had to come from one of them. The Negroes in America had emerged from some jungly mish-mash of invented heritages. They had lost their culture and their tribal links and their tradition. They ran around the streets in dashikis printed in some White person's factory and jumbled together a bunch of bright colors, because White people told them that was how they should look. And did they help each other? No; those that escaped the poverty and suffering society had provided them by abridging their rights took their professions into the White world. They aspired to be doctors in White hospitals and professors at White colleges, rather than starting their own institutions and returning to their own communities to enrich those around them (though she could not see herself returning to eastern Europe with Benjamin to spread his talents in some Jewish ghetto).

One or two of the women she associated with had children that had had dalliances and liaisons with the Colored; they had never worked out well. Usually they resulted in a large sum coming out of a bank account to fund an abortion or a hasty trip abroad to get that brand of fever out of one's system. As she slipped into her coat for the drive into the city, she wondered if she should have brought along the checkbook. She couldn't see explaining this chocolate-brown child to her friends; and what if he decided to call her Grandma? She decided she would never allow him to do that; and she determined to be as hard-nosed and disagreeable to this woman as she could be.

CHAPTER NINETEEN

Odelle was no Auschwitz-skinny crack-whore. She was a college graduate with a real career and her own money. Her ex-husband, the only man she had ever lived with, had left the religious life that had brought them together and now spent his time roaming the world in search of other women. Her faith seemed genuine and strong, but she did not attempt to foist it on her in-laws. As his father was also of European stock, the little boy was, in a word that fell from Beryl's lips involuntarily, "adorable". Odelle was mixed heritage, and the child, with his lush honey-colored curls, eyes the color of Benjamin's and skin that looked well-suntanned, was a racial Everyman.

Benjamin found himself hoping that *she* would stay interested in *Danny*. The boy—well, as his father, it was hard for him to think of him as a man—could be obdurate, even when he was clearly wrong. What if they disagreed about the child? What if one or both of them decided that marriage was not in the offing? Odelle moved with little Stephen into Danny's bachelor apartment, and the next time Benjamin saw it, the woman's touch—re-painted walls, lace curtains, and a refrigerator and cabinets filled with something more nourishing than tomato soup and Bumble Bee Tuna—was everywhere.

And Stephen! He was an articulate, polite, curious, well-behaved, beautiful boy that had received just the right balance of affection and restraint. He saw neither the need to cling to his mother nor to run around in an undisciplined way. Benjamin could not help but think about how much his mother would have enjoyed Stephen.

But Eliana, his mother, was dead, and Elie was dead. Elie had not told anyone for some time after Eliana fell ill that she was not going to recover; he feared the knowledge would be too unsettling for his children. When he finally told Herschel, Elie had begged them not to tell Benjamin. That his letters to his mother went unanswered was not unusual; she seldom responded, except occasionally through a footnote at the end of Herschel's carefully crafted missives. He had continued to read, "Mother sends her greetings" for months after it was not possible for her to do so. Then Elie himself, long a spokesperson for the advantages of a good cigar after breakfast, lunch, and dinner, had developed a nagging cough. Herschel was of the opinion that his father knew well what it was, but without Eliana, whom he loved more than he gave indications of and certainly more than she knew in life, and without his beloved Cologne, which he could have returned to, but refused to, he found no reason to remain alive. He therefore did not seek treatment for a malady that could have responded well to prompt treatment until it was much too late.

Benjamin had asked Beryl to accompany him to Uruguay to stand over his parents' graves. Andy had begged off, blaming a surfeit of issues at work demanding his attention as the reason he had not been able to free himself for such a long trip. Danny had overdue term papers, or so he claimed; he had, after bringing his undergraduate studies to a startlingly sterling conclusion, decided to delay work and go straight to graduate school. He had completed one year, and was almost through the second, putting him within striking distance of a Master's degree. Benjamin and Beryl had both agreed not to press him; he was, after all, at last, it seemed, on the very path they had wanted him to go.

Still, Delsey, as Danny called her, was a delightful person. Beryl had, at first, hesitated to introduce her to her friends. What would they think of her? What would they think of *Beryl*? And what would they say about her behind her back? Her friends' comments changed from, "She's nice, for a Black girl" to "She's a really nice person" to "You are *so* fortunate, Beryl! I wish *my* daughter-in-law was..."

Then Beryl modified her theatergoing. She began looking for Black films, Black productions to take Danny and Delsey to, and followed them up with meals at ethnic restaurants. She looked for gospel performances and jazz concerts to attend. Delsey endured her efforts to relate, but allowed that she had been quite immersed in her own culture and would like to experience theirs more.

Danny resented the curtailment of Black culture a bit; he had quite an interest in anything Black. He wished Stephen was a little less international looking and walked with a bit more of a Black swagger. He bought Delsey a colorful caftan and persuaded her to stop straightening her hair, but her natural hair did not evolve into dreadlocks and she insisted her office was too conservative for the caftan. He could not say he was *sorry* that he married Delsey; he would just say he wished she and Stephen were more like the Black people he was used to hanging out with. Delsey had never smoked weed. She certainly had no street life, and had been religious all her days. She had worked her way through college and gone into the workforce. Her only misdeed, if he could even call it that, had been her first marriage. He had known her ex, although he had not met her during that time; and was more than surprised when he heard about the other man's messy exit from the union.

Danny developed his own brand of Negritude. Even though he did not have a drop of African blood that anyone knew of, he felt it important that be not only acknowledged, but accepted by the heavyweights among the Black people with whom he was working. A vendor sold him a

Malcolm X ball cap. It was red, yellow and green, with a big **X** embroidered in black. He absolutely prized it, and wore it as a token of acceptance into the larger minority community, oblivious to the stares—and glares—of Blacks and Whites around him.

Delsey told him one day in her most diplomatic tone that not every African American might appreciate his wearing that hat. She said some people might feel he had no right to wear it, because, sympathetic with their cause as he might be, he was not actually Black. As well, she said, some White people might feel Malcolm's philosophy did not reflect their thinking, and might view him as a rabble-rouser, intent on bringing about some long-delayed global Diasporic uprising, and consider Danny a troublemaking agitator. She begged him not to wear it, especially at night, when even a brisk walk home from the subway just might be his last. He laughed at her temerity and told her she was being 'ridiculous'.

Stephen came up with another solution. After telling him, "Daddy, don't wear that hat. I don't want somebody to hurt you!" and seeing his father leave the house with that hat on anyway, he did not bring it up again. A few days later, however, Danny, who was not the most careful in keeping track of his belongings, found himself searching for his beloved cap. Delsey said she had not seen it. Stephen, now nine years old, said he had not seen it either, but there was something in his voice that made Danny suspicious. Danny loved the boy, but he hated the lies; as a perennial seeker of truth, he found himself enraged by deliberate lies. Stephen stuck to his story, though; and no amount of cajoling, warning or punishing would move him. Even when Danny got down to his level and glared at him, Stephen just glared back. "I don't know where your hat is, so you can buy another one or you can find it. Stop asking me; I don't *know* where it is!" Delsey finally told Danny to leave the child alone; she would replace the hat. However, she did not; she bought him a Kangol hat, which, while it did not carry the same flair for him, kept him safer on the subway. Stephen would be much older before he finally admitted that he had secreted the hat out of the house and given it, along with a dollar, to one of his buddies to hide "anywhere", provided he never told Stephen where it was. Ultimately Danny came to understand that his son had done it out of love; a love for which he was willing to endure any punishment if it kept his father safe; that took awhile.

CHAPTER TWENTY

Beryl could not deny that she enjoyed Delsey; she lived close enough to drop in almost any time and she didn't mind sharing a cup of coffee and conversation. She also never brought up personal issues. Her discussions centered around how fast Stephen was growing and current events. Only once did she ask an *inquisitive* question. She had, she said, met Aunt Ayelet before she died, and she had a good relationship with LiLo. She spoke with Shoshana and had hosted her around the town when she came up from Uruguay once or twice. But she had met only Marta, Peshella's daughter, and wondered if Beryl had any other relatives. Beryl, usually so open, had given her only a curt, "It's nothing you need to know about!" and beat an abrupt retreat to her bedroom.

Delsey learned from Danny what he knew about his mother's family, which was basically nothing, excepting one event: Danny, who could leave nothing alone, always wanted to find out about Beryl's missing family. He had discovered Marta only by chance. She was in his French Literature class, and was the spitting image of photos of Beryl from 20 or 30 years ago. It was hard for Danny to hear that Gershom, the grandfather he had never met, had died. He would not be able to query him as to why his mother had never been 'right'; why she broke down or quivered with fear or withdrew a thousand miles away into herself without preamble. Together they had come up with a scheme for him to meet Malka, and he had to put it into effect soon: she was dying.

Malka had lived eighty-one tumultuous years as a pampered young princess, a deceived and betrayed wife and a bereaved mother whose dead child was still living somewhere in the world. She sometimes wondered where, but whenever her thoughts drifted to Beryl, the Rabbi's face flashed into her mind, along with his voice, saying, "She has betrayed her family, her faith and her tradition. She has no part in your inheritance or your life. Cast her from you as you would the worst vileness. She is a disgrace; a pestilence, that has no place among us." And so Malka had flung Beryl from her thoughts. Still, she could not get her out of her feelings. Beryl was hard to forget. She recalled her sparkling eyes, her vivacity, her brilliance; all which had dimmed the more she prepared for her bas mitzvah. At times, Malka wondered—but no; Beryl was just a bad girl; Rabbi Feuerstein could never have wronged one of her children. Had he not counseled her on every aspect of her life, including how she should deal with Gershom during his wild years and how she should handle her finances? Had he not come to see her in the hospital, not once but many times? He was an old man, now, true; but old in that elegant way that the fortunate few of men age. His skin was still smooth and suntanned, even in the cold of a Camden winter. He had not bent with age, nor had he become infirm in his step. Unlike her other idol, Moses, the Rabbi wore glasses, true; but they were wire-rimmed, and added to his elegance. His suits were impeccable, and he smelled slightly of Old Spice cologne. If she caught beneath that scent the mere hint of *schnapps*, she was certain it had been offered to him by others, and certainly not to excess. He was a beautiful man, even in age. No wonder vague rumors, always coming to naught, seemed to follow him! And with his wife, his Gerda, who apparently suffered from some nervous disease all these years so that she rarely appeared even when she was young, dead these last nine years; well, people just *meddled*. Malka put her own feelings toward him into religious wrappings and felt—well, *comfort*—as he squeezed her now wrinkled hands and smiled into her eyes.

The nurse came in and whispered something to him. Looking mildly annoyed beneath his façade of graciousness, he released her hand and rose. "It seems your niece is here to see you," he said in his saccharine voice. "So I will be leaving you for tonight. I will come tomorrow."

The young woman and her companion brushed past him. Feuerstein noticed her well-shaped figure beneath her modest skirt and blouse. His eyes roamed over her and then her male companion. Lucky man, he thought, who could possess that one! And then he caught sight of the younger man's face, and froze. He never forgot a face, no matter how long ago or brief an encounter might have been. He looked from the face of the young man to that of the old woman in the bed. Then he quickly shook his head. Beryl was dead; he had declared her to be so himself. How could her seed come back to this place? He departed quickly.

Marta felt Danny's hesitance through his hand. She tightened her grip on him and propelled him ahead of her toward the form in the bed. Malka looked timidly into his face. He looked a lot like Marta. She couldn't recall her sister having male children, though all teenagers seemed to look alike these days. This one, with his curly russet hair and his hazel eyes with flecks of brown—he put her in the mind of someone. She was about to enquire of him who he was, when Marta spoke up.

"You remember my roommate Carole?" she asked, conjuring up in Malka's mind some vague image of a girl with fuzzy red hair and bad skin. "Well, this is—er—her *boyfriend*. He drove me here." Malka nodded weakly and he responded, stiffly. Marta prattled on for another five minutes or so, while Danny raked Malka's face with his eyes. His gaze made Malka uncomfortable; as if she were looking into the face of the Grim Reaper and the Angel of Life, both at the same time. When, what seemed like a century and a half later to Malka, they rose to leave, Danny

298

gave his grandmother a little bow and followed Marta out without a backward glance. So flummoxed did he leave Malka that out of sheer exhaustion she fell asleep, without her sleeping pill. The next morning, however, she awoke, and reported troubled dreams.

"I dreamed of Beryl," she said to Feuerstein. "I dreamed she was in this room; I dreamed she was *this close!*"

It was the first time she had spoken her daughter's name aloud in over a score of years; and it was the last time. She suffered a stroke that night, and died a few days later. Danny thought about going to her wake, but he didn't. He never told his mother what had happened; he never told her that he had encountered her demon face-to-face and, for all he knew, slain her. But he told Delsey, who treated Beryl with a little more deference than she might have otherwise.

Slowly, slowly, Beryl watched her younger son change; and while he was, in her estimation, still a screw-up and a con man, at least his flaws were becoming less obvious. The green parka he had apparently rescued from some trash receptacle somewhere, the one that spewed a cloud of chicken feathers whenever he made a sudden move, had been retired. Delsey had gifted him a new jacket from a reputable store, and Stephen had presented him with a leather wide-brimmed hat. In apparent retaliation (Beryl's assessment), Danny had decided to grow a beard, which Delsey had insisted that he trim, so that he now looked more than respectable. If he did not have the money in his pockets, he at least *looked* prosperous, to the point that Beryl's friends began to comment that he must be over his 'mental issues'. Beryl congratulated Delsey one day "for helping Danny overcome his problems". Delsey had commented only that she had plenty of issues herself, that Danny was helping her to overcome. Delsey had her issues, Beryl was sure; but she did not trouble Beryl with them. Beryl was happy just to have someone around that did not count on her for life coaching.

Benjamin liked Delsey, too, even though she never went up to the college with him after her first visit. She had sat quietly in a rear seat at one of his catered seminars, her notebook out to take notes. One of his graduate students had ambled over to her and, in front of several other students, told her to bring him a cup of coffee. When she had told him that the coffee bar was self-service, he had called her a bitch and told her to get off her fat black ass and get him a cup of coffee *right now,* or he would have her job. Benjamin had strode over and introduced the student to Delsey. "Delsey, this is Carl, one of my graduate students. Carl, this is my daughter-in-law." Carl had blanched and then flushed. After murmuring a polite 'hello', he had gone to get his own coffee.

Benjamin never understood racial prejudice; he supposed, because he had not grown up in America and because in Germany, his people had been the ones under oppression. He knew people had differing views about who was superior and who was inferior when it came to color and ethnic origins. His mother had felt superior to the Poles and the Germans had felt superior to his mother. The Russians had felt superior to the Germans and the Americans had felt superior to the Russians. The English had felt superior to the Americans, and apparently the Japanese had felt superior to the British. One of his African students had confided that he felt superior to Colored people, and when he had asked him why, since they both had dark skin and kinky hair, the student had said because the Colored people were mixed with all kinds of people—Indians and Irish and French and even other African tribes. They could not trace their ancestry back more than two or three generations, whereas his people were pure, seldom marrying outside their own tribes; and could confidently name practically every ancestor as far back as 500 years. Benjamin thought, sometimes, of the debacle at his in-laws' house. To him, religion, or lack thereof, was a personal matter. Since Beryl was considered a dead Jew—obviously a tragedy for her, but not at all disturbing to him—he felt no compulsion to raise his sons to be anything. He observed that Andy did only obligatory things with his wife; for instance, the girls went to Jewish schools, but never had bas mitzvahs, which Beryl would have been very much against. He had not been consulted to make a recommendation pro or con. This both pleased and saddened him.

Danny, on the other hand, included him in just about everything, except what went on in his bedroom. But he was now informing him of a plan that disturbed Benjamin very much: at the age of forty, Danny wanted a bar mitzvah.

CHAPTER TWENTY ONE

To Benjamin's consternation, the bar mitzvah had been Delsey's idea. This surprised him; she was, he had always thought, the sensible one in their relationship. He was even more amazed to discover that Danny was going for it. He was, after all, 'nigga-struck', as he himself said. If something was even remotely connected to Colored people, Danny was interested. He hadn't seemed to want much to do with anything White, and absolutely nothing with Judaica. He declared himself to be emotionally a Black man, and usually, despite Delsey's efforts and the dress code at his job, attempted to dress as one, wearing out-of-style Dashikis and allowing his hair to curl into a 'jew-fro', which he encouraged to snarl and tangle between requisite haircuts. He affected a method of speech that confused those that listened to him for the first time over the phone as to what his ethnicity might be. He declared quite openly to his friends of all hues that he would make an excellent Black man; in fact, he would be better than most, in his estimation.

The story eventually came out. Delsey had told him at one point that he indeed would make an excellent Black man, but such a transition surely required that he know something about his own heritage. He had reluctantly agreed to study Judaism; not just the traditions, but also its underpinnings: the history and the religion. He had begun attending a Temple in the City, which led to his studying Hebrew. And now—

Beryl did not want to go. She felt too much animosity toward her birth religion. "Besides," she said, "you know Danny is just shamming. He has no interest in really becoming a Jew. What is he going to do, after all? Get himself circumcised?" She brought this up, even though she knew that practically every male child born in the Western world, Jewish, Christian or otherwise, including Danny himself, was circumcised at birth.

"I can just see him becoming a rabbi now," she said, her lip curled in contempt. She had no doubt that if he did, he would become a Feuerstein. Not that he had ever shown any signs of pedophilia, but she just could not picture him being legitimate. He would have to be shady somehow; she was convinced of it.

Benjamin, on the other hand, felt differently. It was good, he thought, for Danny, who had been all over the God-search map, to finally come home to what his blood and ancestry dictated. Secretly, he envied his son's assurances about an afterlife; about a just Deity that saw all, rewarded goodness and forgave evil. He wished that he could fall contentedly asleep in the arms of good angels that would wake him tenderly every morning, then hold him close and gentle him unmolested through the terrors of dying and through the imposing celestial gates. Instead, he sometimes lay awake in the darkness of his bed, afraid to place a hand under his head, lest he hear his heartbeat and become alarmed if it skipped a beat. There was no one to whom he could bare his isolation. Andy, he felt, would have little interest, and perhaps no comprehension. Danny would perhaps place his whole mental struggle into the theoretical realm of agnostic existential angst and probably lecture him on a need to seek out spirituality. Jenny was too far away, Delsey he judged to be too gentle to subject to his pain, and the gray creature next to him that flinched if he even brushed against her accidentally in bed could never understand. Insecurity was a weakness he could never bring to his friends. Therefore, he continued to tussle more frequently than not with his nocturnal specters and envy those that could boast belief in something larger than themselves.

CHAPTER TWENTY TWO

Danny stood taller and straighter than Benjamin had ever seen him. He had purchased a new suit for this momentous occasion; and though he was over a quarter of a century older than he should have been to hoist the Torah and carry it against his shoulder, to march behind his rabbi into the packed Temple, to read the holy words and place adoring lips to the scroll that gave structure and meaning to his life, his very stance caused an electric streak of involuntary pride to surge through Benjamin. He could not help but feel that this was, indeed, a day like no other. He took his seat behind Delsey and Stephen, who sat with Marta and a young neophyte on the second pew. Danny and Delsey had invited a number of people from their offices, church group and even from Stephen's school. Fearful that there would still be a dearth of people to fill the Temple, they had asked the Rabbi to invite other members of the Temple to attend.

Beryl sat beside Benjamin during the entire service, staring into her lap. He could feel the warmth emanating from her body through her clothes, but otherwise she was as still as a statue, as cold as stone. Benjamin commented to her on the size of the congregation, but she did not lift her head and she gave no response. She rarely talked about things beyond travel, campus gossip and general enquiries as to his satisfaction with a meal, some artistic acquisition or 'new' slacks that she had reclaimed for him from some thrift shop or another. Particularly she said little about anything concerning religion, unless it was to add to a negative consensus, or about Danny, unless it was to deride him.

Discreetly, he leaned over the pew and tapped the Rabbi on the shoulder. "So nice," he said to him, "for you to invite your congregants to our son's bar mitzvah. Having the temple full really makes it an event."

But the Rabbi turned to him in surprise. "I've got no more than twenty people here," he said. "I don't know these other people."

More puzzling for Benjamin was when the Rabbi addressed the congregation and asked those who would to come forward to support the life of this new Jewish male. Usually a father or an uncle or a few elder cousins came forward to stand behind the fledgling man. The Rabbi's assistant rose, and Marta's husband, and LiLo's husband, and Ezra, who had come from South America for the event. They made their way to the stage. But a **host** arose to stand behind the new Jewish man, Daniel Rosenthaler: people unknown to everyone in the hall; unknown to everyone but Marta—and Beryl.

She recognized her elder brother and sister. The others, she assumed, were her other siblings, an aunt that had survived Malka, nephews and nieces she had never known, old family and friends that she had not heard from since she had risen befuddled from her mother's dining table. She looked around fearfully and scanned the crowd, but Feuerstein was not there.

The service was suddenly over, and the crowd bustled into the Fellowship Hall through the sanctuary's side door. People bustled to find seats, but not Beryl's family. Her three brothers, her two sisters and their spouses, her aunts and uncles and cousins and friends all lined up at the doorway through which she had to pass. Eldest to youngest, each took her in their arms and held her close. "Beryl," each muttered, "We thought you were dead. But you have a son; a Jewish son, born since they told us you died. He could not have life if you were not alive. You are alive, Beryl. Welcome; welcome back to your family. Welcome home."

Beryl, so long bereft and adrift from her people, so long dead, found herself as did the New Testament prodigal: safe among her own. True, her

308

mother and father had both slipped away into that dark night, still willfully estranged from her, still bemoaning her death, even though they realized that she was alive. Still, there were others—

"...Uncle Lenny died last winter", Miriam was saying, "and Rabbi Feuerstein; you remember. He is gone,".

Dead?

The bugaboo, the dybbuk that molested her again and again even in her dreams, that leered at her from her husband's eyes and thrust himself in front of Benjamin when they were abed? *That* Rabbi? He that flooded her mind with fear and self-loathing and drove her to pills and sharp objects across her delicate veins? Her face flushed. She hoped the devil took him straightaway; that he had no time to repent, and thus basked in the fires of Gehenna. In that moment she wished she had belief; but hadn't he taken that away from her? Now that he was gone—stone dead and rotting, right down to his filthy fingers in some unknown place—maybe even her faith, as her family had, could return to her.

Luncheon was a blur. Beryl's family smothered her with embraces and caresses, as if trying to make up for the last forty-three years of privation. They exchanged addresses and telephone numbers and agreed that Danny's bar mitzvah should be declared a family holiday that they would celebrate annually, or at least periodically.

Beryl hugged Delsey. "I don't know whether God exists or not," she said, "but if He does exist, He sent you to our family." Delsey just smiled and looked down. She, too, saw the Universe at work, far beyond her simply wanting to help Danny find himself.

All the way back home in the car, Beryl was silent. Benjamin wanted to say something, but he thought that anything he said would be wrong. He had no idea what was going through his wife's head. Now that her family was back with her, what was she feeling? Had she managed to slay her demons, or had new monsters come to populate her dreams? Bemused, he pulled the car into the garage and turned off the motor. She opened and closed her door, went into the house and straight into her bathroom. He went to his office, took off his suit and hung it in his closet. His linens he sent down the laundry chute. He slipped on his bathrobe and slippers and shuffled into his bathroom. With the warm shower hazing the day's events, his thoughts turned to tomorrow. His Core Engineering class was overdue for an examination; he must construct one in the morning. The gutters needed cleaning; Beryl had been needling him about having it done for several weeks, now. He would have to start looking for someone to handle it. His desk needed attention, too; he should get to work on it before he started misplacing things. He turned off the shower and set to work on his teeth. He hated flossing, but it beat having to handle false teeth, and he had some gum problems already. He stroked his chin, shaven only hours ago. He supposed it was a part of aging, that he grew stubble so quickly. Deodorant, unguent for a small pimple on his neck, a hairnet to hold his graying mane of hair that the mirror told him was slowly thinning, his gray cotton pajamas—and he was ready for bed. He shuffled slowly back to the bedroom.

But he did not lie down. The sound of the shower in the en suite bathroom drew him like a north-poled magnet to its southern counterpart. Through the thinly frosted glass, he caught sight of Beryl, her figure still sleek, her skin soft and pink and soapy. Her silvered russet hair was caught up high on her crown in a clamp and cascaded down to her nape. She had her back turned to him, and had no idea of the scene she was providing him. He felt himself growing warm under his pajamas. The water shut off suddenly, and he dashed for the bed before she could grasp her towel to wipe her wet face.

"It was a nice service," he said as she slid in next to him. She said nothing, but moved closer to him, and with a very large sigh, into his arms. Anya, Hitler, the stomping Nazis—tonight they fled, and went in search of somebody else's bedroom to haunt.

And that was extraordinary indeed.